AUG 2 6 1997

stt to Jdd
lve 04/98

W/11

D0341327

POSTSCRIPT TO MURDER

BY THE SAME AUTHOR

TOUCH AND GO
THIS BLESSED PLOT
A LOOSE CONNECTION
A MOUTHFUL OF SAND
A WORM OF DOUBT
IN REMEMBRANCE OF ROSE
THE SPLIT SECOND
HANG THE CONSEQUENCES
THE SITTING DUCKS

Daly City Public Library
Daly City California
DISCARDED

POSTSCRIPT TO MURDER

M. R. D. Meek

St. Martin's Press ⚲ New York

W

POSTSCRIPT TO MURDER. Copyright © 1996 by
M. R. D. Meek. All rights reserved. Printed in the
United States of America. No part of this book may be
used or reproduced in any manner whatsoever
without written permission except in the case of brief
quotations embodied in critical articles or reviews.
For information, address St. Martin's Press,
175 Fifth Avenue, New York, N.Y. 10010.

Library of Congress Cataloging-in-Publication Data

Meek, M. R. D.
    Postscript to murder : a Lennox Kemp mystery /
M.R.D. Meek.
        p.   cm.
    ISBN 0-312-15626-X
    I. Title.
PR6063.E35P67   1997
823'.914—dc21   97-5497
                                                      CIP

First published in Great Britain by Collins Crime,
an imprint of HarperCollins*Publishers*

First U.S. Edition: June 1997

10   9   8   7   6   5   4   3   2   1

Postscript to Murder

CHAPTER 1

'Someone is trying to kill me,' Lennox Kemp remarked conversationally to Detective Inspector John Upshire.

'Oh, aye? D'you want the other half?' Without waiting for an answer, the inspector scooped up both their glasses and ambled over to the bar, using his big shoulders to get through the crowd but without unnecessary impact, easy as an animal in thick undergrowth. Kemp watched him with mingled affection and exasperation, and sighed. The laconic reaction had been much as he'd expected.

'So, what's new in that?' Upshire's baby-blue eyes were bland as milk. He put the two half-pints down smoothly and settled his bulk into a chair designed for someone of lesser size. 'You've been an unpopular bastard in the past, and there's probably still folk around would be happy to see you interred.'

'Thanks, John. How well you put it . . .' Kemp took a long drink of the beer which somehow tonight didn't taste so good. 'But I meant what I said.'

'Not threatening letters again?'

'Those, too . . . But they're common enough.'

'Disgruntled clients? What else do you expect? You know, Lennox, it always surprises me that you lawyers don't get more of them. Look at it this way . . . Every time you've a court case there's bound to be a loser. You've said so yourself. Even in what you call civil suits – and pretty uncivil some of them are the way I hear it – one party comes out feeling he's been kicked in the teeth.'

'That's just our adversarial legal system,' said Kemp, doggedly, 'and they should know all about that before they even get into court. We do warn people if they've got a weak case. If they insist on going ahead against our advice it's no use

7

them foaming at the mouth and vowing vengeance on all lawyers when they lose the battle . . .'

But Upshire had warmed to his theme, and ignored the comment.

'Same thing in criminal cases . . . You get one of my known villains off the hook on a technicality and the men on my patch who've sweated their guts out just to bring him up before the bench, they're mad as hell . . . They'd like to see you roasted . . .'

Kemp looked startled. 'Not to the extent of trying to set my house on fire?'

John Upshire drew the back of his hand across his lips, and gave Kemp a sharp glance. 'H'm . . . I think you'd better tell me about it.'

'Somebody pushed petrol-soaked rags through my letter-box this morning, followed by a lighted match. Luckily I was in the kitchen at the time and saw the flare-up. I stamped out the fire and we only lost the doormat. I did report it, John. Your desk sergeant has the details, and the debris. You weren't around.'

'I've been up at the Bailey all day helping to put away the Clayton brothers. My God, Lennox, why didn't you tell me straight off?'

'I'm telling you now. And it wasn't the first attempt. My car was rammed out on the London Road on Saturday night. An unidentified van drove into me, reversed smartly and accelerated away leaving me on the edge of a ditch. It was a wet night, and I thought he'd just skidded, didn't want to face the consequences and got the hell out . . . Now I'm not so sure. My car's still in dock, that's why I walked here tonight.'

'We're both walking,' said Upshire, tersely, 'and this calls for something stronger. Whisky, eh?'

'Sounds like a good idea. I'll get them.'

As he threaded his way through the brass-topped tables Kemp was reminded of the many other nights he had spent with John Upshire in the Cabbage White, turning the small coin of their shared experience. For it was only here, away from the strictures of their respective offices, that they could, as it were, unbutton and let their tongues go free. Lawyer and policeman, they might be said to have the same end in view, but Kemp's way was not Upshire's and they both knew it, warily skirting the difference when occasion arose.

It had been a long friendship of benefit to each of them in their lone years when neither had other companionship, the inspector a widower, Kemp unmarried and with no clear plan to alter that state. Despite careful adherence to, on the one hand professional ethics and on the other the rules of police procedure, such meetings were mutually enlightening and sometimes their outcome had played havoc with the lives of those socially malfunctioning members of the community who had criminal tendencies. It was of these that Upshire now spoke.

'You've helped put away a few in your time, Lennox. Their families, now, they've not liked it. When some of our old East Enders came out here for a new start they thought they'd find us less on the ball than our colleagues in the Met. Well, they learned different . . . But when someone we've nabbed is doing his stretch he gets to brooding . . . Mebbe he comes out with a grudge . . .'

'You know we solicitors don't prosecute nowadays, John. That's all up to the Crown Prosecution Service . . .'

'Five or six years ago you were doing it. Put a few behind bars in those days. Some got ten to twelve . . . With remission, they're out now, prowling the streets, God knows what in their twisted little minds. You thought of that?'

'I've not had time to think of much . . . Anyway, it would be your lot who finally put them away, my part was small . . . Why don't they have a go at the police?'

John Upshire grinned – a rare occurrence. It split his chubby features like a half-opened bun. 'Because, my lad, we embody the law. We're a force to be reckoned with. They can't point the finger at one individual in a team. But you, you're out on your own . . .'

'Which I feel most acutely,' said Kemp, not heartened by the turn in the conversation. 'Believe me, I've been searching my conscience since this morning . . .'

'Then you're in the wrong area. Conscience has nothing to do with it. If you've nailed some rogues in your time, and even a few murderers, you did it in the course of duty . . .'

9

'And in answer to the call for justice . . . I know all the high-sounding words, I just wonder sometimes as to their meaning . . .' Kemp felt it was probably the spirit of the grain which was beginning to fuel their terms of expression. John Upshire was normally a man of some reticence in speech, more at home with official prose than abstract concept. Only with Kemp did he sometimes relax sufficiently to reveal an inner depth of understanding, a cognisance of other issues beyond those contained in police dossiers. Kemp was surprised that he had not been made superintendent by now. The local force respected him for his fairness, the knack he had of seeing their point of view, his sympathy with raw recruits doing a difficult job in hostile circumstances, he backed them to the hilt against all criticism while at the same time upholding strict discipline, that first tenet of his belief in the system he had to operate. Perhaps the powers that be had never interpreted correctly Upshire's inherent loyalty to the men serving under him, and his refusal to bend even when it went against the wishes of his superiors. There would have been conflict there; perhaps it had not helped him in the promotion stakes.

'I'll run a routine check,' the inspector was saying, 'to see if there's anybody just released or out on parole who might fit the bill.' He paused, and shook his head. 'But it's a long shot. Most of them steer clear of trouble – at least for a month or two. And we keep a close eye on them if they've been part of one of the organized-crime rackets. This kind of petty revenge isn't nearly as common as you might think . . .'

'I don't see anything petty in an attempt on my life. It's the only one I've got and I'd like to hold on to it for a while yet.'

'I bet you do – particularly now it's changed. You got married . . .'

Upshire could not keep a slight resentment from edging into his tone. He too had savoured these nights spent mulling over cases, the relationship which had brought comfort to them both when neither could find it at home. Now things would be different. Kemp had acquired a wife – and not one John Upshire would have chosen for him. Mary Blane, her name when she was single, though she had had others, had

10

a past which the inspector considered to be dingy if not downright disreputable. He could not help commenting on it, even at the risk of putting strain on a friendship he cherished.

'Have you thought that it could be your wife they were getting at? She had some pretty weird connections back there in the States.'

'Come off it, John. Matrimony hasn't quite blighted my wits. Of course I've wondered about that, but it just isn't on ... These letters I've had, what they say, they're aimed at me alone. They hint at things that have happened only to me, either here in Newtown or even further back ... I haven't any ideas yet as to what they're getting at but I'm working on it. But it has nothing to do with Mary.'

Upshire grunted. 'Whatever you say ... I'd better have a look at them. I suppose you've kept the stuff?'

'Have you ever known a lawyer throw away anything that's written down? And, talking of Mary, she'd like you to come to supper on Saturday night. She feels it's time she got to know you better and, frankly, I think a closer acquaintance with her will modify your view.'

If John Upshire's acceptance of the invitation was grudging that was only to be expected. Kemp was well aware that the inspector's opinion of Mary Madeleine Blane, now Mrs Kemp, was bound to be coloured by her involvement in a recent case which had put her by Upshire's reckoning in that grey area between legal right and moral wrong, or perhaps the other way round. As an upholder of the law, the inspector didn't like grey areas; he preferred to see people in black and white, and possibly with little captions under them saying guilty or innocent. Kemp's work, by its very nature, forced him to dig deeper into the character and motive of his clients so that his attitude to their frailties tended to be tolerant and sometimes even ambivalent.

The two men parted at the corner, Upshire to go back to the empty suburban house he and Betty had bought when he was first posted to Newtown. His daily housekeeper would have left him his supper, and be gone till the morning. He would eat it in the kitchen, lock up and go round putting out the lights, but the bedroom would be cold and unwelcoming ... Kemp watched him stride off, and felt a pang.

11

He knew that life only too well. For years he also had returned late at night to a sterile lodging, the flat above the builder's yard he had inhabited for so long with its folk-weave curtains drawn against the dark and the drab furniture staring up at him . . .

All that had changed, and Kemp had sensed the under-current beneath the inspector's guarded: 'Well, if nothing comes up I'll be round on Saturday . . . Seven-thirty? Right . . .'

It was inevitable that the relationship between them would never again have the old easy familiarity. Professionally they would meet as before and have the same respect for each other's work but that other bond that had drawn them together, two men of single status in a society seemingly composed of couples, that bond was broken.

Well, it wouldn't be the first time a friendship had foun-dered on the rock of a marriage . . . Kemp's mind was caught up by a half-remembered jingle, something from the Chinese:

> 'The single man can never know
> The ins and outs of marriage . . .
> The envy that the coachmen know
> For those within the carriage.'

Despite the serious nature of the matter which had made him seek out Inspector Upshire tonight, Lennox Kemp was smiling as he went home to his wife.

CHAPTER 2

As Kemp put the key in his own front door he was reminded of another complaint by John Upshire.

'I don't know why you had to stick yourself in this end of town anyway . . . It's too near the centre – what with that bowling alley and that so-called youth club – a lot of mindless do-gooders doing no good at all to them that's going to the bad anyway, like rotten apples in a barrel . . .'

Upshire's rare excursion into metaphor owed more to the quality of the malt being drunk than an attempt at humour, but again behind the words there had been resentment. 'Why didn't you and your new wife take a nice house in a quiet suburb instead of down there in that troublesome spot . . . It's no wonder you get things put in your letterbox.'

The inspector probably guessed that it had been Mary's choice, the large Victorian leftover in a terrace beside the station.

When the railway had first come to Newtown it had not impinged on the original village but discreetly held to the banks of the Lea where the river-barge traffic had once flourished. But the Victorians too were entrepreneurs in terms of their future and soon houses were needed to accommodate those whose business interests might lie in the City of London but whose horizons encompassed a wider land of England beyond the green woods and sleepy hamlets of the home counties. Railways brought trade and prosperity till even the squat little widow of Windsor was moved to approve, and with that blessing of crown and country, villas rose fast along the new steel lines which conveyed not only freight to the Midlands but also ladies eager to sample the delights of shopping in Oxford Street.

George Meredith's heroine, Diana of the Crossways, complained to one enthusiast: 'How I hate your railways . . .

Cutting up the land and scarring its countenance for ever, its beauty will never be the same again . . .'

If these, not unmodern, sentiments had echoed over the century they had never struck any chord in Newtown, which had gone on grasping at commercial straws, both long and short, right down to the present recession. However, No. 2, Albert Crescent had not been one of the victims of this particular turn of fortune. There had never been money enough to convert it, unlike its neighbours, during the upsurge of the eighties, into a gold brick of plush offices for financial consultants and insurance brokers. Under the heel of circumstance these now had a tarnished look, gilt peeling from gingerbread, while No. 2 still stood in all its decayed splendour, an honourable relic.

'I like it,' Mary had said as soon as she saw it. 'Far better-looking and half the price of those awful boxes on the estate where your friends the Lorimers live, and just look at the length of the back garden . . . Why, it goes right down to a river . . .'

'Once you've fought your way through the undergrowth, yes, that's the Lea, all right. A puddle of slime enriched with beer cans . . .'

'You've never seen the Liffey,' said Mary, complacently, 'nor the East River for that matter. I guess we can clean up a little brook like the Lea. If we buy this house, Lennox, I'll go half on the purchase price . . .'

'You bloody won't . . .' But of course he'd been overruled, despite the fact that when she had stood up at the altar Mary Madeleine Blane had promised to obey.

He should not have been surprised, for this woman he had married – perhaps against his better judgement – was still an unknown quantity. When he asked her to marry him he knew it went against all his reason to do so; had he stopped to think he never would have made such a proposal . . .

But he had not stopped to think because he was caught up in the age-old folly which had nothing to commend or excuse it, except the fact that he was in love.

She came out from the drawing room when she heard him in the hall. Her kiss of greeting was by no means perfunctory.

14

'You told John Upshire?' she asked. 'What did he have to say?'

'Not a lot. You know what policemen are like.'

'Oh, I do, I do . . .' When she smiled, as she did now at the thought behind his words, her plain features lit up like a glint of sun on a cloudy day. 'They've the face on them puts us all in the wrong. Let's have some coffee, it's just made.'

'Does he think it's me that's to blame?' she said later, as they sat by the fireside.

Kemp held nothing back from this new wife of his. 'He did wonder about the possibility but I soon scotched that one. You and I have seen those letters, it's me they're aimed at.'

'But why now, Lennox? Whoever's writing them, they're obsessed with some grievance against you.'

'Well, I only wish they'd come out in the open with it.'

'But that's not the way it is with an obsession. It blocks the light of day for people, like a great wall. And it's a wall that's maybe been building up over a long time.'

Kemp looked across at her. She sat holding her coffee cup in both hands, frowning slightly at the effort of putting thoughts into exact words because when she was serious only the right words would do. It was one of the first things he had noticed about her during the short time she acted as his secretary, her way with words. Later, of course, he had realized that such adroit handling of the tools of speech could be put to many uses.

'That's why I'm wondering why they're being sent now,' Mary went on, 'because something must have triggered them off, and the only thing I can think of is that you got married. Is there some woman in your life who might resent it?'

'Whom I have cast aside like a worn-out glove?' said Kemp, airily. 'Oh, they must be thick as autumnal leaves that strow the brooks in Vallombrosa, the women I've abandoned . . . Come off it, Mary, the only woman who has been affected by my marriage is yourself, and if I may say so, you've taken it rather well.'

'You mean I have bettered myself, being rescued from a life of crime and marrying the boss into the bargain? Sounds

15

quite a romantic fiction . . .' But he could see she was only laughing at him as he went over and sat on the hearthrug at her feet. She curled her fingers in the tufts of hair on his forehead. 'You're getting a bit thin on top,' she said. 'I don't see you as a breaker of hearts, Lennox, but I was serious about the letter-writer maybe being a woman, it's a way women have . . .'

'Willing to wound and yet afraid to strike . . . I don't think that was said of a woman.'

'Oh, you and your quotations . . . I'm serious, Lennox. You've been involved with women in a lot of your cases, not only the matrimonial ones. There must be someone out there who is bitter.'

'It wasn't a woman in the van that skedaddled the other night, and I don't see a woman pushing firelighters through a door at seven in the morning. Much too obvious.'

'She would have help, of course. Women don't often act alone.'

'You did, Mary Madeleine . . .' Kemp could not see the point of never alluding to her past life; it was there before them both and, as he had accepted her, so it had become part of his life also.

'I had grown used to being alone. It was the only way to survive . . . then . . .'

'And now?'

Her face glowed in the firelight as she looked down at him.

'Ah, now I've found a better way . . .'

'No more talk then . . .'

But when he kissed her eyelids he saw first the fear in her eyes and knew what she was thinking. As he had once been afraid for her life so she was now for his.

Perhaps he should take more seriously what she had been saying, perhaps he should look back over his past cases, ransack his memory to find cause enough for someone to send him such poison through the post. He knew many of the phrases by heart, so often had they been repeated.

'You'll get your comeuppance, never fear . . .'

'You wrecked lives, Kemp, let's see yours get wrecked . . .'

'I'll get even if it's the last thing I do . . .'

'Vengeance is mine. I've waited long enough . . .'

Such sentences recurred over and over again in the six letters he had received during the last months, interspersed with more specific threats, a knife in the back, a breaking of bones, death by a variety of methods, all violent, couched in language not easily identifiable. There were misspellings, of course, but they could have been deliberate. 'Comeuppance' – not a word in everyday use – had been spelt correctly, as if a dictionary had been used but if so, why make other mistakes? There was a certain literary quality about the style, even semicolons were scattered about, and the grammatical errors looked false. Despite such contrivances the words flowed as if the writer knew very well what he or she was about, and feeling came through almost too well – a spillage of hate bursting its banks.

The letters were typewritten on plain paper torn off the kind of pad available at any stationers. The typing had the pepper-and-salt look made by a two-fingered typist, but that too could be misleading – any expert can imitate an amateur. The machine was manual not electronic, black carbon ribbon, the alignment fairly even with no smudging of the e's and o's . . . Someone who kept the keys clean or did not use that particular typewriter very often?

Except for this kind of muck . . . Kemp sighed. He would hand the lot over to John Upshire tomorrow and let the police get on with whatever analysis they could make of such unpromising material. He had already made photocopies for himself. He shovelled the letters back into their envelopes, plain brown manilla, all addressed to himself, Mr Lennox Kemp, at his new home. He studied the postmarks, all different, all districts of London from the City to outlying suburbs, the malevolent missives had obviously been simply popped into pillar boxes wherever the writer fancied. None had been posted here in Newtown, but there was local knowledge; references to 'your posh office' . . . 'I seen your glossy girls go in and out' . . . (That had an almost poetic ring to it.) 'Choke you to death in a gravel pit' was an obvious pointer to the main industrial activity along this stretch of the River Lea . . .

Kemp tossed the bundle into his briefcase and put it in the hall ready for the morning.

Mary was down first. She felt the draught halfway up the stairs and saw that the front door was standing wide open. It was a strong old-fashioned door of solid oak but the lock too had been old-fashioned and all too easily shattered, expertly done – and quietly. Where the wood had burned in the previous day's fire the bolts had not drawn across properly.

Kemp surveyed the damage, and shook his head.

'We kept open house last night,' he observed, gloomily.

His briefcase had gone. It was all that had been taken.

CHAPTER 3

'So you've lost the evidence?' John Upshire sounded more scornful than sympathetic.

'Evidence of what? That someone hates my guts? I know what was in those letters – that's enough for me. But there's plenty of evidence for your men to get started on – a broken lock, an arson attempt and a stolen briefcase.'

'All my sergeant's got is a sackful of ashes . . . As for the breaking and entering, why'd they only pinch your case? Anything in it apart from the letters?'

'Luckily, no.' The inspector was just the man to assuage anger, it was part of his job. But even that habitual stolidity could do little to take away Kemp's sense of outrage at what he saw as the violation of his home. He had been burgled before, both at his flat and in his office, and had accepted such happenings as part of modern living, but then he had been a single man . . . What rankled now was that he and Mary had been upstairs in bed, wrapped in sleep or other blessedness. It was as if a stranger had stood and watched them . . . He shook off such unproductive thoughts. 'I don't take so much work home with me since I married, and all our thief got was a pocket calculator and a folder of brochures on – of all things – security systems.' He laughed. 'Talk about locking the stable door – Mary and I were just about to have the whole house done.'

'Well, it looks as if you'd better get on with it. I've had a word with the officer on patrol. Constable Barnes was in Station Road about midnight. There was a bit of a fracas at the Victoria pub but he soon cleared that up, and his beat would take him round your crescent in the early hours and he saw no one acting suspiciously – in fact, he saw no one at all though there's the usual number of cars and vans parked . . . He wouldn't have been able to see your front door anyway for all those damned bushes in your garden. Yes, I take your point about the fire, I don't believe in coincidence either. Someone wants to scare you, they begin by letting you know how easy it is to get at you and your house is the obvious target. That and the letters . . . Just our luck they managed to pinch them back.'

'Pure chance,' said Kemp. 'There's no way they could know where they were. I think you're right, breaking in that door and leaving it open was just a bit of showing off. They never went further than the outer hall, they spotted the case and simply lifted it, probably thought it would cause me embarrassment if I had clients' files in it. Anyway, apart from the writer, no one knows such letters exist except Mary and myself, and now you.'

'And I've not mentioned them to anyone on the force. I was waiting to get them to put them under the usual analysis. Well, we'll just have to bide our time and see if you get any more of the same.'

'I hope not,' said Kemp, fervently. 'Such vicious stuff has an unnerving effect on one. You and I can handle break-ins and burglaries, even that knock to my car if it was part of the whole scheme, because it's men's hands that wield the chisels or turn the steering wheel . . . Even pushing fire-lighters through the letterbox makes a loutish kind of sense. Plenty of our minor criminals get a kick out of bashing property – makes them feel bigger than they are. Vandalism grown up. But the letters, that's something else again, the sheer malice behind them, the anonymity . . .'

'Let me see your copies on Saturday evening,' said John Upshire, briskly. 'I'm still to come, am I?'

'Of course you are. Mary's not the kind to let this business get her down. Nor am I, if it comes to that – which is just as well for I've enough obsessed clients without becoming one myself.'

As he returned from the police station to his own office Kemp attempted to switch his attention from personal matters to the more pressing affairs of the practice. Despite recent shake-ups in the profession, Gillorns remained the eminent legal firm in Newtown, with a high reputation for probity and fairness, and Kemp was determined to keep it that way.

Having over the past few years gathered round him not so much a team as a coterie of lawyers who worked in their separate fields but could stand together when required, he knew that he was the pivot of the firm, he held it together. Like John Upshire, not all of them had approved of his marriage, perhaps sensing a change in him. Despite their being friends as well as colleagues, he had spoken to none about the letters, for the animosity displayed in them seemed too personal – at least so far. But he knew how easily the reputation of a legal firm can be damaged when the character of any member is impugned, and there had been more than a hint of that behind the writing.

Had Kemp confided in anyone it would have been Tony Lambert of his Trusts department, who had a wise head on young shoulders, but Tony had recently become engaged to a pretty law student from Australia and it did not seem fair to intrude upon his present starry-eyed contentment. Michael Cantley's insight into the thought processes (where such could be discerned) of Newtown's up-and-coming young criminals might be of help should the scaring tactics be repeated, but in Kemp's view the mind of the anonymous writer was of a different generation. Cantley had been with the firm for many years; he might yet have to be consulted if old files were to be exhumed. So might Perry Belchamber who had come over from the Bar and specialized in matrimonial matters; if, in the past, a troubled family had eaten bitter fruit, their children's teeth could be set on edge . . .

Kemp couldn't find the right quotation for that so he dismissed the whole matter of the letters from his mind and concentrated on Friday's business.

There was no lack of it, despite the recession having trailed its dusty underskirts over all aspects. Instead of houses happily changing hands weekly on the new estates built in the boom years, now the property files were full of repossessions, and anguished cries from the building societies. 'Ignore them as long as you can,' Kemp told Charles Copeland, his conveyancing clerk. 'Where there's a roof there's hope . . . I'd rather be blamed for the law's delay than have families out on the street.'

It saddened Kemp to handle the failures, the flow of

bankruptcies, the winding up of small firms set up in the good times with such high hopes, those who had ventured too far, been too sanguine in their expectations and now found themselves facing a harsher reality.

Surprisingly, the figures for divorce had gone down. There were still the inevitable matrimonial disputes – paired-off humans being what they were – but couples were tending to stand together in adversity, or, as a cynic might have it, they were looking more closely at the financial consequences of splitting up one home and providing for two. A statistician might have an interest in this effect of hard times but there could be little comfort in it for moralists.

One of Kemp's cases in court that morning brought him up against an old adversary, Nicholas Stoddart, who had been a colleague in the firm some years ago. Stoddart had left Gillorns in a move which was of benefit to both parties. Kemp had discovered in the past of this envious man a shady episode which might never have come to light had Stoddart not attempted to smear someone else, thus showing himself as not only untrustworthy but vindictive also. It was upon this latter ground rather than the misconduct itself – which could be seen as merely an ambitious young lawyer's attempt to outsmart an opponent – that Kemp had accepted Stoddart's resignation.

Nick had taken his undoubted talents as a bold litigation man to the City for a while, but now even there the sturdiest of companies were shedding twigs like trees under storm, and Stoddart was back in Newtown. Not that he would have it that way. According to Nick Stoddart, the local firm of Roberts could hardly wait to engage his services.

Watching him now, on his feet before the Bench, Kemp felt a grudging admiration for Nick's powerful presence and skill in argument. He should have been a barrister, he thought – not for the first time – and indeed, Stoddart's appearance would have been the better for a wig. As it was, his heavily handsome features seemed to be tacked on to a head too small to hold them and the brow which should have been impressive failed at the low hairline. To make up for this disunity – of which he must have been aware since he had once confessed to Kemp that he practised his important speeches in front of a mirror – Stoddart employed a trenchant style which had put the fear of God into many a hapless witness.

In today's case there was no need for such histrionics. A mere neighbourhood dispute about barking dogs, bad feelings, bad language and some bad law; in Kemp's opinion it should never have been brought before the Bench. Getting to his feet and saying so succinctly he caught the nods of approval from the magistrates and heard them dismiss the claim of Nick's client, with costs against him. Those who had retained Kemp grinned all over their homespun faces, despite their Worships' admonition for them too to go away and try to get on better with their neighbours.

That was entirely Nick's fault, thought Kemp, he went at it as if it was a murder trial at the Bailey.

Kemp stuffed the folder into the tattered old satchel he was using in place of the stolen briefcase, and bowed his way from the court. On the stairs he met Stoddart who, not surprisingly, was in a black mood.

'Damn that office at Roberts,' he fumed. 'They never get things right . . .'

'Hullo, Nick,' said Kemp. That's what you've always done when you lose a case, blame someone else. You should have advised your client properly, taken a closer look at the papers instead of indulging your penchant for bully-boy tactics . . . But Kemp knew better than to voice his thoughts; he didn't want a brawl on the steps of the court.

'What sods we've got on that bench . . . Soapy shopkeepers who don't know their arse from their elbow when it comes to law . . .' Stoddart was still splattering blame around like hailstones.

Kemp shrugged. 'Some you lose, some you win. Don't take it to heart, Nick, you've had victories in your time.'

But Stoddart only glared at him. 'I can do without your advice, thank you, Kemp . . .' He muttered, 'You . . . you just watch your own step . . .'

He swung away across the crowded floor of the entrance hall cannoning into a hapless usher on his way to the door. She was not the only one to stare after him in surprise. Kemp had long since buried his hostility towards Stoddart. There had been a future for the man with Gillorns, he had been well thought of at the London office. Did he still blame Kemp for what had amounted to dismissal? It had all happened years ago and he and Stoddart had met several times since Nick's return to Newtown, yet until today he had never wondered about any lingering bitterness . . . Those blasted letters . . . They were making him look askance at everyone.

On Friday evenings Kemp closed the office early, a custom which pleased the staff mightily, though it was not intended solely for their benefit. But it enabled the partners, the qualified assistants and the articled clerk to reserve a table in a local hostelry for refreshment and an informal chat about the week's work. There was little enough time for them to meet during office hours, each being in a sense compartmentalized within their own sphere, so it was an opportunity to raise issues, air particular problems and give voice to complaints on a more personal level than was possible within earshot of the clerical staff.

It was from such meetings that Kemp took his soundings as to the health, or otherwise, of his small establishment.

For the most part they were congenial get-togethers; policy decisions might be taken or abandoned, tricky points of law argued where diverse opinions were better than just one; occasionally, as on this evening, they were merely social. Now it was congratulations to Tony Lambert upon his getting engaged.

Glasses were raised to him. 'Never thought you'd get round to it, Tony . . . What brought you to the brink?'

Tony pushed at his large spectacles, a habit he had when embarrassed. The gesture tended to draw attention to a certain owl-like solemnity he had, an asset with his elderly clients. 'I suppose it was meeting someone like Anita,' he said, simply answering the question.

'Miss Allardyce . . .' Michael Cantley turned to Kemp. 'You've met her?'

'I've seen her about,' said Kemp. 'I gather she's at Guildford studying law.'

'She comes down here weekends to stay with her brother. He works for the Development Corporation . . . That's how we met.' Tony was flushed and happy. 'Which reminds me,

24

I hope you're all coming to our party on Tuesday night out at The Leas – that's Zachary Allardyce's place . . . He and Anita got together on the invitations . . .'

'Glad to see you settled at last.' Kemp meant what he said. He valued his young colleague highly, and knew his circumstances. Tony was a native of Newtown, his parents on the lower end of the local gentry, owning land in the original village. Tony, their only child, had lived with them, succoured them in their old age like a dutiful son, and mourned them when they died within months of each other.

In the past Tony had been seen around with various perfectly proper young women but the relationships had somehow never quite 'taken' . . . He was a serious type, though not a prig, and modest about his considerable intellect. It was said the Allardyce girl was bright . . . Kemp wondered if it was loneliness after his parents' death that had brought Tony to take this step towards marriage. At least people can't say that about me, he thought – I'd been on my own for so long I'd got used to it. He looked across at Tony who smiled back as if they followed the same line of thought.

'I'm only following your example, Lennox. Taking the plunge doesn't seem to have done you any harm . . .'

'I'm not so sure about that,' said Sally Stacey, 'I don't get the tax figures from Mr Kemp as quickly as I used to. I think his mind's on other things . . .'

'And I had to remind him about a maintenance hearing last week which he forgot,' said Perry Belchamber. 'Time was when it was him did all the reminding round here.'

'You have been distrait . . .' Michael Cantley had been happily married for years, and was prepared to make allowances. 'You did rather take the whole place on your shoulders before this, and now you have your own worries setting up home and all that . . .'

This was surely the time to tell them . . . Explain that the reason his mind had not been entirely on business lately had nothing to do with Mary or his marriage. They had the right to know about the letters, these colleagues and friends of his . . . They would exhibit astonishment, outrage, but he would have their sympathy.

But Franklyn Davey, their young articled clerk, was rather

nervously putting a question about a recent case in the Court of Appeal, and as everyone clamoured to give their point of view, the moment passed.

Kemp was to regret its passing . . .

'You'll be sure to bring Mary to Anita's party next week,' Tony said to him as the meeting was breaking up. 'We've seen so little of her, and I always liked her when she worked in the office. She might find it a little awkward, of course, seeing us all again in such different circumstances . . .'

Kemp laughed.

'I've come to the conclusion that my wife can handle any situation, but thanks for the thought. We'll both be delighted to come . . .'

Once again he would like to have drawn Tony aside and told him about the threats and the break-in, if it was only to share the burden with someone . . . Yet he hesitated, unwilling to strike a sour note on the evening of the younger man's celebration. In the past it had been Tony Lambert who had shared his confidences when Kemp felt it necessary, now the timing for such things was all wrong . . .

Yet as he walked home through the darkening streets he had a premonition that somehow he had missed a chance which would not be given again. He should have grasped it firmly when it was to his hand, not let it be whisked away in a moment of indecision.

One of the maxims by which he lived was never to lose control of events; he had the uneasy feeling that that was exactly what he had done.

CHAPTER 4

No day in the week separated the married from the single as much as Saturday. Hitherto, Kemp had taken the cessation of work lightly but by Sunday evenings, he had tended to return to the office, if only in spirit, out of a certain deprivation, though he would not have called it boredom. He was not a man of hobbies; what went on under the bonnet of his car was a mystery to him and he had never owned a garden until now.

Since his marriage, however, he looked forward to the weekends, and the time they allowed for him and Mary to be by themselves, enjoying each other's company and planning expeditions into the country. It was a felicity he had long forgotten.

This particular Saturday started off as no exception. Rising late, they were lounging about in their vast sunny kitchen, he drinking coffee at the table, she idly questioning whether soup or smoked salmon should begin their evening meal – idly, because she had already decided.

Newtown's local paper plopped on the new doormat, through the new letterbox in the new door – one hastily put in place the previous afternoon by a carpenter who said the old one was a fine bit of oak he could use on his garden shed.

'I like your *Newtown Gazette*,' said Mary, bringing it in. 'It's all so nicely irrelevant to the national news. All these pictures of happy brides with flowers in their hair beside bright-eyed boys, bashful in their collars and ties. And right next to them there's more bashful boys up in court for brawling in the pub. Sometimes the names are even the same . . .'

'That's Newtown for you. All human nature in a nutshell of newsprint. I have to read it to keep up with my clients, they only give me expurgated versions of themselves and I learn far more from the press . . .'

Mary was turning the pages. Suddenly, she stopped.

'Lennox . . .'

'What is it?'

She put down the paper on the table in front of him.

It was a headline, not on the front page, but a headline just the same.

Local Solicitor Threatened

It was divulged yesterday that Mr Lennox Kemp, of Gillorns, Solicitors, The Square, Newtown has been the recipient of 'poison pen' letters from an unknown sender. We understand that several of these have been received by Mr Kemp and that not only do they contain threats of personal injury but also imputations affecting Mr Kemp's professional reputation. On contacting the police we were informed by Detective Inspector John Upshire that the matter was already under investigation.

Kemp was still staring at the item in disbelief when the telephone rang.

'You can take it as fact it didn't come from the station.' Upshire was in a barking mood.

'Well, it certainly didn't come from me,' said Kemp.

'I couldn't be sure of that . . . Thought maybe you'd jumped the gun. I had to think fast when the *Gazette* got on to me asking if it was true you'd had letters. All I said was that if you had then we'd investigate.'

Kemp took a deep breath.

'It's damnable,' he said at last. 'Whoever pinched that briefcase leaked those letters to the press . . . Might not even be the sender. The *Gazette* phoned you? Why the hell didn't they get in touch with me first?'

'Would you have denied it?'

'I'd have said, no comment. That probably wouldn't have stopped them. It's damaging, though . . . That bit about reputation . . .'

'Was there something like that in the letters?'

'Enough.' Kemp was terse. 'Look, John, it's urgent you get moving on that break-in. I'll have a word with the editor. Alf Grimshaw's always played fair with me in the past. I'll see what I can get out of him as to source.'

'A journalist's source? No chance . . .' Upshire didn't sound hopeful as he rang off.

It was obvious at the *Newtown Gazette* that Alfred Grimshaw was expecting Kemp's call.

'Tried your office around five last evening but couldn't get you. It was too good an item to miss and the paper was ready to roll. You know how it is, Mr Kemp.'

'All I want from you is where the hell you got your information?'

'OK. OK. Keep your hair on. There was a phone call earlier. First thing Friday morning. Came in to the desk. The reporter who took it thought I'd better see it . . . Half a mo . . . I've got the note here. It was a man's voice, no name, of course. Said Mr Kemp was getting threatening letters, that it was in the local public interest for people to know, etc., etc. Well, I wouldn't have touched it with a bargepole, you know that, Mr Kemp. A delicate matter, and from an anonymous tip-off . . .'

'Then why the hell did you print it?'

'Because we got proof it was true. Came in later . . . A packet of letters in their envelopes, postmarked and addressed to you – and opened.'

'How many?'

'Three . . . That's why I tried to phone you . . . But the story couldn't wait. My reporter called Upshire. He's a friend of yours, isn't he? We reckoned if there was anything in it he'd be the one to know. My man was sure he did.'

'I suppose that packet came by hand and nobody saw who brought it?'

'Right. Dropped in the outside box Friday lunchtime. Look, Mr Kemp, it was an item of local interest, besides having the makings of a good story. We might even be able to help in following it up . . . And we certainly wouldn't print what's in those letters. It's vicious stuff. I think perhaps you ought to have them back.'

'I think so too. After all, they are my private correspondence,' Kemp said, with some sarcasm. 'Who's seen them at your office?'

'Only myself and the reporter who took the call, Dan Frobisher. I can vouch for him keeping his mouth shut, but, as I've said, the *Gazette* may be able to help . . . Sometimes these things are better out in the open . . .'

'The voice of the press in the interests of the great British public . . .' Kemp could not help the sardonic note, but he had to admit that Grimshaw had a point. 'Could you send Frobisher round here with those letters before they go any further? And I'd like them in the same packet in which they were delivered. Your item was correct, the police are investigating and John Upshire will soon spike your guns if anything else gets printed in the meantime.'

'Right-oh . . . Just so long as we get the full story in the end, Mr Kemp.'

Mary looked at him closely when he came back from the phone.

'More coffee?' She was calm, she was rarely otherwise.

She put two fresh cups on the table, poured and sat down opposite him.

'What harm can it do?' she asked.

'The bit about reputation is nasty . . . and I'd rather I'd told my colleagues about the letters than have them read about them in the *Gazette*. I've had letters before threatening to have me struck off, usually from people who think we've overcharged them or disgruntled husbands who're sure I'm having it off with their wives . . . But these are only crackpots getting something out of their systems, and they soon stop. This joker's different, he or she is relentless – and they hark back to the fact that I'd been struck off before . . .'

'But that was nearly twenty years ago, and you've said yourself anyone in the legal profession can look it up.'

'Mud sticks, Mary . . .'

'Only if you let it . . . I grew up in so much of it I never noticed. But I can see how it might be different for you. All the same, I am more concerned with the death threats. Your reputation is important to you but I don't want to read about it on a tombstone.'

30

'I think that's one of the nicest things that's ever been said to me.'

Kemp spoke lightly but the underlying meaning was clear to both of them; when people come together in their middle years the relationship is deepened by knowledge of the fragility of such a merger. They were still holding hands when the doorbell rang.

Daniel Frobisher was not what Kemp expected; he thought of reporters as eager young men in leather jackets. Frobisher was in his fifties and soberly dressed in a grey suit. He was a stocky man of good features. Glasses did not quite conceal a cast in his left eye which gave him a slightly sinister look until one became reconciled to it.

'Mr Kemp? Of course, I've seen you in court. Mrs Kemp, we haven't met?' His glance swept briefly over her. 'Sorry to intrude on your Saturday leisure.'

He was already in the hall. 'Nice house, this. Glad to see you've not altered it. A good period for architecture.'

'Do come in, Mr Frobisher,' Kemp told him, rather belatedly. 'We can talk in the study.'

He led the way into the small room designated as such, though so far unused since the habits of a single man had been already cast off by Kemp, without regret.

Mary hovered for a moment in the doorway.

'I have to shop, Lennox, or there'll be no meals in this house today. Nice meeting you, Mr Frobisher.'

'She's an American, your wife?' asked Frobisher as soon as he heard the front door close.

'Is she?' said Kemp, pleasantly. 'I hadn't noticed . . . Now, Mr Grimshaw said you had a packet of letters for me.'

'Sure. Sure. Here it is.' Frobisher struggled with an inner pocket and produced a brown paper package. Kemp took it from him. It was unmarked, unaddressed and had been originally sealed with Sellotape. He shook out the contents which he recognized instantly: three envelopes postmarked and bearing his address. He was aware of the reporter's eyes upon him as he carefully scrutinized the letters.

'All present and correct, squire?' It was a sobriquet which Kemp particularly deprecated, but here the style bespoke the man: Frobisher was the sort who would see himself as equal in any company.

'I think so. Will you thank your editor for me? I understand from him you will keep your discretion.'

As if on cue, Dan Frobisher laid a surprisingly well-manicured finger along the side of his nose. 'Mum's the word. You can count on me. Is that all, Mr Kemp?'

'All for now, Mr Frobisher. What else did you have in mind?'

'I'm a reporter, squire . . . Just doing my job, like you do yours . . .'

'Look, there's nothing further in this for you – at least for the present.'

Frobisher walked round the big desk, looked down at its bare surface, then transferred his gaze to the bookshelves where Kemp had begun to arrange his literary treasures. 'H'm . . . the classics . . . I'm a great reader myself, Mr Kemp . . . "A Good Book is the Precious Life-blood of a Master Spirit" . . . I remember that from my schooldays . . . You've a nice set of Disraeli there . . . Who do you think wrote them?'

Kemp stopped himself saying, 'Disraeli, of course.' He knew exactly what Frobisher was up to – the man must have been studying the techniques of television interviewers.

'I've no idea,' he said, smoothly.

'Oh, come on, surely you haven't got that many disgruntled clients.'

Frobisher turned from his contemplation of the Victorian brown-and-gold bindings, and grinned at Kemp.

There was no doubt here was a man on the make. He had scented a good story, perhaps one of the few to come within the orbit of a small provincial paper, and he had decided to milk it for all it was worth. Kemp was wary of journalists, but they were a breed he had no wish to antagonize.

'Shall we just say the question is an open one? Your editor has suggested the services of the *Gazette* might be used . . . These services at the moment require you to keep your mouth shut, Mr Frobisher. When the writer of these letters is discovered Inspector Upshire will issue a statement. In the meantime I have no comment to make.'

'Now there's a phrase sticks like wax in the ears . . . Mine, I keep 'em open, Mr Kemp. That little item this morning, you may not like it but it'll get people talking . . . Stir things up a bit. Might make it easier for the police to get their man . . .' He had turned to the bookshelves again, peering at the titles. 'Lord Lytton, eh? That's turgid stuff . . . D'you suppose anybody reads him now?'

'Not as many as read the *Newtown Gazette*. Did it never occur to you that the reason those letters were delivered to your paper was simply that, to stir things up? The publication of that little item, as you call it, has helped neither myself nor the police to find the culprit.'

Kemp disliked talking to any man's back so he opened the study door and walked into the hall, leaving Frobisher no alternative but to follow. Eventually he did so, but with reluctance.

'I like your taste in houses, Mr Kemp, like your choice of books, old-fashioned but very correct. A good image for a solicitor . . . Can't afford a blot on the escutcheon. Leatown, wasn't it?'

If it was meant as a disabling shot it misfired – Kemp was ready for it.

'A good reporter does his homework, Mr Frobisher, and I can see you've done yours. But that story's been dead for twenty years, and if you're thinking of bringing it back to life I would remind you of the little matter of difference between libel as a tort and libel as a criminal offence. You're a well-read man, Mr Frobisher, so I shall detain you no further on the subject – nor on any other.'

'No offence meant, squire – and none taken, I hope. Homework always was a bind but it had to be done. From what I gathered, you had a rough time of it back then . . . And you've helped put away a few villains since you came to Newtown. Don't think I don't appreciate that.' There was even a hint of admiration in Frobisher's voice as he flipped out a card. 'Call me any time.'

'Thanks.'

Slightly mollified, Kemp took the card as he opened the front door.

'That's a fine new bit of timber you've got there, but it's

not a patch on the old one,' Frobisher remarked as he went down the step. 'Some say we need neighbourhood-watch schemes . . . Newtown's always had 'em, neighbours watching robberies like it was television only not so exciting . . .'

Though cynical, the observation was apt. Kemp had also found the people of Newtown anxious to keep themselves to themselves, like the three monkeys, when it came to cooperation with the forces of law and order, an attitude which did little to diminish the crime figures.

He thought of this, and of other things, as he closed the door and went back to his study to ponder on the interview. Was Daniel Frobisher as smart as he made out, or had he merely picked up a few tricks of investigative journalism with which to dazzle the natives? At his age he should have wider scope than his present job on a local weekly mostly given over to weddings and obituaries, and only occasionally enlivened by reported rows in the council chamber.

'He was thorough,' Kemp told Mary over lunch. 'I'll say that in his favour.'

'Thoroughly bad.' Mary held to a definite opinion. 'I didn't like him one bit.'

'You hardly saw him.'

'I saw enough. He gave me a passing glance and decided I wasn't pretty enough to bother with . . .'

'He didn't get as far as your ankles. Anyway, you can't blame him for simply overlooking you. I wouldn't want someone like him taking an interest.'

'Neither would I. It's lucky for you, Lennox, that you married a plain woman. Those who are fair of face have significance for men, they start wondering where the husband got hold of her and what's she like in bed.'

Kemp watched his wife as she peeled an apple. Everything Mary Madeleine did she did with the same quiet intentness, as if all that mattered was the here and now. She was the most concentrated person he had ever met. Yet she could let her mind fly, and her words, too, when the fancy caught her as it had just done.

'Do you know who he's married to?' she said.

'I never thought to ask.'

'Amy Robsart.'

'Not Leicester's love? Shut up in Cumnor Hall so lone and drear?'

'I don't think so.' Mary went on cutting up her apple. 'I've no idea what you're talking about. Amy's the daughter of the Robsarts at the corner shop where we get our papers.'

Kemp had to shift gear to keep up with her.

'Someone else has been doing their homework . . . How did you come by this gem?'

'I was paying our account when Mrs Robsart did a tut-tut about that item in the *Gazette*. Terrible thing, Mr Kemp getting them poison-pen letters . . . So I said we'd a Mr Frobisher in the house right now helping us with our enquiries. Don't they call that a euphemism?'

'They do, and it's got nothing to do with euphony, which means harmony.' He knew Mary's concern for the niceties of the English language, a topic barely skimmed in her American school – admittedly a fairly low-grade one where her attendance had been erratic. Coming late to academic learning, she was saved from error by natural wit and from pretensions by wide experience of life at ground level. She thought of herself as a slow thinker; in Kemp's view she could outstrip the field if the stakes were the survival of the fittest.

'Well, there was little harmony in the Robsart household when Mr Frobisher seduced their youngest a few years back. Apparently he fought shy of fatherhood but Mr Robsart's an ex-boxer himself so the nuptials duly took place. Naturally, it's no good word they're saying of their son-in-law.'

'How did you get all that out of Mrs Robsart? She's always been pretty taciturn with me.'

Mary considered it for a moment, then she said: 'People in Newtown don't know how to place me – in the English sense – so, because I'm ordinary, and nothing much to look at, they take me as one of themselves . . . They like to talk and I'm a good listener.'

And you have the common touch, thought Kemp. Loving her as he did, he meant nothing derogatory, rather that it was an attribute too rarely given the place it deserved. He had had it once himself when he had been struck off by the Law Society and the only job he could get was as an enquiry agent in the East End of London. He wouldn't have survived for long in Walthamstow had he lacked the common touch.

'And I got more . . .' said Mary, as she piled the plates neatly, one on top of the other. 'I was asking Mrs Robsart about the times her boys deliver the papers in the morning, and she told me one of the lads saw a person at our door last Thursday about half past seven but they scuttled off so fast he couldn't say whether it was man or boy, or even a girl . . . What it is, there's a bit of rivalry in the paper rounds, the newsagents from up in the town trying to butt in. The Robsarts get up in arms if they think there's poaching on their ground so the paperboys are told to report back if they see anything . . .'

'Why the hell didn't they tell the police?'

'Oh, Lennox, when will you ever learn? They don't talk to the police. Some of the lads, they'll be underage . . . But they're desperate for the job.'

'All the same, I'll pass the word . . . Might get a description. Boys have bright eyes.'

'They'll keep them skinned in future; Mrs Robsart, she'll see to that. All this one got was a glimpse of a flapping raincoat and a cap pulled down over the ears.'

'Still, it's better than nothing. Tell your tale to John when he comes this evening, and I'll give him those letters handed over by our friend, Frobisher.'

'Let me have a look at them when I've finished the washing-up.'

'They're not the most dangerous,' she decided, when Kemp had spread them out on the study table. Nevertheless, she shuddered. 'I hate to think of that Paul Pry reading them, especially that bit . . .'

She pointed to it:

You was found wanting once before. Sticky fingers in the till, wasn't it? You got six years for that. Nothing to what you'll get from me one dark night . . .

'Might be worse,' said Kemp, grimly. 'Whoever the mischief-maker is who dropped them in on the press he probably hoped they'd print the lot . . . Make people think I'd gone to prison for a six-year term . . . Thank God Grimshaw has a healthy respect for the laws on libel.'

'And Frobisher?'

'He checked up on my record, of course. Well, it's his job. I'm only angry that my colleagues at the office had to find out about the letters this way. I should have told them earlier . . .'

They had all been on the telephone that day, and Michael Cantley had called round. He was appalled when he saw the contents of the three letters.

'Are they all like this?' he asked.

Kemp nodded. 'Some of the others were more specific about the way I should be dealt with. What do you think, Mike, of the letters themselves?'

Cantley read them again, carefully.

'Someone who goes back a fair way. A case that went wrong, the injustice thing comes through. Real bitterness . . . But, I don't know, Lennox, there's something funny about the actual phrasing, the vagueness . . . I'd like to have studied them all. Why on earth didn't you tell us?'

'They were too personal. It's only the more recent that hinted at a slur on reputation . . . It was then I began to think of damage to the firm . . . And now there's this item in the *Gazette*.'

'Oh, we can ride that one out, though I don't think the paper should have printed anything without checking with you first. If you like I'll have a word with the local Law Society . . . See whether we should issue a disclaimer.'

'I'd be glad if you would, Mike; it would be better done through the firm. I've got photocopies of the others, by the way – these are originals.'

'You got these from Dan Frobisher? I know him. He's a bit cocky but he's a good reporter, does most of the court stuff for the *Gazette*. I think he'll be discreet if there's something in it for him in the end. He's been around Newtown longer than you have, Lennox, though I can't imagine why he stays . . . He and Nick Stoddart used to be thick, possibly still are now that Nick's back.'

'That's a combination I can well do without.' Kemp sighed. 'But it's time I stopped getting paranoic about everyone I meet.'

37

CHAPTER 5

John Upshire set off for dinner at No. 2, Albert Crescent in the mood of a man with nothing better to do on a Saturday night. It was preferable, marginally, to eating a takeaway meal in front of the television. He was uneasy, however, at the prospect of again meeting Kemp's wife who he still thought of as Mary Madeleine Blane because of the file on her he had once received from the New York Police Department. That nothing in that file had ever been proceeded with had come as a relief to Inspector Upshire who had no wish to get embroiled in matters best left to the American authorities.

In the event the case had been satisfactorily dealt with by some tricky footwork on the part of Lennox Kemp, the legal complexities of which the inspector did not wish to know, and would not have understood if he had. All the same, Kemp did not have to go and marry the woman . . .

As Upshire strode through the streets of Newtown he made up his mind that he would distance himself from the new Mrs Kemp. Although this might be construed as resentment at the marriage, it was more a question of how he felt about her as a person. Upshire was not given to analysing his feelings; all he knew was that tonight he had the hump.

Halfway through dinner he realized that he was enjoying himself as he had not done for years. The atmosphere was relaxed, there were no signs of tension between them (he was the only guest), the conversation was agreeable and the food delicious.

John Upshire was amazed to find himself talking to Mary about Betty's last illness, a thing he had never spoken of before. Mary had nursed many such patients and understood. She listened with quiet sympathy but a calm detachment, showing that her interest was in him rather than the

38

circumstances since his wife's death had happened some seven years ago.

It was not that becoming Mrs Kemp had changed Mary Madeleine's appearance. Upshire had considered her a plain, unprepossessing woman the first time he met her, and she still had the same too-wide brow, a narrow, rather stubborn chin, and a general colourlessness which did not make for beauty. But she gave a straight look from her pale grey eyes, and she smiled a lot . . . It's the Irish in her, thought Upshire, who was well aware of her parentage, and he admired the way her soft brown hair was cut in a bob so that it swung out like a bell when she turned her head.

She had forbidden any mention of the letters during the meal.

'My cooking would not be getting the full attention of your mouths if I allowed it,' she said. 'Taste first, you can talk afterwards.'

'Take your port into the study like gentlemen,' she told them as she began clearing the dishes. 'I'll be bringing coffee in a while.'

Kemp spread the letters out on the table, smoothed the brown paper they had been wrapped in, and added his photo-copies of the others.

Upshire studied them all closely.

'I've sent a man to fingerprint the *Gazette* staff – though Mr Grimshaw says only the office boy who took it from the box, himself and Dan Frobisher actually handled the package. It was Frobisher who opened it. And I've got a transcript here of the note he took of that phone call. Apparently whoever it was asked for him.'

'Asked for Frobisher himself?'

Upshire shrugged. 'It's well known he's their crime reporter. He sees to it he gets his by-line . . .'

'You know him, John?'

'Over the years, yes. He's in and out of the station – that's his job. Never given us any trouble, though . . . My men get on with him . . . Doesn't badger us, like some . . . He'll push for a story if he thinks there's anything in it . . .'

'He's already tried pushing me,' said Kemp, grimly.

He told Upshire about the reporter's visit, at which the inspector raised his eyebrows, sceptically.

'But that's a dead duck. Why'd he bring it up now?'

'Presumably because our secret scribbler has already done so.' Kemp pointed out certain parts in the letters.

'H'm . . . they only hint at something . . . But surely anyone could find out?'

'If they thought it worth their while . . . So far as my profession is concerned, it's over and done with long ago. But the slur is there . . . If they had been specific it could do less harm.'

'I see what you mean.' The inspector looked again through the letters for a moment. 'You think this chap's clever? I think he's a nutcase.'

'I'll not be agreeing with you there, John,' said Mary Kemp as she brought in the tray. 'I wish I could . . . If a person is mentally deranged, they'd give themselves away by doing other crazy things than just writing letters. It's the sane I'm afraid of.'

'Mary thinks they could be written by a woman,' said Kemp.

Upshire shook his head. 'Looks more like a man to me.'

'When Michael Cantley read them,' said Kemp, slowly, 'he thought there was something odd about the phrasing. The same thing had struck me. It's as if ideas had been tossed about before being committed to paper, like people do when there's two of them working on a script . . .'

'You think there's two of them?' exclaimed Upshire.

'That's it,' said Mary, eagerly. 'A man and a woman. That would account for the use of phrases that don't seem to me to quite match up.'

'You've got me out of my depth.' John Upshire accepted a cup of coffee, piled sugar into it, and drank. 'When the analysts have done with them, mebbe a shrink should have a look . . . There's some nasty threats in there, Lennox, and I don't mean the ones about revealing your murky past. It's your immediate future I've got in mind . . .'

He got a grateful glance from Mary for that.

'It's what I'm always telling Lennox. If this person, or these persons, really want to harm him, then he's in danger. That stuff put through our letterbox . . .'

She told the inspector about what the delivery boy had seen, and he promised to look into it without upsetting the Robsarts. Then he turned to Kemp.

'That accident to your car, Lennox, we haven't a hope in hell . . . The London Road on a wet night, people are skidding all over the place . . . and you never got a proper look at the van. No, what I have to concentrate on is the theft of your briefcase, and how that ties in with the letters being leaked to the *Gazette*.'

'Goes with my theory that there's more than one person involved . . . If their object is just to cause me embarrassment, maybe lose me a few jittery clients, they've picked the wrong man. I'll not be done to death by slanderous tongues . . .'

Mary smiled at Upshire. 'That's the wine speaking out of him,' she said. 'He's started on his quotes . . .'

But Upshire, more perceptive now, saw the disquiet in her eyes as she went on: 'Yet I don't like to hear the word death on anyone's lips . . .'

'Don't you worry, Mary . . .' It was the first time the inspector had used her name. 'In my experience real killers don't send letters about what they're going to do. You can take my word for that. And we'll catch this joker before he does any more damage. You can count on me . . .'

As he left the Kemps' house John Upshire wished he could be as confident as he hoped he had sounded. He hated cases like this where there was nothing really to get hold of; burglary, theft, attempted arson, these were run-of-the-mill petty crimes in Newtown . . . And, digging deeper, he had no doubt that there were families in the town with enough hatred in them to conspire at mailing poison-pen letters like those his friend was getting – John Upshire would put nothing past some of the crooks he'd known.

Dismissing such thoughts from his mind – for surely an examination of them and some slogging by his own men would bring up something – he walked with a lighter step than he had earlier in the evening. Whatever her past, Mary Kemp was a pleasant woman of more than ordinary gifts,

41

and he could understand now why Kemp had married her.

Watching her moving about in the big old-fashioned draw-ing room which, despite its spaciousness, she had contrived to make cosy, he had seen how, when their eyes met, she and her husband had the glowing look of people in love. Upshire felt a pang, a memory of something long forgotten. As the evening had gone on, and he knew he had been accepted not only as Lennox's friend but as hers also, his unease had vanished. When she assured him on leaving that he would always be a welcome guest in their house he knew she was not simply mouthing civilities.

John Upshire was a policeman, not given to much intro-spection. In his job he felt he was like the soldier, his not to reason why, his priority to investigate the crime, search out the criminal and hand him or her over to the law, for he was neither judge nor jury – though often he questioned the decisions of both, but only in the privacy of his own mind. He was well aware of the limitations imposed by his work, the lack of social life, the occasional distrust of acquaintances . . .

So, he was all the more grateful tonight to find himself quite uplifted. Wine, good food, congenial company – and friendship – he valued them for they were rare in his experience.

Having accepted their marriage, he wished well for the Kemps.

CHAPTER 6

It was Tuesday evening. Mary Kemp turned from the dressing table and looked at her husband.

'Glum-face,' she said, 'you're not really wanting to go to this party, are you?'

'I suppose not. I'm not easy with the people in the office at the moment. There's an awkwardness between us because of the letters – the way they found out. It's only natural, they have the firm to think of and their own careers. Mike Cantley's all right, and probably Belchamber . . . he takes the broad view, and, having been a barrister, he's never taken by surprise. For the rest, well, I simply don't know . . . Tony Lambert of course is up on cloud nine because of his love life, but I'm sure that nasty item in the paper shook him, he's very conventional, our Tony. Because he always does the decent thing he expects everyone else to do likewise.'

'A vain hope in a naughty world,' said Mary, smoothing her dress. It was a misty blue which deepened the dark brown of her hair, and for once she had used eyeshadow. 'How do I look?'

'Like a mouse in blue spectacles . . . No, don't brush it off, it suits you . . . I think that's the cab at the door.'

Kemp was still without his car, which irked him. Lorimers' Garage had had it over a week but had just taken delivery of a spare part damaged in the incident on the London Road and had told him it would not be ready until tomorrow evening. Kemp had been perverse about not accepting their offer of a hired car; he thought the walking would do him good, though he was not overfond of the exercise, and after a week he'd had enough of it.

'As soon as I pass my driving test I'm going to buy a Mini of my own,' said Mary, as they were being driven off. Although she had never possessed a motor vehicle in her life

43

– an odd distinction in an American – Mary was a very competent driver; Kemp had not asked her where she got the experience. 'And then we shall be a two-car family like those people everyone tries to keep up with, the Joneses, isn't it?'

'Never heard of them,' said Kemp, 'so we'll just have to make do with the Allardyces. Tony says they have quite a place . . .'

It was indeed. Even Kemp was startled at the size of it. Simply called The Leas after the original meadows upon which it was built, the sprawling modern bungalow occupied a large area with plenty to spare for wide lawns and winding walks through newly planted shrubberies. The drive was brightly lit by spotlights fixed on iron standards.

'Well, I do believe these are old streetlamps,' said Kemp, peering out. 'I wonder where young Allardyce picked them up? Probably perks from the Development Corporation he works for. How very ingenious . . .'

The word ingenious is not one readily applied to an Australian sheep-shearer, and that is what Zachary Allardyce looked like. Tall, bronzed and blond, any typecaster would have swooped on him for the part.

He was not immediately introduced to Kemp, who only came upon his host after doing the dutiful circulating expected of guests at these affairs. When Anita's brother was eventually pointed out to Kemp by Tony Lambert he was deep in conversation with Mary Kemp. As Kemp approached them he heard the true twang of Australian vowels.

'Zachary's a crazy name. I mean, who wants to be called something out of the Bible these days . . .'

'I rather like it,' Mary said. 'The biblical thing . . . Back in the States now, they go in for it too, call their sons Seth or Joshua, Daniel or even Jeremiah . . . as if it sets the seal of the Almighty on them . . .'

Allardyce laughed – as indeed she intended him to.

'I shorten mine to Zack . . . One-syllable names are easier to yell out over a great distance.'

'And I'm sure there's plenty of that where you come from.'

'Yes, ma'am . . . The old man – that's my dad – he still runs the sheep station, but Anita and I, well, we quit . . .

44

Wider horizons, you know ... Like in your country, the young must branch out ...'

'They surely do.' Kemp could see that Mary Madeleine was enjoying herself; she was using one of her many voices. 'Either they end up wealthy on Wall Street or broke in The Bowery ... Oh, have you met my husband, Lennox Kemp?'

Zack Allardyce gave Kemp a handshake that would have pulled his fingers out of shape had it lasted longer.

'Mr Kemp. We've not spoken but of course I've seen you around Newtown.'

It was the second time recently someone had said that to Kemp; more folk know Tom Fool than Tom Fool knows, he thought. He must have gone around with his eyes shut to miss so large a specimen.

'At various planning enquiries,' Allardyce explained. 'I remember you represented that little parish council – Amwell, wasn't it? – when our Development Corporation took over the gravel pits.'

'And won a famous victory ...' It had not been that for Kemp, nor for the villagers of Amwell. They had had this pretty spot with a flowing brook and a deep, translucent pool. Kemp remembered there had been words carved on the little bridge, and he murmured them now: 'Sweet Amwell, Blessed Be Thy Stream ...'

All gone now of course under the desert of the diggings.

'Progress, Lennox ... Can't be stopped, you know.'

'Someone said progress would be wonderful if only it would stop,' Kemp remarked, with a smile. 'I notice the Corporation's gravel workings have fallen on lean times of late.'

'Recession. Hits everybody ...' Zack Allardyce waved at a tray of wine which was passing, and had their glasses replenished. 'I liked your style, Lennox, you put up a good fight for the place, but my Corporation looks to the future, you know ...'

Kemp didn't like being patronized, nor the inference that he had somehow been relegated to the past. Although Zack was at least ten years older than his sister, he was still a young man and it might be that he yet had much to learn about his adopted country.

As if picking up her husband's thought, Mary turned

the conversation by asking how long Zachary had been in England.

Some considerable time, it seemed. He had come as a student, taken his degree here – he did not specify at which university – and, after a stint in local government, he had been, in his own words, snapped up by the Newtown Development Corporation some three years ago.

'Planning's my forte,' he told them, 'so I stick to working in the new towns. Gives me scope for my ideas . . .'

'You'll not be wanting to go back to Australia, then,' said Mary, innocently. 'There can't be much need for planning there with all that empty space to fill and no historic ruins to knock down . . .'

'I don't intend going back. That's why I advised my sister to come over and do her law here. We're both staying in your tight little island, you can bet on that . . . Ah, here's Anita . . . I expect you've already met Lennox Kemp. This is his wife.'

Anita Allardyce was also fair-complexioned but in no other way did she resemble her formidable brother. She was a small girl, chunky rather than slim, with intelligent blue eyes set wide apart. She had the bouncy look of one in perfect health, and attractive because of it.

'I didn't recognize you at first,' said Mary, 'but I've seen you jogging in the local park. You wear a bandana thing round your hair . . .'

'But not tonight.' Anita laughed, and shook out her red-gold mane which was waved and frizzed in the present dishevelled fashion of the young.

'Why, you're a right little lion cub!' exclaimed Mary, who sometimes said exactly what she thought.

The two ladies went off together, Zack abandoned Kemp and moved away through the crowd like a tall ship in a fishing fleet.

'I see our friend Stoddart's here.' Mike Cantley had come up and was whispering in Kemp's ear. 'How's he connected to the Allardyces?'

'Well, Roberts get most of the Corporation's legal work when we are on the opposite side – which happens quite often these days.'

'Letting Nick loose on planning must be like sending a bull into a china shop,' Cantley muttered. 'Look out, he's heading this way. I'm off . . . I don't want my evening's enjoyment spoiled.'

'Hullo, Lennox, Gillorns in full force tonight, eh? Nothing like presenting a solid front . . .' It was obvious that Stoddart had already imbibed more than his share of the wine.

'It's Tony's engagement party, Nick,' said Kemp, smoothly, 'so naturally the firm is here to help him celebrate.'

'The Allardyce kid? She'll eat him alive, that one . . . Great chap, her brother Zack . . . Did you know he's now a high-flier with the old Corp? And nearly was a corpse that esh-establishment till he took over . . .'

'Its work was done,' said Kemp, shortly, 'the town's built. All they're doing now is scrub round the edges.'

'Which don't suit you conservash . . . conservationists . . .' Nick had trouble with the word, so he changed the subject, at the same time modifying his voice and mien — a good barrister's trick if done swiftly enough to disarm an opponent. Unhappily for Stoddart, alcohol had slowed him down and the effect was merely clownish. 'You need friends, Lennox, at a time like this . . .' He went on nodding solemnly like a drinking duck. 'Of course, we in the profession know all about your bad time, but no shouting it from the rooftops, eh?'

Usually Kemp could be amused by Stoddart's antics but tonight he was not in a forgiving mood. He was saved from throwing something bitter in Nick's face — vermouth by choice but probably only words — by the appearance of Mary at his side. She must have heard at least some of the conversation.

'They are serving supper, Lennox,' she said, taking his arm, 'in the conservatory . . . As near as the Australians can get to the great outdoors, I suppose, but it will be chilly . . .'

'So, this is the little lady . . .' Stoddart bent his huge head down towards her, and his loosely held wine glass spilled out a few drops on the shoulder of her dress.

'Not so little, and certainly no lady.' Mary fixed him with a direct look. 'Nor are you so great as a man that you can't carry your liquor either inside or out . . .'

47

As she gently towed Kemp away she continued in a clear, carrying voice: 'And it's better manners than that I've had from the drunks on Skid Row . . .'

It was the kind of party where by suppertime those who had indulged themselves too freely were loose of tongue whilst those who had remained sober were grown embarrassed and lacked conviviality. That there had to be the two camps arose naturally from the presence of so many lawyers who knew the extent of police surveillance on the roads home. The various couples split fairly amicably along the line between drinking and driving but the resulting disunity hardly helped the party spirit. Fortunately no expense had been spared, so the food was some consolation.

The members of Gillorns drifted together in an unconscious gesture of solidarity with Tony Lambert. Zack Allardyce dominated the other end of the long table set out under a glass roof among a jungle of potted plants in various stages of greenness and demonstrating verdant health in some, despondent wilt in others.

Sally couldn't take her eyes off Zack. 'He looks like a TV ad for Fosters . . . You can almost see the wide open spaces between his ears . . .'

Young Franklyn had been at the wine. He gave a loud guffaw – brought on as much by surprise than anything else; he was rather in awe of Miss Stacey as he was finding revenue law beyond his powers. Besides, she didn't often make jokes.

Nick Stoddart looked up from where he was sitting mid-table next to Anita. 'I recognize Gillorns's virgin tax expert,' he muttered, 'and I think she of all people should keep her lip buttoned . . . Who's the whipper-snapper who thinks she's funny?'

'Franklyn Davey . . . He's their articled clerk,' Anita told him. 'Since your time, I expect. Didn't you used to work at Gillorns?'

'Long time ago . . .' Nick's voice was blurred . . . 'Before I went on to better things . . . Just like you're doing, honey . . .'

Anita went rather pink. 'Oh, it's not fixed yet . . .' she began, but found her companion wasn't listening. He had found something more interesting going on further up the table. Zachary had tackled Lennox Kemp on the subject of the item in the local paper.

'Hi, there, Lennox . . . Are these real poison-pen letters?'

'Not up for discussion, Mr Allardyce,' Kemp said firmly. He was damned if he'd get on first-name terms with the man.

Nick leaned forward so that his chin was level with his fruit salad.

'That's right . . . No dirty linen, if you please . . .' He wagged his finger in the air. 'Anonymous . . . synonymous . . . And your sins will find you out . . . Y'know what they say . . .'

'What does synonymous mean?' asked Mary of the table in general. 'I don't think it's got anything to do with sinning.'

'And you'd be right, Mrs Kemp,' said Franklyn, eager to be of help. 'It only means equal to . . . on a par with . . .'

'Young Mr Bloody Know-all . . .' muttered Stoddart. 'In my day articled clerks knew their place . . .' He pawed Anita's arm to bring her attention back to him. 'You thinking of getting your articles with Gillorns?'

She coloured slightly, but whether it was at his touch or because of the question an observer could not have known. 'I hope so,' she said, rather primly, 'once I've taken my Part One exams this summer.'

Kemp was surprised; the subject had not been bruited before – at least not in his presence. He looked round for Tony but he was already at the door saying goodbye to the Cantleys.

The party was breaking up. It did not seem the right time to ask Tony whether it was his suggestion that Anita Allardyce should join the firm. Kemp doubted it; Tony was a stickler for doing things the right way, he would have spoken to Kemp first. It looked as if the lion cub – as Mary had called her – had a way with her . . .

Later, Kemp found himself next to Tony in the hall. Around them the departing guests were jostling for coats, calling up taxis, looking for their spouses, arranging lifts for those unfit to drive, and taking farewell of their host and hostess. For a few moments there was a revival of the original happy atmosphere.

'You still without your car, Lennox?' Tony asked him.

'Get it back tomorrow night, thank goodness . . .'

'You know I'm up in town all day tomorrow? It's to do with my parents' estate, and I've got several other little errands' – he looked across at Anita, meaningfully – 'including a present she doesn't know about yet . . .'

'That's all right, Tony. Your department runs itself anyway. You'll miss that Law Society Branch meeting on the budget but Sally can fill you in later.'

'Pity about the meeting . . . I'm afraid I'd clean forgotten . . . But this business in town can't wait. As you know, I'm sole executor and it's the final winding-up . . .'

'You won't be missing much. It's a nuisance for me, too . . . I'd meant to pick up my car earlier but Lorimer says it won't be ready till after five and that's when the Branch meets. Sally's going to take me in her car and then she'll drop me off at the garage later. The way some of these old boys drone on it'll be after eight before we get away. But David Lorimer will leave my car out back as he usually does so I'll just pick it up there after the meeting.'

'You still go to Lorimers'? Bit out of the way, isn't it?'

'David Lorimer's an old client of ours. Besides, he's always given me good service. As you know, I'm hopeless with what goes on under the bonnet . . . Hey, I think that's my coat you've got there.'

'Gosh, I thought it was mine,' said Tony, handing it over. 'I've never known you wear an overcoat . . .'

'Comes of getting married, and coddled. As a single man I never felt I needed a coat, but now Mary insists . . .'

'Well,' said Tony, 'it looks as if you and I go to the same outfitters.'

'Difficult not to. Newtown's hardly the metropolis . . .'

'That reminds me,' said Tony. 'Do you want any errands run while I'm up in town tomorrow? I could call in at Clement's Inn –'

'Definitely not,' Kemp interrupted with some fervour. The last thing he wanted was for Gillorns Head Office to get wind of any trouble at the Newtown end. 'I'm keeping a very low

50

profile as far as they're concerned until this nasty business blows over – as I'm sure it will . . .'

The good wine had got to him, and the effect was to make grave matters seem of less moment.

Young Lambert, on the other hand, had been anxious under the eye of his beloved, and therefore somewhat abstemious. 'I hope so, Lennox, indeed I do. Doesn't do the firm any favours this thing getting out.'

Had Kemp been his usual discerning self he would have recognized a fair comment from one who was both colleague and close friend. In his present euphoric state, however, he only grinned and said: 'Nothing for any of us to worry about – certainly not you. Have a nice day in town. Did you say something about a present for your fiancée? I hope she likes it, women can be difficult to please . . . Ah, here's my wife with that expression on her face which says I'm talking too much . . .'

'Our taxi is here, Lennox,' said Mary, squeezing his arm. 'Let's go and say the proper things to the Allardyces.'

But Zachary had loomed up behind them, and he laughed.

'Don't spoil yourself by being proper, Mary,' he said. It was obvious that he was rather taken with her. 'All these English, now . . . they're too damned polite. Except when they drink, of course. You were a bit hard on old Nick Stoddart, but then you're a pretty direct lady. Comes of you being an American, I suppose . . .'

'Comes of me being me,' said Mary, firmly. 'Thank you for a very enjoyable evening. Now I must have a word with your sister.'

Zachary seemed anxious not to let Kemp go. He began a rambling account of a recent planning appeal which had been settled in favour of what he called 'his' corporation, dropping some influential local names along the way and making much of his own contribution. Kemp listened politely but with no great interest in the matter, although he was intrigued by the Australian's self-esteem and could see that it could have impact in some quarters.

He was about to turn away when Allardyce stopped him again. 'I say, Lennox, I'm sorry if I was out of line asking about those letters . . . But that piece in the paper did make the thing public. Have you really had your life threatened?'

'We all step on someone's toes from time to time. When we deal in controversial issues there are always people who get upset.' Kemp tried to turn the conversation. 'You must have met a few angry protestors in your line of work, Mr Allardyce.'

'Sure, I've been threatened by farmers' dogs and looked down the barrel of a shotgun. Folk don't always like what we do, but at least they meet us face to face . . . Anonymous letters, now that's something else again. That's sneaky. You've not been attacked physically, have you?'

Kemp shook his head. He had no wish to share his experiences with Zachary Allardyce, though the man would make a formidable bodyguard should he ever need one. Fortunately he was rescued from this disturbing thought by the reappearance of his wife and they went out together to find their cab.

'These people, Lennox . . .' Mary Kemp sat contentedly in her own sitting room with a coffee cup in her hand and a glass of cognac on the table beside her. '. . . They don't act real . . .'

'Parties are all the same in Newtown – and in the whole of England, too, for all I know.' Kemp, back in his home, was apt to be philosophical.

'Are we holding a postmortem on social events?' she asked.

'We do appear to be doing so on this one.'

'Well . . . Should I be giving you my impressions of it? From an outsider's point of view, an American for instance . . .'

'For so they took you . . .'

'Being not one of them . . .'

'Nor an Australian from the outback . . . Come on, Mary, you're dying to tell me.'

She took a drink of the brandy although she didn't need it for the words to come.

'Zachary Allardyce is on the make. I don't believe his old man ever owned as much as half an acre, and only counted sheep as an aid to sleep . . . Little sister, Anita . . . she's out on the prowl and your Tony's a toothsome morsel . . . Nick Stoddart's on the slide, pushed down by that chip on his

shoulder the size of an oak tree, and his tendency to tipple
... Your office colleagues, they'd sure like to be loyal but
... self-interest takes the heart out of that ...'

Kemp sat up.

'You were listening to them?'

'I have good ears. Nondescripts like me get overlooked
when people are talking ... Same as the servants in
eighteenth-century novels ...'

Kemp looked across at her fondly, but with some apprehension.

'You've been doing some fast reading, Mary.'

'And why not? The Irish have always had a way with
words. It's not difficult to catch up. Tonight I was hearing
the hesitations, the spaces between the words ... When you
listen to the silences you know what's at the root of the talk.'

'And that is?'

'There is mistrust of you, Lennox, because of the letters
... Of your position as head of the firm. Of course, they are
all of them lawyers so they're careful in their speech, for
ever looking over their shoulders for fear they'll get sued for
slander ... That's where what they don't say matters more
than their words ...'

She drained the brandy in her glass.

'Mary Madeleine Blane, I think you're tipsy ...'

'And what of it? Isn't it the truth I'm telling you?'

Going upstairs with his arms around her, and comfortable
in all else, Kemp hoped it was not so.

53

CHAPTER 7

Wednesday was an ordinary day. The morning post brought few surprises: fiscal reminders, conflicting claims, routine conveyancing, fervid complaints from dissatisfied clients, the odd appreciation for services rendered, building society cheques towards impending completions, notice of meetings, appeals for charity, and letters from rival firms competing in the matrimonial stakes.

Kemp dealt with them all, distributing among his colleagues their particular headaches for the day, and taking to himself those in which he was concerned. He dictated, saw clients, drafted documents, perused and completed the various forms required by bureaucracy to ensure every citizen's right to be heard, to be tried, to be scolded, solaced or compensated according to the law. It was Kemp's framework, the narrow space in which he operated and within which he fervently hoped his intelligence and expertise might make for, at the very least, a happy compromise – justice was too often a will-o'-the-wisp and hard to catch, an abstract concept only possible in an ideal world . . .

It was already five o'clock when Sally Stacey came into his office.

'We're late, Lennox, we'll miss the sherry . . .'

'If it's what the local Branch usually provides it's no great loss . . .'

As he had predicted, the meeting went on and on, petering out finally just after eight when the old-stagers had run out of steam – and their reminiscences of times past when the budget meant little more than a change in tax without the modern complexities brought about by political expediency.

Sally Stacey did not say much at the start of their drive back to Newtown, which was unlike her for she was normally quite a talker. Kemp was reminded of what Mary had said about the silences . . .

'Lennox, there's something I have to tell you . . .' When Sally spoke at last she had her eyes on the road, her hands firm on the steering wheel. 'It's about those letters . . . Of course we were all shocked to see that bit in the *Gazette* . . . I got to thinking . . . You know the reporter, Dan Frobisher?'

'I've met him.'

'What you probably don't know is his background. You remember when I came to Gillorns four years ago? You had me doing matrimonials . . .'

'I'm sorry for that, Sally. We just thought . . .'

'Because I was a woman solicitor, the first you'd had, you thought I'd naturally go into that department . . .'

'It was a mistake. I know that now, and I took you off it as soon as I realized you'd a business brain . . .'

'You were the only one who guessed . . . And I'm grateful. What I wanted to tell you was that while I was doing what everyone expected me to be good at – the social welfare thing – one of my clients was Amy Frobisher – well, she was Amy Robsart then . . .'

'I didn't know she'd been your client.'

'To put it bluntly, what she wanted was a bastardy order. She was pregnant. She said the father was Daniel Frobisher and he wasn't keen to marry her.'

'And?'

'She was quite a tough little piece. It was either get him into court or she'd have an abortion.'

'I see.'

'No, you don't . . .' Sally's hands were gripping the wheel very tightly. 'She came for legal advice . . .'

'Which you gave her?'

'Well . . . up to a point . . . But when she talked about abortion, I was in a quandary . . .'

Kemp waited for her to go on. When she didn't, he said, gently: 'I know that you are a Roman Catholic, Sally, and I appreciate that you might have strong views on abortion . . . but you are first and foremost a lawyer.'

It was some time before she spoke. They were by now on

Newtown's ring road and the high lamps shone brightly into the car so that he could see the strain in her face.

'I told her she should on no account abort the child.'

Kemp leant back in his seat, and watched the highway so brilliantly lit, the way forward so clear. Eventually he said: 'And she took your advice?'

Sally nodded. 'She said she would have the baby . . . In the end the court papers weren't needed. Her parents made him marry her . . .'

'So the child was born in wedlock?'

'The child was born mentally defective . . .'

Kemp heard the indrawn breath that was almost a sob. He took his time before he spoke.

'It wasn't your fault, Sally. These things happen . . .'

But Sally Stacey would not listen to any words of consolation.

'She burst into my office,' she went on, bleakly, '. . . it must have been about six months later . . . She just stood there like a wild animal . . . and she hurled abuse at me . . . Because of me, she said, she was stuck with a husband she loathed and a thing she couldn't look after . . . She called it a thing . . . She was only nineteen, Lennox . . .'

'Have you seen or heard from her since?'

'No.' Sally shook herself. 'I had to tell you now because of the letters . . . just in case there is a connection.'

'I don't see how there can be. This happened, what, two years ago? And anyway, the letters are coming to me, not you.'

'Amy Frobisher said that day she wished all lawyers would burn in hell . . . we were all liars and cheats, we wrecked people's lives and didn't care . . . I could only sit there and hear her out. Afterwards I wrestled with my conscience . . . Had I really done wrong?'

She was talking now to herself and although Kemp could have answered her, he chose not to. He could have told her she had been wrong, not in her personal conviction, but in allowing it to intrude upon her legal judgement. She would have been very persuasive with Amy Robsart, the strength of her religion lending sincerity and force to her argument, and the young girl in no state to withstand that persuasion.

Sally had forgotten that the girl had rights too. The lawyer in Sally should have warned her she was stepping outside her brief; she ought to have stayed within the legal frame, offered advice only on that.

Kemp could see why Sally Stacey had not liked the matrimonial side of their work: too many messy lives, too many divorces, split homes, custody cases, in short, too much human misery. Given the scope of her mind it was better employed in arranging clever little tax-avoidance schemes for well-heeled clients where the moral line need not be too finely drawn – in fact, could be ignored altogether. As this was neither the time nor the place for further discussion of professional ethics, he contented himself by saying: 'Don't think about it any more, Sally. I'm glad you told me. It does mean you can appreciate my feelings when I get these letters . . . Now, we have to turn off here, Lorimers' Garage is on the other road.'

When they pulled in, the forecourt was flooded with light from the neon signs above and from the lamps left on in the showroom.

'I'll wait till you get your car started,' said Sally as Kemp was getting out. 'I've had a few bad experiences with garages.'

Walking round to the back of the buildings, Kemp was plunged into darkness, the deeper for the brilliance he'd just left, and it took him a minute to adapt his eyes. David always put his car in the same place, against the far hedge, and as Kemp began walking carefully across the rough gravel he saw its grey outline over to the right some distance from the breakdown truck and the usual huddle of lorries. One thing David Lorimer couldn't complain of on his premises was lack of space.

Kemp got out his keys. The other set would have been left hanging up in Lorimer's office for him to pick up later.

Beyond the hedge a faint glow came from the lights on the ring road across the intervening fields, throwing black shadows along the ground. Kemp had almost reached his car door when he stumbled over one and saw it was more substantial than a shadow.

The body lay in a humped position along the driver's side

of the car on the darkest area of the gravel. Kemp dropped to his knees, looked first, then felt gingerly for the neck above the coat collar, the skin beneath the ear. There was no pulse. His fingers came away sticky with blood. Gently he turned the face and peered down in the dim light. He knew he had a torch in the glove compartment. No need for that. Tony Lambert.

Kemp got to his feet. The blackness that came over him had nothing to do with the night, the silence, or the shadows cast by the bushes in the hedge . . .

Act first, think afterwards . . . He was running.

'Sally! Call the police, and an ambulance . . . There's been an accident . . . That telephone kiosk at the last roundabout . . . Quick!'

Sally stared for a second, but the urgency in his voice, the look on his face, prevented questions. She accelerated out of the forecourt and on to the road with a squeal of tyres.

Kemp walked back to his car. This time he heard his feet crunch the gravel like ice breaking, all his senses now so alert, his eyes darting to the side at every flicker of shadow. He thought, I must keep my head, not let go, not stop to think, only do those things that have to be done, above all, stay in control.

So that the ground near the body should not be disturbed, he opened his car from the passenger side, took out the torch, and stepped with caution.

When he shone the light in Tony's eyes he felt his own heart die within him . . . Hopelessly, he felt along the jawline, then let the head rest back on the ground. He touched nothing else, nor did he allow his eyes to linger on the massive wound, the splintered skull. Others would deal with that. All he must do was observe, note and wait.

He timed his arrival at the garage: eight-thirty, and the body found within minutes. It was a cold night and his touch on the skin had found a little warmth, but the heavy coat had been rucked up round the neck . . . That coat . . . He winced . . . No more of that, he told himself, there'll be time enough for that.

He walked carefully over to the lorries, swung his torch around. No movement, nothing. He hadn't expected there would be . . . An isolated spot, perfect timing . . . There would be no witnesses.

Another hour had passed by the time Inspector John Upshire came to Kemp and found him slumped in his car which had been moved to let the scene-of-crime officers nearer the body. By now the place was alive with lights, headlamps, arc lights and, eeriest of all, the glow as from a camper's tent from the roped-off area where figures went to and fro about their grisly business.

'I got Dr Albury out of a dinner party,' said Upshire. 'He'll give us some idea of time of death . . .'

'That won't be difficult. I'm no medical expert but I'd put the time of d-death . . .' Kemp stopped, stammered at the word and tried again. '. . . time of death at about eight o'clock. Just before I got here . . .'

Upshire cleared his throat. 'Let's have some facts. I've taken a statement from your Miss Stacey and sent her home. You arrived at about eight-thirty and she called us within minutes. She took a chance running her car up on that pavement but it was an emergency . . . She says you were away behind the garage no more than a few minutes before you came back shouting. So, I don't think you had time to do it . . .'

He met Kemp's glare stolidly. 'We have to consider it. My men searched your car, no bloodstained instrument . . . And they searched you, too? Right. It's all procedure, Lennox, as you damn well know so don't go all prissy on me . . . They're going over the ground with a toothcomb, of course, but whoever did it was up and away . . .'

'It was timed . . .' said Kemp, dully. 'My car was left here for me to collect – anyone in Lorimers' knew that – probably half Newtown knew it . . .'

'What are we talking about here? It was Mr Lambert got killed.'

'It was meant to be me . . . He died for me.' There was almost relief in getting the words out. He turned in his seat and the inspector saw his face. 'Can't you see it, John? Tony was murdered in my place . . . It's my body should be over there being mauled about by Albury!'

Upshire was jolted by the raw emotion in Kemp's face, the

desperation behind what he was saying, but the words were coming out cold and hard.

'Because of the threats in those letters?' the inspector said, slowly. 'You think someone made a mistake?'

'I don't think . . . I know . . . They were out to get me tonight . . . Probably just hung around waiting for me to turn up . . . They could have been anywhere − in the hedge, behind those lorries . . . The fact that I was late was a godsend to them . . . nobody's around, the place is closed, all it needed was a heavy spanner, an iron bar . . . anything. He . . . Tony . . . may never have even heard them . . .'

Upshire had his notebook out but he wasn't writing.

'You gave a statement to the sergeant − there's none of this in it.'

'I told them all that was needed. Times, what I'd seen, what I did . . . Why I moved the head . . . and that I recognized him.' Kemp passed a hand across his eyes. 'At first it was just a body I'd stumbled over. I had to find out if it was still alive . . . then I saw the face . . . And I ran . . . What does Sally say, five minutes? I couldn't have said − time stood still.'

Waiting for them to come he hadn't even glanced at his watch. When he said now that time stood still he'd meant it no longer had any meaning.

'The ambulancemen say they got here just after nine,' said Upshire.

Kemp nodded. Their shaken heads and pursed lips as they bent over the body had told him nothing he didn't know already.

'And my men were on the spot by nine-fifteen . . . It's a good start to any operation, Lennox . . .'

The bleak look he got from Kemp showed that the phrase was hardly well chosen.

Upshire snapped his notebook shut.

'Come on . . . there's hot tea going in the garage office. We got Mr Lorimer down to open up. It's a damn cold night out here . . .'

Kemp climbed slowly from the car, his limbs like lead weights. He felt his brain too had stopped functioning, forward thought impossible, while thinking back was blocked as if there'd been a landslip.

He had already met David Lorimer, looking somewhat dishevelled, for he had been taken almost literally out of his bed so that the facilities on the premises might be used by the investigation. What David had said to him hadn't helped.

'My God, Lennox, it could have been you!'

It was from the washroom adjoining David's office that Dr Albury emerged a little later, drying his hands.

'They can take the body, Inspector, I've finished for now. You'll get the postmortem report in due course.'

Upshire handed him a mug of tea. 'Can you give us something to be going on with, Doctor? Oh, this is Mr Lennox Kemp, who found the deceased.'

'We have met before. This is a dreadful business, Mr Kemp . . . I understand Mr Lambert was your colleague?'

'My partner, yes . . .' How quickly the tenses change . . . But perhaps to police pathologists such things came easily.

'No doubt about the cause of death,' said Dr Albury, warming his hands round the tea mug. 'The first blow to the back of the head probably stunned him. He might have turned slightly, and the next blow cracked his skull. He died on the spot where he was found, there was blood on the gravel under the head, and pieces of gravel in the wound. I would say that death was almost instantaneous.'

'Weapon?' asked the inspector.

'Something fairly heavy. Sharp-edged, possibly metal. I'll know more when I've done the PM.'

'And the time of death?'

Dr Albury turned to Kemp. 'You found the body just after eight-thirty, the blood was sticky, and you felt a little warmth on the skin. He could not have been dead long . . . Half an hour perhaps . . . I'll try and be more accurate in my report, but I would say he died about eight o'clock. I don't suppose five or ten minutes either way is going to matter much, eh, Inspector? Anyway, I'm off . . .'

'It's time you got home, too, Lennox,' said John Upshire. 'Mary will be wondering what's happened to you.'

'I used the phone in the office here when David Lorimer arrived . . .' He couldn't remember what he had said to her, how he had told her, just the bald facts. What she had answered was also a blank. An impenetrable darkness had taken hold of his mind, muffling voices, suspending all feeling. When he got up from his chair he stumbled into the table like a blind man.

John Upshire was startled. He had never seen his friend act like this before. It was almost as if Kemp had been the one struck down out there . . . At a loss for words, the inspector took refuge in practicalities.

'Sorry you can't have your car back yet, it's part of the scene of crime and they'll want to give it another going-over. There might be prints – maybe the bugger leaned on it. I'll give you a lift. There's nothing more you can do here tonight.' He could see that Kemp was reluctant to leave. He blundered against the door going out, then he stood on the forecourt as if he didn't know how he'd got there . . .

Kemp was indeed lost. He looked out over the scatter of men and vehicles to where the sodium lights on the ring road flushed the frosty air. They had been driving along that road, he and Sally, such a short time before . . . A little time? No, it was long, long ago . . . A time when he'd been innocent of another man's death . . . Upshire caught his arm. 'Get in the car, for God's sake, man. Think, you could be dead . . .' If he spoke roughly it was only because he could not think of any other way to deal with this new, and frightening, aspect of Kemp. It hadn't been the happiest comment to make.

'I think that's exactly what I am,' said Kemp.

CHAPTER 8

The inquest on Tony Lambert had opened and been adjourned, the verdict the one everybody expected: murder by person or persons unknown. Life in Newtown continued as normal; the food shops thrived, the big stores offered gifts to increase trade, companies failed and the banks flourished, people got married and some separated, house prices dropped and electricity bills went up, babies were born and baptized, there were two ruby weddings and a woman broke an ankle on a paving stone and sued the Council. In short, nothing happened that was worth writing home about.

A week after the inquest, Inspector John Upshire was surprised to find Mary Kemp sitting in his kitchen when he came home in the evening.

'Mrs Furness let me in,' she said, going to the oven and taking out a casserole. 'I hope you'll not be minding. I've done the vegetables and they'll keep hot while you have a wash.'

Upshire eyed her curiously. 'You're quite the little manager, aren't you? How'd you know I'd be in tonight?'

'That nice Sergeant Cribbins told me you were coming straight home. You left your house number.'

'You know, you'd make a good policewoman, Mary, you've got an eye for detail . . .'

'Funny you should say that. There was a man from the Mafia once said I should be working for them . . . Now, don't let your supper get cold, John.'

When he came downstairs the table was laid, the meal steaming, and there was a hearty smell of onions.

'You don't object to shirtsleeves?' he said, pulling up a chair.

'My father never wore else but a dirty sweatshirt, but he

was a pig of a man anyway . . . Which reminds me, there's beer in the fridge.'

She poured it for him as he watched her going about, neat, quick, competent.

'Are you not having something yourself, Mary?'

'I'll not be spoiling your meal by taking a share of it . . . I'm here to talk.'

'I didn't think you'd come for the company. How do you do these fried onions? I don't get the like of them from Mrs Furness.'

'I'm not competing. She's a nice woman. My mother showed me how. She learned the trick long ago at Jamets in Dublin. You'll not have heard of it.'

She let the inspector eat while she sat at the end of the table, her chin cupped in her hands, and spoke of what was on her mind.

'He goes around like a sleepwalker,' she said. 'It's as if something's died in him. There's a blackness in his mind I can't get at . . . Oh, he's off to work every day all right, but it's like he's a mechanical man, and I'm thinking he's the same in the office. They tell me he tears through the paper-work as if it was the last day, and if he stopped for a minute the whole world would collapse. He never talks to anyone unless he has to and no one sees him smile . . .'

The inspector wiped his mouth with his napkin, and put it down carefully folded beside his plate. 'Not even you, Mary?'

'Me least of all . . . Sometimes he looks at me as if he didn't know who I was. That's the worst part. I thought I could comfort him but I've not been a wife long enough to know how . . .' She turned away to fetch a bowl of fruit. 'Have you been seeing him?'

'Once or twice. There wasn't any need but I thought I'd be doing him a favour by keeping him in on the investigation.'

'And are you any further forward? He tells me nothing.'

In the line of duty the inspector had seen all manner of sorrowing women, some distraught by the loss of loved ones, some with hearts broken by the delinquencies of children, or seeing their menfolk locked up. If his senses were blunted it was no wonder. But Mary Kemp was different. He knew she had been through hard times, spent what youth she'd had in rough places where poverty and violence went hand in hand on a scale to make the good citizens of Newtown blench. He could only speculate on that background but it was enough for him to give her credit, to come out of it as she had – a serene and capable woman, owing everything to character, nothing to circumstance. He wished he could reassure her . . . She wouldn't want the usual police platitudes – they were following up leads, and hopes of an early arrest – she wasn't going to believe that old flannel, not the wife of Lennox Kemp.

So he told her what they had so far, which wasn't much. They couldn't even be sure of the weapon . . . '. . . builders had just finished that new extension to Lorimers' showroom. They were clearing the site, and over near where the body was found there was a heap of scrap waiting for the skip. Stuff from the old sheds they'd pulled down, lengths of piping, iron bars from windows, bits of guttering – enough sharp-edged metal to fit out an army of hooligans . . .' He broke off, and sighed. 'All he had to do was pick his piece, use it, wipe it clean and stick it back in the pile. My men have been through the lot, but what's the use? It was a frosty night – even honest folk would be wearing gloves, and chummy would be sure to have his on . . .'

No, he told her, there wasn't a trace of anyone else's prints on the car save Lorimers' mechanics' and Kemp's own. The car had been sitting there by the hedge since five o'clock. No one had been seen going anywhere near it. The statements taken from the garage attendants, the lorry drivers and David Lorimer himself had provided no clues. One of the drivers, returning to the site about quarter to eight to get something from his cab, thought he'd seen someone crossing the field but it was misty and he couldn't be sure. His piece of evidence, however, was vital to the time of death for he swore there was no body lying beside the isolated car over by the hedge. Like all the drivers he was wary of anyone lurking in the lorry park . . . He'd had to admit the car was in the shadow and some distance from his own vehicle . . .

'Fits in with what that doctor said at the inquest, though,' Mary interrupted. 'That Tony was killed about eight o'clock, or just after.'

65

Upshire sighed. 'That's the only sure thing we've got – the time of death . . .' He stopped, and looked at her. 'For heaven's sake, why am I telling you all this?'

'Because it's your help I'm wanting, and even if you are an inspector of police, you're going to give it. Would you be wanting your coffee now?'

'What d'you mean, you want help?' He found himself talking to her back.

'Lennox is on the verge of a breakdown. He's not going to last for much longer the way he is. He's given up on thinking, so someone else must do his thinking for him. Now, hasn't he helped you on cases in the past?'

'Yes, he has . . .' Upshire had to admit it. He thought about the past for a moment. 'Yes, I owe him that . . .'

'Then help me with this one.' Mary set the coffee percolating. 'Could it have been an ordinary mugging?'

'There's no such thing as an ordinary mugging. They're all bloody different . . . My Super would like to go along with the idea that it was that kind of attack, and they got interrupted so they got away with nothing – neither his wallet, money, credit cards, nor the Rolex watch still on his wrist . . . In many ways' – Upshire sighed – 'I'd like to go along with the Super . . .'

'So would I,' said Mary, fervently, as she set out cups on the table. They rattled for her hand shook. 'Because the other is the unthinkable . . . It's what's eating the heart out of Lennox. The night it happened when he came home all he could say was, "He was killed for me . . ." '

John Upshire swallowed hard. He was uncomfortable with that kind of language, he found it emotional, melodramatic, not something he was easy with.

Neither of them spoke while she poured out, pushed across the milk and sugar. She took a cup herself, sipped and sat back.

'Why was Tony there?' she asked.

'Ah . . . there's the nub of it . . . Your husband swears there was no reason for Mr Lambert to be there.'

'He knew where Lennox's car was, and the time he would likely be dropped off at the garage by Sally Stacey. He knew exactly where to find Lennox if he'd wanted to speak to him.'

'But why go there? He could just as easily have gone to your house and waited for him. Anyway, Lennox says he knew nothing that urgent would have cropped up in the space of only a day . . . nothing in the office, that is . . .'

'Tony was going to be in town all Wednesday. I heard him say so. Perhaps something came up that he wanted Lennox's opinion on.'

On firmer ground now, the inspector gave her the gist of Lambert's movements on the day he had died. They had been checked meticulously by members of the force.

Tony had taken the ten o'clock train to London, called at Medway, Austin & Co in Chancery Lane, the family solicitors, for an eleven-thirty appointment. He and Donald Medway had gone for lunch together at the Law Society between one and two. Tony had said he had another call to make in the city before catching the five-thirty train to Newtown, and they had parted in the Strand just before three. Several people who knew him by sight had seen Tony on the evening train, and Zachary Allardyce, who had been up to town at a planning enquiry, travelled back in the same compartment.

'The Allardyces . . .' said Mary, putting a hand on her mouth. 'That was terrible . . . Lennox said, who would break the news to her? He'd not told you Tony was engaged to Anita Allardyce . . .'

'Well . . . we knew there was no next of kin to be informed. A WPC went round to his house to tell the house-keeper, Mrs Crabtree, in case she was expecting him home and was worried. She's an elderly lady who used to look after his parents. We reckoned there wasn't anybody else . . .'

'Bad news will keep till morning, that's what I said to Lennox . . . We'd not go upsetting the girl . . . But we didn't want her hearing it on the news, so Lennox phoned early. I think it was the hardest thing he'd ever had to do.'

She remembered how his face had looked, grey and stony, how he had stammered into the phone. She'd never heard him stammer before, the man she'd married, the glib talker . . .

67

It was then she realized it was going to be far worse than she'd imagined. It was not just poor Anita . . .

She said nothing of this to the inspector. Instead, she went on in her flat expressionless voice: 'The next afternoon Miss Stacey came and asked if I'd go with her to give some comfort to Anita Allardyce. I could see why. The child was alone, her folks are all in Australia, she'd have no other women around . . . and she's only young. We both felt someone ought to go.'

'Yes, of course.' John Upshire hadn't known of the engagement but he could appreciate it might be a kindly gesture.

Mary Kemp put her cup down. It rattled in the saucer.

'It was not pleasant, what happened. Her brother, Zachary, came to the door, and refused to let us in. We could hear her crying . . . He said things . . .'

'What things?'

'Well, it was mostly at me. How I had the nerve to come calling when it was all my husband's fault that Anita had lost the man she was to marry. That it was Lennox who'd put Tony in danger so it was Lennox that was to blame for what had happened . . . Oh, and a lot of other things were said, none of them nice. Then he slammed the door in our faces.'

'But that's ridiculous!'

'No, it's not, John, and you know it. I can understand how they feel, and what they think . . . Everyone else thinks the same — including Lennox himself . . . Of course I'll not be telling him what happened, and you must not.'

'Mr Allardyce knew about the anonymous letters?'

She told him about the remarks which had been passed at the party on Tuesday night.

'Bloody tittle-tattle!' Upshire's face had reddened. 'And I suppose they think the police are doing nothing?'

'To find who wrote the letters? Well, are they?' She wasn't exactly standing akimbo, hands on hips, but there was challenge in her attitude.

He took a deep breath.

'We're not fools,' he said, testily. 'Before this happened there hadn't been much time . . . Now finding the writer is part of the murder investigation. If there's a connection, then

68

we'll find it, and him . . . or them . . . The psychoanalyst who examined them, he's sure there's more than one person involved. I don't understand the lingo those fellows use, but it seems there's one with a real grievance, and another who's just a troublemaker – one eggs the other on. That's supposed to give us some idea of the characters . . .'

'Big deal,' she said. He'd forgotten how American she could sometimes sound. 'What about the paper and the type?'

Upshire spread his hands. 'Nothing so far, but we're working on it. That's the material evidence I'm looking for. I don't go much on all this psychological stuff . . .'

'You think it's crap?' She smiled at him. 'But I don't . . . Could you let me have a read of the analyst's report?'

He hesitated.

'Why're you doing this, Mary?'

'I told you. I'll not be standing around watching my husband lose his mind because some nutters have been playing games with him. It's a precious mind to me and I'll not see it wrecked . . .'

She washed up the dishes before she put her coat on and went to the door.

'I'll leave that report at the desk,' he told her. 'The facsimiles are with it if you want to look at them again . . .'

'Thanks, John – for everything.'

She'll go her own way, the inspector thought, I should have warned her there could be danger in that . . .

He had already felt frustration at the lack of progress his men were making, now Mary Kemp had added a new, urgent dimension – a personal appeal for a quick result. He was suddenly angry; he threw his bag on the table and got his head down to study the notes he had made on the murder investigation.

As he had told her, he owed Kemp.

CHAPTER 9

Kemp was in the study when Mary returned. He said he'd brought home some leases to draft. He hadn't touched the cold meat and salad she had left out. She sat down calmly and ate her own supper; when she was a child there had never been enough food, when she became a nurse she learned the need for not shirking it. Kemp didn't ask her where she had been, he seemed to have lost all interest in her comings and goings.

She had a fire burning in the sitting room. She took the coffee tray in there, brought out drinks from the cabinet, and at ten o'clock she went to him.

'Coffee's ready,' she said.

He glanced up briefly. She could see he had been writing furiously in his neat hand all over the draft documents in front of him.

'Stop that right now,' she told him in a voice she hadn't used in a long time, a small voice, sharp as the blade of a flick-knife. 'What do you keep an articled clerk for?' She went round the desk snapping his books shut. She gathered up all his papers and shovelled them, willy-nilly, into his old satchel. 'Time you got a new briefcase. You can well afford one,' she said as she took the bag out into the hall and dumped it on the table.

Then she walked into the sitting room, and waited.

He came in at last and sat down, flexing his fingers. But at least he was looking at her. It had taken a sharpish instrument but she thought she had prised open a crack in the carapace. He hadn't liked being spoken to in that tone – she hadn't liked using it either, it made her feel like a shrew.

She set the cups out with a steady hand.

'You'll be having a brandy?'

'No . . . I'll get myself a Scotch . . . Looks like I'm going
to need it.'

He looked bemused, but that in itself was nothing new.
As he squirted the soda he knocked the edge of the glass,
stopped and stared at it as if surprised by his own clumsiness.
In the last two weeks he had been responsible for a lot of
chipped and broken china . . .

She put the coffee on the table beside him and poured
herself a large brandy.

'We have to talk,' she said, kicking off her shoes and
stretching her toes to the fire.

'Do we? What about?'

'Well . . . not the ozone layer . . . What married couples
should talk about when there's a crisis in the home – themselves.'

'Is there a crisis?'

'I think there is.'

He said nothing. She saw that his eyes were unfocused,
drifting, as can happen when a person is drunk, but she knew
that Lennox never sought refuge in liquor. She suspected
that if he did have an inner landscape into which he retreated
it would be a dry area. She, who had little imagination for
that kind of thing, thought of it as a desert.

Now she allowed the silence to lie between them for so
long that it was he who had to break it.

'I feel I'm about to be criticized . . . Is that what this is all
about, Mary? You're going to give me one of Mrs Caudle's
curtain lectures . . .'

'Don't come the clever words with me, I don't have your
literary background . . . I only want you to talk to me, tell
me what you're thinking.'

'The psychiatric sofa, eh? I'm to have one of those little
spells of therapy all good Americans run to for the good of
their souls?'

'You know very well I don't go in for that sort of thing
. . . Anyway, you'd twist the head off anyone who tried it
on you. No, all I think you need is a good dose of common
sense, and maybe a few home truths . . .'

'Ah, the social-worker angle, the pull-yourself-together

71

routine? I'm the idiot patient and you're the nurse who knows it all.'

Mary took a drink of brandy without taking her eyes off him.

'You have a mean tongue, Lennox, but you should know better than to give me the edge of it. I was immunized long before I met you . . .' She paused, then she went on, quietly: 'We're going to talk about Tony's murder.'

She was prepared for the reaction, the arm that flailed, the swept-away glass, the smashed cup. She put on her slippers, picked up the bits of broken china and went to the kitchen for a cloth. When she came back she wiped the table top, mopped the carpet, got out another glass and cup and asked him if he wanted more coffee. He was crouching forward in his chair as if ready to spring and, for one brief moment, she did wonder if he might strike her. She could sense the anger in him for the very air between them seemed to vibrate with it.

Gently now, but still implacably, she carried on speaking. She reminded him she was his wife, not a well-meaning friend nor a doctor concerned for his mental welfare, above all, not a prying nobody wanting to wheedle out his secrets; she was the woman he had married . . . She also told him, in passing, that he was an arrogant bastard, and a low-down heel . . .

At that point she realized she was getting mixed up, and had run out of steam. 'Both of us have been on our own for too long,' she ended, wearily. 'We're used to solving problems without help from anyone else . . . I don't know the wifely words . . . they don't come easily to me . . . And as for you, you've been such a solitary creature, you'll not be letting even your heart be shared with me . . .'

She tried to swallow the sob that had risen in her throat but it stuck there. She didn't believe in giving way to tears; they had been dried up in her since childhood when they had proved of no avail. When she found she couldn't stop them running down her cheeks now she started to wipe them off with the dishcloth she had in her hand.

It was the sight of her holding a washing-up rag to her eyes that brought him to her side. 'Oh, Mary Madeleine, you little goose . . . What am I going to do with you? You turn me inside out like an old sock . . . Come on, here's a proper handkerchief, dry your eyes and let me look at them . . .'

He could never bear to see a woman cry and had thought this one incapable of that soft option. The harshest of words would have been preferable. She had been right in the way she had gone about jolting him out of his misery, even though she had no cure for it. At least now he had to make the effort to talk about Tony.

It didn't come easily. From the moment he had recognized the face on the body he'd stumbled over a blankness had settled on his mind so that, since then, he had acted like a robot, looking neither to right nor left because on one side there was a gulf of guilt and on the other the pit of an inconsolable loss.

'That it should be Tony . . .' he raged now. 'Tony of all people, who harmed no one . . . With a future before him, and a new happiness in his life. To be done to . . . to . . . death like that . . . a d-death which should have been mine.'

The stammering was coming less often as he talked.

'Can we be sure it was meant to be you?' Mary was trying desperately to be practical.

'There's no doubt in what's left of my mind . . . That coat so similar, the place, the time . . . things known to anyone who wanted to find out where I was . . .'

'But why was Tony there at all?'

'God knows . . . Something must have come up he wanted to see me about and he knew I'd be at my car sometime after eight. Or perhaps he was lured there by a telephone call . . . Perhaps he was supposed to find my body . . .' He stopped, unable to follow any coherent line of thought. He jumped to his feet. 'But this is nonsense . . . the kind of thing you get in detective fiction – gives a new turn to the plot . . .'

He began to stride up and down the room while his wife listened, and tried to understand what to her were wild words.

'There has to be a body to thrill the readers, whether it's real in a newspaper report or a figment of the writer's imagination. A body in the library, a body in the gutter, what's it matter? But a body that was living flesh only minutes before

73

. . . a body that talked and laughed, had a jaunty step and wore brightly coloured socks . . . someone you knew . . . Ah, there's the difference . . . That's the d-death that stops thought . . .' His voice had grown savage when he went on: 'A corpse in a casebook you can leave for the crows to pick or forensics to claw at, then you can get on with solving the murder, and have neat little contrived conversations with the police about clues. I've done plenty of those and enjoyed them . . . like enjoying a book you helped to write . . . But grief, what happens to grief? You can't describe that, it won't go tidily into the narrative, it's too raw, it won't conform, it bleeds into the brain and clogs the works . . .'

'Like an aneurysm,' Mary had said, bringing him down on to her more material plane. 'When it bursts it leaks blood into the tissues surrounding it, but a good surgeon can nip the neck of it, and the patient gets better . . .'

'A metaphorical diagnosis, Mary? Or just another gentle reminder that I'm only human after all?'

Although she was pleased to hear him laugh, she knew it was going to take time and patience to get his wits going again. In the meantime she must use her own.

CHAPTER 10

Mary Kemp had not known exactly where Tony Lambert had lived so when she telephoned the housekeeper, Mrs Crabtree, she asked for directions.

'Mr Kemp has asked me to collect some law books Mr Lambert had from the office library,' she explained, mendaciously. It was true Tony did keep certain textbooks on Trusts at his home – Sally Stacey had told her that – but they were rather specialized and rarely in demand by anyone else.

What surprised Mary was how close Copt Lodge was to Lorimers' Garage, one field away and on the far side of the ring road. It had been on the edge of the old village which was itself now sadly isolated, cut off by the proliferation of new motorways, and the low grey stone house stood within its own trees some distance from the nearest housing estate. It was not large but must have been a pleasant dwelling for Tony and his parents, the garden well tended and secluded.

'Of course it was a wrench them giving up the old Hall but they were getting on by then, Mrs Kemp, and the place was far too big . . .' Mrs Crabtree, who was not young herself, bustled about, glad to have the chance of a chat over tea and cake.

Mary praised the latter. 'I thought nobody baked like this any more,' she said. 'You'll have steeped the fruit to keep it moist?'

'It was a favourite of young Tony's . . . I still called him that for I'd known him since he was a lad. He was that good to his parents – the nicest family you'd get hereabouts . . .'

Emily Crabtree it seemed had worked at the Hall when she was a girl, married the head gardener and, when widowed, had come back to housekeep for Mr and Mrs Lambert some ten years ago. Death was no stranger to her but she was more taken up with the passing of the elderly couple, being within her comprehension, whereas she found it hard to cope with the fact that the son too had gone.

In the manner of her kind she filled the space not only with chatter about the past but also with surmise as to the future, for she was a practical woman and aware of the things that mattered in life. Besides, this Mrs Kemp was such a friendly visitor and had a sympathetic ear. Not that she was much to look at, and she dressed plain for someone in her position, but that only made Emily think the more of her. You could see she'd be a good wife, the interest she took in the domestic duties involved in looking after a bachelor man.

'He said to me when his parents died, would I stay on a while; well, of course I said yes. Mind you, he'd no thought of getting married then, but I could see it would come . . . Such a nice, steady young man and with a fortune at his fingertips, you might say, as well as a career. They got a fine price for the Hall and the grounds when it went for development . . . and so they should – the Lamberts were squires here once.'

' 'Tis the same story in the west of Ireland,' said Mary, 'the old places going, and the bungalows being built . . . Well, maybe some of it's for the best . . .'

They shared a moment's talk on the changing times until Mary asked if Mrs Crabtree would be staying on at Copt Lodge.

'Bless you, no . . . Young Mr Tony has seen to that. When he told me he was going to marry Miss Allardyce, he says to me: Emily, you'll not have to worry about a place. There's that cottage over Ember Village you've always wanted. I've bought it, he says, and made it yours . . . whenever you want to go . . .'

'A very decent man,' commented Mary.

'Always the one to do the right thing, Mr Tony. He'd not want me staying on when he brought home his bride, though I'd have stayed to see them settled, like . . . That poor lass . . . I only met her the few times she was here . . . Bright, like they all are these days, and her to be a lawyer too . . . She'd a good look round the place, said it could do with a bit of modernization . . . Ah, well . . . she can have it now . . .'

'Sorry, I don't quite see . . . ?'

'Did you not know? He's left her everything. That Mr Medway from London, he's been to see me. I've to have an annuity under the will as well as the cottage at Ember – in recognition of my services to his parents, Mr Tony said.' Nothing in Mrs Crabtree's life had made her proud but she was nevertheless pleased that what she had seen as her duty had been rewarded.

'And quite rightly, too,' said Mary. 'You have earned it, Mrs Crabtree. It's rare these days for people to think of those who serve them. I suppose Mr Lambert had no one else to leave his property to except his fiancée . . .'

'He'd no kin . . . Mr Medway says he made the will when he got engaged. But who would have thought he'd got so little time left . . . That was a dreadful thing, him getting mugged like he was . . . They'd be thinking he'd money on him, I suppose.'

Brushing crumbs from her lap, and accepting another cup of tea, Mary steered the conversation gently in the direction of the night Tony had been killed.

'My night for whist at the village hall in Ember,' said Mrs Crabtree. 'I allus go on a Wednesday, it's the regular night. I leave here at six and get back on the bus before ten. If Mr Tony's to be in he knows his supper's in the oven, or in the fridge . . .'

'Did he eat it that night?'

'Never a scrap. He'd been in, I knew that, left his briefcase on the table but he must have gone out again straight off, still in the coat he went to London in . . . It was a cold night, coming over frosty . . . I thought mebbe he'd been called for by someone in a car because his own was still in the drive outside. Gone out for a walk, says that inspector. Not on your life, I tells him, Mr Tony's no great one for walking.'

'Nor is Mr Kemp,' said Mary. 'It's a car every time for him. So you wouldn't be worried at first when Mr Lambert wasn't in when you got back at ten?'

'I was puzzled . . . The house was so cold. He'd left that little window in the hall half open . . . Well, we leave it that way sometimes for Timmy – that's my cat. And when I come in, there's Timmy right enough in the kitchen washing his

77

paws. But Mr Tony wouldn't have left that window open if he'd meant to be gone long. Not on a cold night, like that one was . . .'

Mary put the heavy textbooks into her shopping bag when she left, and thanked Emily Crabtree for her hospitality.

'You've come on the bus, then,' the housekeeper said, surprised to find no car at the door.

'I've not learned to drive yet,' said Mary, 'and I don't mind using public transport . . .'

'Not like some,' said Mrs Crabtree. 'Now, Miss Allardyce, she's got no car either, but she can't abide the bus 'cos it takes so long going all round the council estates instead of straight into the town.'

Mrs Crabtree liked people who travelled on buses; it brought them within her own orbit, and so she warmed to Mr Kemp's wife and invited her to visit again.

Mary replaced the books in the library at Gillorns that same afternoon, confident that her husband was in court and would not see her. She was about to slip out quietly again when she met Sally Stacey in the corridor, case in hand, outdoor jacket round her shoulders. 'Why, Mary . . .' she said, 'how nice to see you. You wouldn't like to come for a drink, would you? Tea – or something stronger?'

'It's awash with tea I am already. But I'd like to come . . . Aren't you busy?'

Sally grimaced. 'I should be but I can't get down to it here in the office. The atmosphere is stifling, and I don't mean the heating. I'm going home to work but I'd be glad of the company. Come on, my car's out at the back.'

Sally's flat was like her mind, a tidy, well-organized place with few feminine touches. The pictures on the walls showed she had a good eye for art but little sense of adventure.

She immediately brought out gin and bottles of tonic.

'I'm no great drinker,' she said, 'and it's not six o'clock yet . . . If it wasn't that I had to talk to someone, I'd call it sinful . . .'

Despite their shared experience at the Allardyces' front door – which had shaken Sally more than herself – Mary

78

was uncertain of Sally Stacey, though she was at pains to hide it. When Mary had been Kemp's secretary their relationship had necessarily been a distant one, reflecting the gap between those in the office who drew salaries and the others who were paid wages, but Mary was also aware that Sally's own position in the hierarchy had never been easy. As the only woman lawyer she missed out on the male camaraderie, the beer in the local at lunchtime, the retelling of court exploits, the essential masculinity of the talk; even at the Friday-night sessions her participation was meagre, her voice thin. Another kind of woman might have ridden over the gulf by strength of personality or bridged it with feminine guile but Sally, an only child brought up in Kensington and privately educated, was inhibited by a set of principles too high for everyday use.

I catch a whiff of the convent, thought Mary, as she listened to Sally's obvious need to unburden herself of Amy Frobisher's unhappy history.

'I was sure Lennox would have told you . . .' Sally sounded surprised that he hadn't.

'He never betrays a confidence,' said Mary, rather primly, but thinking he should have made an exception of this one, 'and of course a client of yours was involved . . .'

'There wasn't much confidentiality about the way Amy yelled at me that day,' said Sally, bitterly. 'She was loud enough to be heard by anyone . . .'

'But it was years ago, Sally, and people do come to terms with even the most tragic things in time. What did happen to the child?'

Sally shook her head, pursing her lips. 'I've no idea. I know it sounds hard but I put the case right out of my mind. I didn't want anything more to do with the girl . . .'

You lack normal curiosity, thought Mary, who had plenty – particularly about Amy, her parents, and her husband.

'I only told Lennox because of those awful letters,' Sally went on, 'and because when I thought about it again I realized there might have been ethics involved . . .'

'I wouldn't know an ethic if I met one in my soup,' said Mary, briskly. 'Where I come from it was hard enough telling good from bad without going into the theory of it all . . .'

Had Sally Stacey imagined they might have religious views in common because Mary was half Irish? Fat chance of that; Mary's childhood faith had died with her mother a long time ago, and any beliefs she had formulated since were only catholic in the widest sense.

Unlike her husband, however, she saw no reason to let Sally off the hook entirely, this was no time to pander to some folks' delicate sensibilities – there was too much at stake . . .

'Tell me again the phrases Amy Frobisher used. You've got a good memory, Sally, can you remember the exact words?'

Though she had done her best to forget, the episode had seared itself into Sally's conscience and her legal education had taught her the value of accuracy in recall.

Mary tucked away the things that had been said, and the manner of their saying; she may not have been an expert in hypothetical questions, like how many angels could dance on the point of a pin, but she had an excellent mind for facts.

Her arrival home to Albert Crescent coincided with that of her husband.

'You've been out late,' Kemp observed, as she brought her basket to the kitchen table.

'Supermarket's open till half-seven,' she said, thankful that she had just managed to catch it after nipping into the police station on her way from Sally's flat, thankful too that she could throw a meal together without fuss and by the shortest possible route.

After dinner she produced the bundle of copy letters. Last night Kemp had been disposed to talk; she was determined to keep up the pressure for otherwise he would slip back into that dark place where she could not follow.

As it was he frowned when she laid the package in front of him, along with the analyst's report.

'Two people,' she said, 'just as you and Mr Cantley thought . . .'

Had they? Kemp couldn't remember talking about the letters to Mike but he supposed he must have done. He knew he ought to show some interest in the report, just as he knew he ought to feel anger at the sight of the letters . . . He felt nothing, only a dull nausea.

'I won't touch that filth,' he said, pushing away the large brown official envelope marked in John Upshire's writing: 'For Mrs Kemp. To be called for'. 'What the hell do you think you're doing?'

'Finding out who wrote them.'

'What good will that do? It won't bring Tony back . . .' Nor take away my guilt for his death, he thought. The pain was still there, and all the talking in the world wasn't going to assuage it . . . 'We catch those responsible and close the book on the case, is that what you want?'

'Yes,' she said, simply.

She sat across the table from him, and spread out the letters.

He turned his head away, and said, in desperation: 'Can't you see, they've done their work, those letters . . . They've destroyed me as surely as if it was my s-skull that was broken that night. They've wrecked my life like they said they would for I've to go on living with Tony on my conscience for ever . . .'

She heard the bleakness in the voice, and tried to understand. Though she lacked imagination, she had a wide capacity for compassion, but reined it in most of the time lest it interfere with seeing things as they are rather than how one might wish them to be . . . Unused to a close personal relationship with anyone, she was now faced with conflicting emotions, her love for her husband, and her own curiosity and need to set things straight.

Press on, she thought grimly, he can't be worse hurt than he has been already.

She chose her words carefully. 'You are alive, my dear . . . and so are those who killed Tony . . .'

'So easily you say it . . . A murder enquiry . . . Find the clues, arraign the suspects, get the evidence, and everyone goes home happy . . .'

One part of Kemp's mind – the irrational half – was behaving badly, the other half was telling him so. To have two voices in his head was an experience new to him; it only made him irritable.

Mary persevered. 'All I'm trying to do is to make you think, Lennox. You seem to have given up on that, and you're

81

supposed to be a hotshot at it. I want you in that game again, the game of finding out . . .'

Aware that he was barely listening, she began to read out the analyst's report on the texts of the letters.

'". . . an hysterical note . . . juvenile, possibly female . . . trauma of some kind . . . phrases from films or out of magazines . . .

'". . . An older person . . . probably male. Literary . . . resentment rather than anger . . . careful attention to detail . . . particularly the threats . . . intention to cause fear and apprehension. Lack of specific facts . . . hints more damaging . . . A complex personality. No psychopathic tendencies in either . . . But . . . textual discrepancies show more than one hand . . ."

'Then there's a lot of psychological stuff about ids and egos that I don't understand,' Mary finished. 'Don't you want to read it?'

'All that pseudo-psychological jargon and analysis of word frequencies in the text? No, thank you . . . Of course it was obvious there were two people, one with a grudge, the other with a mischievous need to fuel it . . .'

'You never said that before,' she accused him. So, he had been thinking after all.

'I did have my own ideas, and didn't take them seriously . . . Look where that got me . . . Tony's dead because I played it cool instead of going all out to find who was writing them . . . I was more worried about my bloody reputation than the actual threats . . .'

She knew it was true, he had only got angry when the item appeared in the press. Why couldn't he be equally angry now with the killer? She asked him that.

Kemp found he could not answer. When a friend is murdered, anger should follow as the night the day, it would be the natural thing, anger and desire for revenge. But because it had been through his neglect, his careless insouciance, that the death had happened, the empty knowledge blocked all outlets for emotion and had set up barricades against the normal processes of thought, leaving his mind in a state of torpor.

'Leave it to John Upshire,' he said, wearily. 'I want no part in it.'

Mary knew she'd lost him again. There was no way she could move into that desert he had made for himself. If only we had been married longer, if I had got to know him better . . .

She knew her limitations. She too would have to go her own way.

CHAPTER 11

Mrs Robsart was drinking tea in the room behind the shop.
Mary was by now familiar with the great propensity of the
English for cups of tea. They indulged it, she had heard, in
great houses in the afternoon with fine china and old silver,
while the lesser breeds made do with mugs at any time of
the day or night. She would not have called Florrie Robsart
a lesser breed had she not been one herself. It made things
easier.

'I'll not say Dan Frobisher's been a bad husband what with
all he had to put up with. He's good to our Amy . . . This
job he's taken up on Merseyside, it's promotion but what he
says to me is it's a change that's needed for her . . .'

'I didn't know he'd left the *Gazette*,' said Mary.

'Just last week it came up. Mind, he's been after a move
for some time. It's on the *Liverpool Post*, a daily, and he could
have gone there years ago but of course he wouldn't, not
when they had the little boy . . .'

'And now you tell me the child's dead,' said Mary, gently.
'I'm so sorry . . .'

'The Lord gives, and the Lord takes away,' said Mrs
Robsart, piously. 'Not that it wasn't a blessed relief . . .'

Mary waited. Florrie Robsart could talk about it now, put
behind her what had been a running sore, a lingering
hurt . . .

'He wasn't quite right, Mrs Kemp, when he was born . . .
mentally, I mean. He was put in an institution up Cambridge
way . . . Well, they had to, didn't they? Amy couldn't cope,
and there was nothing we could do what with the rest of
the family and all . . . It was for the best, they said . . .'

'I'm sure it was, Mrs Robsart. Comfort and care they'd be
giving him there . . . It would be too much for a young girl.'

'You understand, Mrs Kemp – there's some that wouldn't

. . . said she ought to keep him, she was a bad mother . . . a lot of nasty things . . .'

'People should know better,' said Mary firmly, with the full strength of her own convictions. 'Your Amy had had enough pain when she didn't give birth to a perfect child . . . How easily some folk bear the sufferings of others!'

Mrs Robsart liked the emollient sound of the words, recognized a sympathetic soul and extended her confidence. 'She went berserk, Amy did . . . We could do nothing with her, and she'd doctors and social workers swarming all over her as if she weren't right in the head!'

'When all she was, Mrs Robsart, was angry — like she wanted to kick the cat . . .'

'Now, that's just what I told them . . . Amy'd always get in a tantrum if she didn't get her own way, even as a little girl . . .'

'And this was something so important to her . . . It would be like a blow in the face. Poor girl, I can understand how she felt . . . But time has passed . . . Do you think she has got over it?'

Mrs Robsart didn't answer directly. Perhaps her hope was stronger than her knowledge of her daughter. 'We've not been seeing so much of her lately. Well, Mr Robsart, he thought she was upsetting the family. Mind you, it were him she upset most times she were here.'

Mary crumbled a biscuit, drank her tea. Mr Robsart didn't sound as if he was much of a listener, and it might well be that the other son and daughter had gotten fed up with the troubles of Amy. Mrs Robsart was a talker by nature, and now was glad of a kindly ear.

'There was an awful thing about six months ago,' she was saying, 'when Amy's best friend Sharon got married — not before time — and she had a baby boy. It seemed to bring it all up again . . . Amy turned right nasty to Sharon. She kept dropping notes in the pram whenever she met Sharon out with it . . . I never seen what she wrote but Sharon's mother, well, she got wild and took them to a solicitor to make Amy stop . . . It were lucky for Amy that Dan knew him and they got it hushed up . . .'

Mary shook her head. 'It was only anger, Mrs Robsart . . .

her way at hitting out. But maybe it's for the best that Mr Frobisher has taken her out of Newtown.'

But Florrie Robsart still fretted. 'There's such a difference in their age,' she said. 'Sometimes I wish they'd never got married . . . For all that he's stuck by her, I never really took to him . . . We thought we were doing what was best for her. She was such a pretty girl and so lively . . . Done well at school, too . . .'

From the way Mrs Robsart was speaking she was back in happier days when Amy had been their pride and joy.

'A lovely girl,' Mary agreed, looking at the photograph she'd been given. 'A pity there was no one of her own age . . .'

'Amy was a sight better than most of them round here.' Florrie sniffed. 'That Daren, he were sweet on her, but he's one of them Roddicks from the council estate and we all know what *they* are . . .' She broke off, leaving Mary uncertain whether it was Daren himself, his family or where they lived that was at fault. Knowing something of the smaller snobberies, she decided it was probably the last.

'A new life in a new place will work wonders, Mrs Robsart,' she said, 'and your Amy is still young. From what I hear of Merseyside, it might just be the very place for her to find her feet again.'

Mrs Robsart nodded. 'Better that than have her take up with young Daren again . . .'

So that's the way things were running, thought Mary. Perhaps Daniel Frobisher had more than one reason for whisking his wife off to pastures new. Well, there might indeed be music and dancing and love and romance up there in Liverpool for Amy, but possibly not with her husband.

'You know, your visit's really cheered me up, Mrs Kemp,' Mrs Robsart told her at the door. 'No one else wants to hear about our Amy these days. It's done me a power of good just talking about her . . .'

And no harm either, I hope, Mary thought. She had found out what she wanted to know – the feminine side. It would be the weaker element, of course, which would be why it now had to have protection, and be kept at a distance. She could almost in her heart feel sorry for Amy. Something Mrs

Robsart had said . . . 'It's like Amy can't stand people being happy, getting married, having babies . . . as if they've got no right to a normal life . . .'

'Dan Frobisher's left the *Gazette*,' she remarked to Kemp when they were having dinner that evening.

'Has he? Can't say I'm sorry . . . I noticed he didn't even write up the inquest. Perhaps he was warned off.'

'He's gone to Liverpool.'

Kemp permitted himself a small grin. 'A hard city, it'll keep him on his toes.'

'Did he have friends in any of the law firms in Newtown?'

'We don't call them law firms . . .'

Mary wasn't going to be put off by the diversion. 'Well, had he?'

Kemp looked warily at her. When Mary was in her American mode she was at her smartest.

'I think he knew Nick Stoddart,' he said, cautiously.

'Ah, the wine-spiller . . . So those two were buddies . . .'

'What are you getting at?'

'Stoddart has a grudge against you.'

'What of it?'

'I'm thinking of the letters . . .'

Kemp stopped her with an impatient gesture. 'Not that again! I tell you I want to hear no more about the damned letters . . . They're a dead end . . .'

'Not to me . . . Look, Lennox, what if Stoddart and Frobisher were in it together?'

'Why on earth should they be? I've never done Frobisher any harm.'

'His wife might think your firm did.'

Kemp frowned. It seemed a very long time ago since Sally Stacey had told him that story. He could barely remember what it was all about. They had been driving under the big lights before they turned off to the garage . . .

He brought his fist down hard on the table.

'Stop this, Mary! You go on and on about the letters as if they mattered. They don't any longer. They're just a bundle of scribbles with no more reality in them than a bad dream. Whoever wrote them was living in a fantasy world . . . But

Tony's death took place in the real world, the world of facts. And death is the hardest fact of all . . .'

She was not going to be put off.

'And you think because you face that fact there's an end to it.'

He answered her tacit criticism as truthfully as he could. 'I can see nothing beyond Tony's death. I know I ought to be angry, curious as to who did it and burning to help the police . . . But I can't . . . Tony is dead by some senseless mistake, a cruel twist of fate for which I am ultimately responsible . . .'

'So you do concede that the killing is linked to the letters? That there must be a connection?'

'Between the thought and the deed? Between the acting of a dreadful thing and the first motion?'

'You've lost me . . . I suppose that was a quote . . .'

'Yes . . . though I don't know why it cropped up . . . Can't we talk of something else, or perhaps not talk at all if you can't stop being obsessed with those damned letters . . .'

She heard the bitterness in his tone, and went no further.

The conversation broke off. Like all the others they were having these days it had been brittle as thin ice. She knew he could skate rings round her on the surface when he chose, while all she wanted was for the ice to crack so that she could jump in and rescue him.

This discrepancy in their attitudes to the situation did not exactly promote marital harmony. But it did make Mary think long and hard about the man she had married. He had taken up a stance; he would shut his mind against participating in any enquiries concerning Tony's murder – perhaps out of a real fear of deeper psychological damage, perhaps from simple inability to see beyond the death because of what he saw as his guilt for it, perhaps from the knowledge that his mind was for the moment flawed . . . Whatever the reason, she would get no help from him, and in the meantime they were drifting apart.

To hell with that, an inner voice told her, the stubborn voice that had gotten her through the bad times, and was surely not going to give up now she had fallen into easier ways . . . Thrown back on herself – an entity of which she had little opinion – she knew she could cope; she had always done so. She might not be up in all the psychological jargon, nor did she know the banal words of comfort owed to a husband troubled in conscience and low in spirit, but she was single-minded when she had an aim.

She washed up the dishes, and thought about her next move.

She lacked the imagination to visualize terrors ahead; her upbringing had taught her to accept the here and now, and prepared her to take the way forward no matter the consequences. She had had to always live in the present, neither looking back nor envisaging the future, but if the present was untenable then steps must be taken, and, so far, she had found her wits equal to the task.

Something had been said in that last conversation . . . She couldn't recall what it had been . . . If only he didn't use quotations, they flummoxed her, good with words though she was. But an idea had struck her, it had come like a flash and gone again . . . She knew she was a slow thinker – she had been told so many times – but once something got into her head it would stick there until it was needed.

In the meantime, until it surfaced again, she would simply act . . .

CHAPTER 12

'I'll see whether Mr Stoddart is free.' The telephonist at Roberts & Co had a bad cold and sounded as if she didn't care one way or the other. 'Who shall I say is calling?'

'Tell him Mrs Kemp. Mrs Mary Kemp.'

That should get him, she thought, and indeed, he was quick on the line.

'Good morning, Mary. Nice to hear from you. I trust you and Lennox are well.'

'Thank you, yes. I have a favour to ask of you, Mr Stoddart.'

'Anything, dear lady . . .' The air of gallantry was something he used on all his women clients, though it tended to wear thin when they made demands on his patience. This, however, was not a client, unless . . .

'What can I do for you, Mary?'

'I would like to meet with you in private. By that I mean out of your office.'

Oh-ho . . . A matter of confidence . . . Tricky, that. Rival solicitor's wife seeking interview? Scenting possible matrimonial discord, Stoddart was both intrigued and uplifted. He lowered his voice to conspiratorial level. 'Something you wish to discuss of a personal nature? I take your point, my dear Mary, it would not do for you to come here.'

'You catch on fast. Lennox mustn't know I'm in contact with you. Oh, and Nick, I'm sorry about that night at the party. You must have thought me downright rude . . .'

'On the contrary, dear lady, I was myself somewhat under the influence and I behaved badly. You only spoke your mind . . . May I suggest you also do so now?'

'Not on the phone,' said Mary, firmly. 'It is a delicate matter. I wondered if we could meet? Perhaps have lunch . . .'

So it was that husband of hers. Nick dearly loved an

intrigue, particularly when it involved someone he disliked as much as he disliked Kemp.

'Let me look at my diary,' he said, trying to sound not too eager. He rustled the pages. 'As a matter of fact,' he said, slowly, 'it so happens I am free today between one o'clock and three. A conference with Counsel has been unexpectedly cancelled. Now, where would you suggest?'

'Oh, I leave that entirely to you, Nick.'

'H'm . . . The Castle does a passable meal and we could find a quiet corner.'

'You are most kind . . .'

'Not at all, Mary. Shall we say one o'clock in the Castle?'

Mary had dressed carefully. She must strike a balance between appearing inconspicuous yet at the same time be attractive enough to appeal to Nick Stoddart's ego. He would not like to be seen lunching with a frump. The first was comparatively easy since her very plainness and lowness of stature, along with a certain habitual drabness in her clothes, tended to make her unnoticeable in a crowd.

Today, however, she chose an expensive suit, quiet in colour but of good provenance, crocodile shoes which favoured her neat ankles, a handbag to match and a Hermès scarf of the deepest red to set off the large ruby on her ring finger. She figured Nick would be impressed by such things.

He bobbed up smartly from a corner table at her approach. Bet he does it like that in court, she thought, but he looks better sitting down. He certainly had what she considered Roman features, they would sit well on a senator, and he would be vain of them. Pity the rest of the head wasn't up to the job of taking their weight.

'How nice you're looking, Mary. You brighten a dull morning.'

She was nonplussed by compliments; they rarely had come her way.

'Thank you,' she could only murmur in the American mode she had always despised, and biting back her fancied retort: 'You're welcome . . . Have a nice day . . .'

Stoddart made great play of ordering drinks for them, and they proceeded to discuss the menu amicably. That settled, he leant forward in a manner both ingratiating, and sly.

'You know, we did all wonder when old Lennox got married at last – I hope you don't find this impertinent? – what kind of woman he would choose.'

'I'm not minding. You mean he might be a hard man to please?' She looked at him over the rim of her glass. '. . . Or he would be an easy victim?'

Stoddart laughed.

'I'm not saying which . . . We lone men can be either when it comes to the ladies.'

'I'm sorry . . . I didn't know . . .'

'Oh, I've been married, Mary, and divorced. Once burned . . . you know the saying . . . But we are talking about Lennox. How long is it now since you've been his wife?'

'Just over six months.'

'Ah, still in the probation period . . .'

The cream of asparagus was a little too thick. Mary jibbed at the blobs of uncooked flour while they continued a conversation which, to her mind, rather resembled the soup, being put together from scratch and clogged by ingredients of uncertain origin.

The *sole bonne femme* was better, the wine he had chosen light and refreshing. By then they had returned to the subject of her husband.

'I worked with him for a while, of course,' Nick was saying expansively, 'before going into the City where I was given more scope.'

'He does rather take a lot on himself . . .' Mary murmured, thus allowing her companion just that greater scope.

'Far too much,' said Stoddart. 'Just because he managed to climb his way back into the profession by playing detective in some dubious murder cases he seems to think himself above all us ordinary plodding chaps.'

'He's clever all right . . .' Mary toyed with the stem of her glass.

'And doesn't he know it! You knew, of course, that he'd been struck off?'

'It was hardly a secret he'd be keeping from me, Nick.' By now she had decided to get properly on Christian-name terms. But not so close as to divulge that she had nursed

Lennox's ex-wife in New York when she was dying, and was therefore familiar with the whole story. 'Besides, that's all in the past . . . or was until those awful letters started coming . . .'

'I read something about them in the *Gazette* . . . But surely a man like your husband wouldn't take that kind of thing seriously?'

Mary didn't answer. The waiter had brought her escalope of veal and Nick his generous helping of roast beef so that the pause was covered by the laying of plates, and the service of food. When these duties had been accomplished and they were alone again she spoke, in a low confidential voice with just a hint of embarrassment.

'He may not have done, but I did. And that's just what I wanted to talk to you about, because you knew him . . . It's no good me going to the others at Gillorns – they're so loyal to him they'd clam up . . . You see, Nick, I think the letters were written by a woman. Now, I may be Irish but I'm not green as grass . . . It's obvious Lennox had been having some sort of affair that went wrong . . .'

Mary managed a downcast look, a flutter of her fair eyelashes, and the indrawn breath of one who dares speak the unspeakable.

Stoddart was delighted. He put on an expression of the deepest concern and reached across the table for her hand. She let it lie limp in his warm palm.

'How awful for you, Mary . . . Of course, I quite understand . . . To have such a thing come to you, a new bride . . . What was said in the letters?'

She withdrew her hand to take up her fork again – the brave little woman who can still go on eating in the face of disaster.

'Enough for me to know that whoever she was she had been let down by Lennox . . . She must have been so upset when he married me . . .'

'I don't know what to say . . .' Which for once was true of Nick Stoddart. He too resumed his lunch while he speculated upon ways to exploit the situation.

Finally, as he caught and speared the last roast potato, he said, judiciously, as if the words were the residuum of the

93

most profound thought: 'Those cases of his . . . I would not wish to speak ill of him, but . . . they generally did involve women, and I'm afraid Lennox allowed himself to be more emotionally involved than befits a good lawyer.'

'I gathered that much for myself,' said Mary, a trifle tartly, 'and I wouldn't have expected him not to have entanglements before he met me. But then why doesn't he come clean about whoever has been writing the letters?'

'What does he actually say about them?'

'That's the terrible thing, Nick . . . That's why I've come to you . . . Lennox won't speak of them. He slaps me down if I even mention them . . .'

'That's strange . . . He must have some idea. Is it because he's upset over Tony Lambert's murder? I mean, we all are, of course, but Lennox was closer to him than the rest of us.'

Mary raised her pale, anxious eyes.

'That's another of my worries. He simply won't talk about Tony.' She sighed. 'There's times, Nick, when I think he's losing his mind altogether . . . Not to want to help the police investigation into the crime, it's so unlike him . . . It's as if he doesn't want to know . . .'

'Because this woman might be involved,' Stoddart observed, shrewdly. 'In that case, his attitude is understandable. Are you in on the police thinking?'

Mary shook her head.

'John Upshire used to be his friend . . . but now I get the impression they're avoiding each other.'

She had given Stoddart a great deal to occupy his mind, a softening-up process she continued until they were well into their meringue Chantilly. The cream was good but the egg-whites – if indeed they had even started out as such – were baked to rock-like hardness. Mary took her spoon and struck hers a hearty thwack. Here goes, she thought as the sugary shells splintered satisfactorily.

'I think I know who this woman is who's been writing the letters,' she said to her plate.

'I'm sorry . . . I didn't quite catch . . .'

'I've found out who the woman is.'

It was Stoddart's turn to draw in his breath.

He abandoned his meringue, wiped his lips carefully on

his napkin and continued to hold it close to his handsome mouth as he asked: 'Who do you think it is?'

'A girl called Amy Frobisher, Amy Robsart that was.'

Nick spluttered in his anxiety to rid her of such a notion.

'But that's ridiculous . . . Quite preposterous . . . Why, she's . . . she's . . .'

'Daniel Frobisher's wife? I know. They're in it together.'

Stoddart pushed his chair back. His face had gone white, his lips were trembling. With all the powers at his command he struggled to regain composure.

In the meantime Mary calmly finished her sweet.

'You simply can't go around making crazy accusations like that . . .'

'Why not if they're true?'

'But . . . it's . . . it's slander . . .'

'I thought you'd say that, Nick. After all, Frobisher's a friend of yours. But I have to tell you that I'm going straight to Inspector Upshire to ask him to pull them both in.'

She gathered up her bag and gloves, and rose to her feet.

'I won't stay for coffee, Nick. Thank you for a pleasant lunch.'

Stoddart sat on, his face blazing. 'This charade,' he exploded, 'it was set up by Lennox Kemp . . .'

'Lennox had nothing to do with it. I work on my own.'

She brushed past the hovering waiter, thanked him with a smile, and went out of the door without a backward glance. If this were little ole New York, she thought, I'd have been drilled through the shoulder blades by now. That's one very worried man I've just left . . .

Next morning on her way to an appointment at the police station with Inspector Upshire, Mary called in casually at Roberts & Co.

No, Mr Stoddart was not available. Mary gave a small *moue* of disappointment.

'He didn't tell me he was going away,' she said. 'I thought he'd be available.'

Dressed now in a rather dowdy coat and pull-on woolly cap, she had no difficulty in chatting up the languid Linda.

'Got me looking up trains for the rest of the afternoon

while he jumped up and down like a monkey on a stick. Liverpool – of all places . . . God knows what he's doing up there . . .'

Mary had a pretty good idea.

CHAPTER 13

'You've not been round to give me my supper lately.' Inspector Upshire grinned down at Mary.

'I'll settle for a cup of your sergeant's dreadful coffee,' she said. 'As for coming round to your place, I wouldn't want us to get talked about.'

'I suppose your husband doesn't know you're here?'

'Lennox doesn't want to know anything these days except how to get to the office and back. He trots about as if he's on automatic pilot, a mechanical man without a brain . . .'

John Upshire frowned. 'I thought he would have got over it by now, but he hasn't. Any cooperation I've had from him has been strictly on the line, basic facts and no more. None of those intuitions he used to be so good at . . .'

'You'll get no help from him there,' said Mary, decisively. 'You and I, we're on our own. Is there progress your end?'

'On the murder, very little. On the other business, rather more.'

He sorted through some papers on his desk. 'That supposed attempt to run your husband's car off the road, well, we can scrub that one. The driver of a van was brought into a station near Cambridge that night, over the limit, and charged. He admitted that he might have hit another car earlier but swore there'd been no one injured . . . The time and place check out. I'll give you the name and address so that Lennox can get his insurers on to it but as far as being a threat is concerned, it was a red herring . . .'

'And hardly worth him reporting if it hadn't been for the letters . . . They really got him thinking someone was out to get him so that every little incident got blown up . . . Perhaps that's all they were meant to do . . . There's a funny idea I keep getting about them . . .' Again, she was reminded of something she couldn't quite grasp.

Upshire was reading another report. 'As for the fire at your door, and that robbery, there's more from Constable Barnes. That spot of trouble at the Victoria pub the night of your break-in, one of those involved was a young man called Daren Roddick . . .'

'From a family lives up on the council estate?'

The inspector blinked. 'My, how you do get around. D'you mind if I finish?'

'Sorry . . . I shouldn't have interrupted.'

'We know young Daren,' Upshire went on, 'as we know all the rest of the Roddicks. He's got a record of breaking and entering, petty theft and shoplifting – nothing very serious, just following in his pa's footsteps. Anyway, there was a brawl going on outside the pub after closing time, a crowd of youngsters gathered on the pavement so PC Barnes sorted them out and they went off quietly enough, but he did note in his report the presence of Daren Roddick who seemed to have got himself into a fight over one of the girls. She had a car in the pub car park and when the crowd broke up she took Daren off in it. Now, she hadn't been drinking so Barnes had no reason to stop them.'

'Did he get her name?' Mary couldn't help interrupting again.

'Of course not. It's not our policy to go around harassing people. All PC Barnes was doing was keeping public order.' He paused, and went on, rather severely: 'This isn't America, Mary, if young people are out on the streets at night they've a perfect right to be there so long as they're not disturbing the neighbourhood, and as you well know there's darned few good citizens in that locality who'd object . . .'

'Point taken, John.' Mary smiled at him. 'We know it's not the most salubrious place to live but we like it.'

'That said, may I continue? In the light of the break-in on the same night, or rather early the next morning, PC Barnes was asked for further details of anything he had seen on his beat. He recalled that he thought he had seen that same car again, the one the girl drove off in, and this time it was parked down your crescent. Mind you, he's not sure if it was the same car or not for the light wasn't good, either in the car park or down your street. He says in his report there was

98

a couple in it, he heard them giggling and laughing and thought they were snogging. Well, no law against that, even if it was Daren Roddick, so he let them be. He puts the time of that observation at one-fifteen.'

'She would be a bit late getting home,' remarked Mary, 'if someone was waiting up for her . . .'

'It's young Daren we're interested in, the girl's probably not important, though she'd be a good witness as to his presence near the scene of the crime.'

'Oh, no, she wouldn't . . . She'd say she was tucked up in bed with her husband.'

The inspector gave her the full benefit of his bland blue eyes.

'Then you know more than we do. Want to tell me about it?'

'Not yet . . . You get anything on the burnt material in our letterbox?'

'Old rags soaked in petrol, could have come from any source. Would have caused a nasty fire if the house was empty at the time . . . but at that hour of the morning . . .' He shook his head. 'If they knew the premises were unoccupied there'd be nobody hurt, though the house might burn down. If on the other hand they knew you and your husband were in then one of you is bound to be awake – and, remember, the paper round was due . . .'

'I'd worked all that out for myself. So, you don't think it was a serious attempt?'

'Any form of arson is taken seriously by us, but I agree this one doesn't rate high. It was a prankish kind of thing, possibly meant as just a warning . . . Come on now, what's this information you're fairly bulging with?'

Mary looked down at the extent of her chest, which was modest.

'It'll keep,' she murmured, 'until you've quite finished.'

'OK, OK, be like that . . . Well, I had a personal go at young Kevin Brown, the boy who does your paper round . . . and, no, I didn't ask what age he is . . . He did see someone that morning but it was only in the half-light. He thinks the person was youngish from the fast way they moved but to young Kevin anyone over the age of twenty is already old and unfit . . . Whoever it was wore an old trailing coat and some kind of cap, and was of slim build. He was a bit startled when I asked him if they were male or female – I think he's only recently discovered the difference – probably because he did think it was someone poaching on his round and all the newsagents only use boys.'

Inspector Upshire shuffled the various reports together tidily, returned them to his file, clasped his chubby hands under his chin and leant over the desk. 'Now that's all I've got for you, Mary. The usual enquiries are going forward on the murder case, as we keep on informing the press, and some progress has been made, if only in narrowing the field, but at the moment I can divulge nothing more. Now, to a certain extent, Mary, I'm treating you as a privileged person in the same way I would treat Lennox if . . .'

'If he was in his right mind. I do appreciate it, John. I will waste no more words, it's not my style. I do have a lot to tell you and you're at liberty to rap me over the knuckles when I go too far.'

She had to tell it in her own way, the short, flat sentences reflecting how carefully she had marshalled her facts, with the same nicety she brought to piling dishes or peeling apples. She avoided speculation, and stuck to what she knew, but the brief character sketches she gave of the persons involved were pithy and to the point.

It took most of an hour, for there were interruptions, telephone calls and another round of coffee. The policewoman who brought it stared hard at Mary, uncertain as to whether this dumpy female was a suspect or an applicant for the cleaner's job which happened to be vacant. Upshire was a good listener and he had learned in his work to be surprised by nothing so that his face throughout remained expressionless.

When she had finished he sat back and shut his eyes. If it hadn't been for the tap-tapping of his ballpoint on the desk Mary might have thought he had fallen asleep; she had never faced the spectacle of John Upshire thinking.

He was, of course, an experienced officer, used to evaluating facts, reading between the lines of witness statements, sorting out the lies, the evasions and the fumblings with the truth, but he would have no truck with imagination . . . Nor, he surmised, would the woman in front of him . . . She was still a mystery to him. He remembered something said of her in the New York police dossier . . . resourceful, they called her, a fast worker and single-minded . . . As they had been referring to criminal activities they had meant no compliments.

'So,' Upshire said, at last, 'you allege the person who put the stuff in your letterbox was Amy Frobisher because she would know the time of the paper round, and you think Kevin Brown was confused because he half recognized her. The break-in was carried out by Daren Roddick who you say had been her boyfriend. Both offences were done simply out of malicious spite aimed at Kemp because of his marriage and because Amy Frobisher blamed his firm for all her misfortunes. You also say no actual harm was intended and the briefcase was lifted just because it was there and Daren hoped there might be money in it. What happened next you don't know . . . Either Daniel Frobisher found the letters, or his wife handed them over to him and he seized the opportunity to exploit them, or Daniel Frobisher was in it from the beginning . . .'

'Or he was trying to cover up for his wife whose state of mind he knew . . .'

John Upshire put up a hand.

'Wait now . . . Let's get to the letters. You allege they were a concoction of two or more persons, of which Amy Frobisher was certainly one. You believe there was connivance by Nicholas Stoddart, or at the very least, he had knowledge of them . . .'

'He used one of the phrases "your sins will find you out" when he was drunk that Tuesday night . . . He couldn't have known what was in any of the letters unless he'd seen them before, or helped to write them . . .'

The inspector had been scribbling a few notes. Now he looked up.

'These are very serious accusations you're making, particularly about a man like Stoddart. You know very well, Mary, that I can't act on any of this stuff . . .'

'You can pull young Roddick in.'

'I can that. On PC Barnes's report I can bring him in on suspicion of being near your premises that night. He's not the brightest of lads, I'm pleased to say . . .'

'No, it's Amy Frobisher's the bright one of that pair. With her up in Liverpool maybe he'll be at a loss if you get him quick. Can I say a thing about those two?'

The inspector nodded.

'I don't really think they meant any actual harm . . . It was probably put up to Daren as a sick sort of joke, Amy's way of getting her own back at Gillorns, showing Lennox as being vulnerable in his own home . . . And I don't believe she wanted the house to burn down about our ears . . .'

'You can get life imprisonment for arson in this country,' John Upshire growled.

'What I'm saying is, if you put it to Daren Roddick that he's maybe not mixed up in anything worse than the break-in and pinching a briefcase, he might come clean as to what he did with it . . . And that's what is important to us . . .'

'Don't start teaching me my job. We know the way to handle young Roddick is softly, softly, and that's how it will be.'

At least Mary had the satisfaction of hearing that particular order given to one of the sergeants while the inspector motioned her to stay where she was, and to keep quiet.

When they were once more alone he spoke to her sternly.

'I have to warn you, Mary, that all these things you've been saying must not go beyond these walls. And I would suggest that you curb your activities before they land you in real trouble, and that you leave us to get on with the serious work of finding whoever killed Mr Lambert.'

Mary opened her eyes wide at him. 'And haven't I been doing just that? Is it in your mind there's no connection between the threats in the letters and the murder? Surely that takes coincidence a sight too far.'

'You say yourself Amy Frobisher wrote the letters but she meant no real harm . . .'

'And I still say it. I've never met her but unless she's a six-foot Amazon I don't see her striking a man down with an iron bar . . . But there were other hands at work in the

102

letters, maybe they had more sinister business in mind. Or maybe the letters triggered something . . . I get the oddest idea about them . . . Trouble with me is I haven't the imagination to follow my ideas up . . .'

'Glad to hear you're lacking in something,' the inspector observed, drily.

But Mary was off on her own, grasping ineffectually at straws.

'Because if there is no connection,' she murmured almost to herself, 'then that would let Lennox off the hook . . . Oh, if only we could find out who actually helped Amy Frobisher to write them!' She looked up at the inspector pleadingly. 'You will look into what I've told you, won't you? Not only about Amy and Daren Roddick but Nick Stoddart and Frobisher as well? The way Nick took off for Liverpool, there must be something between those two . . .'

Upshire was getting to his feet. 'All I can promise you is that we shall pursue such enquiries as we see fit. You'll have to leave it to us, Mary . . .'

If she left the police station feeling not entirely satisfied, she had at least sown some seed.

CHAPTER 14

Mary was finding that one of the consequences of moving into a more respectable way of life was that her conscience – which she had hitherto treated as a kind of doormat – had begun to squirm and call attention to itself. Now it nagged at her to tell her husband what she had been up to during the last few days. Although she was rather gratified at the results, her methods had scarcely been those of a loyal wife – particularly the clandestine lunch with Nick Stoddart, to whom she had spoken disparagingly of Lennox and even hinted at a fictional and quite improbable affair with a teen-age girl. Matrimonial law was a mystery to her and she had begun to wonder how soon you could get a divorce here in England, and if disloyalty was good cause. She had had her own peculiar concept as to the proper relationship between husband and wife, which she saw as an open one; she had only become rattled when she realized that meant a degree of honesty.

In the end she decided to tell Lennox just so much and no more.

She needn't have worried. Kemp was an old hand at detecting a half-told story – he got plenty of these from his clients – but as his usual sharpness of mind had gone on leave he did not take it upon himself to probe too deeply into the sources of her remarkable assertions.

'So it's young Amy Frobisher you've picked as the fire-raiser, accessory to burglary and writer of malicious letters? You do seem to have got it in for the girl . . .' His summing-up verged on the sarcastic and he didn't like the tone he was taking, but he was in a quandary; he could have worked it out for himself as she had done if his wits had been alert . . .

'She would have had help, of course. I always said if it was a woman she'd be needing help.'

'So you did.' All earlier discussions about the letters had faded in Kemp's mind, overlaid as they had been by weightier matters. Even now the whole subject was wearisome to him. What did it matter who'd written them? He had been the target of their malice but it had been Tony who had died . . . Nothing could change that deep damnation . . .

'Nick Stoddart and Daniel Frobisher, we have to consider these two . . .' Mary's voice was flat as if she was counting spoons.

'What, as first and second murderers?'

'One of them must have had a hand in the letters,' she went on, ignoring his words, 'and Nick's the most likely, he'd seen those other samples of Amy's nasty little habit . . . I somehow don't see Dan Frobisher helping his wife to write such muck, and if he'd even suspected her he'd never have let them get into the *Gazette* . . . Unless he thought if they were brought out into the open it would allay any suspicion she was involved . . .'

'You're getting your logic in a twist,' said Kemp, almost absent-mindedly.

'Better that than my knickers . . . Anyway, logic isn't supposed to be woman's strong point but it is yours. What do you figure happened?'

He could feel her fretting at him like a little hammer on his skull, tapping out the vulnerable spots. She knew he would find it hard to resist a call on his reasoning powers, just as an inveterate crossword solver cannot help being drawn to the puzzle of the black and white squares.

While she supposed he was struggling with a self-imposed lethargy he was instead giving a lot of thought to this new wife of his. He had realized for some time that unlike most people, who considered themselves cleverer than they were, Mary was the opposite; she was cleverer than she knew. In the forcing-ground of her appalling upbringing, ill-educated and totally deprived of any adult appraisal in her youth, she had no opinion of herself and scorned that of others. She had lived by her wits, lying came as naturally to her as breathing, yet she had a hard core of integrity which owed nothing to received ideas or conventional morality. It must have been a toss-up as to whether she would end up a downtown derelict or that fully integrated personality the psychoanalysts hanker after . . . Because she herself had no time for that kind of mumbo-jumbo as she called it, she would not have recognized such a designation, but Kemp had no doubts as to the source of her strength. It was no wonder she had been so excellent a nurse to the elderly, whether they were rich New Yorkers, poor folk from the backwoods, or criminal scum on her own patch; she saw them only in terms of their sickness, their disability, their fear of dying, and she was as untroubled by what they had been as she was by any radical notion of equality. She would have brought to their bedsides not only a patient, methodical care but also a glimpse of Irish charm to relieve the rather prim starchiness of her appearance.

Is that how she was seeing him now, a sick husband in need of succour? Impossible to tell from the calm, grey eyes she raised to his across the table.

'Well, Lennox, what do you think?'

He sighed. She wasn't going to give up, so he set about putting her right on the logic of the facts as they knew them. When he had finished, she nodded.

'That would be the way of it,' she said, 'and you agree it might be Nick Stoddart who encouraged her?'

Kemp shrugged. 'We've no proof of that, nor likely to get it. If he hushed up that affair of the things she wrote to Sharon he might just have got the idea to use Amy in a little exploit of his own. He's got a mind to mischief . . . and a way with pretty, young women who might be impressed by a show of worldly wisdom. Perhaps he told her it would get it out of her system if she wrote it down. They could have cooked up those letters between them . . . But if it was Nick, then he knows the ropes – it'll never be traced back to him.'

'She did the typing. I saw the certificate she got at the school for the typewriting course. Mrs Robsart was very proud of their Amy at the start . . . Said she'd helped out with the invoices at the shop but she took the typewriter with her when she got married.'

'Well, if Frobisher tumbled to what was going on – and

I'll bet he has by this time – then that machine's at the bottom of the Mersey. And my briefcase probably ended up in a gravel pit . . . I still can't fathom Frobisher's part in all this. That day he came to see me, I'd swear he'd no idea his wife was involved. All he was after was a good story with his by-line on it.'

Mary reserved judgement on Daniel Frobisher, but not on his wife. From what she'd learned of Amy, that girl could spin a tale better than most. She was two-timing her husband with young Roddick just for kicks, an affair with Nick Stoddart would be more serious but it was possible, particularly if they were collaborating on the letters. But Amy was not simply out for the excitement a young girl might get from the attentions of an older man, life had given her a raw deal and she still had that anger to keep her warm . . . Mary didn't think Amy cared whether or not Dan knew of her affairs, she was young, he was middle-aged, what else did he expect? But if he had found out about the letters . . . No use her running to Nick Stoddart – he'd deny everything, and the two men would stick together as men do when jobs and reputation are at risk so that it might well be Amy was thrown to the dogs . . .

'It was young Roddick,' said Mary suddenly, at the end of this line of thought, 'gave that packet to the press. Amy egged him on to do a spot of breaking and entering, all part of her plan to harass you and I in our love-nest but she knew better than to be there when he actually did it. He took the briefcase home with him, found the letters, and decided to play his cards real clever – like the big boys do. At some time or other he'd hint to the *Gazette* he'd more where those came from and they could have them at a price, or he might try a spot of blackmail on you if you got anxious about their whereabouts . . .'

'The workings of the criminal mind are clear as daylight to you, Mary. As the man said, you're a loss to the Mafia.'

Mary shrugged. 'It would never have worked in the real world but Daren Roddick doesn't live there. Not the brightest lad in Newtown, our Daren. And of course he'd no idea Amy was involved in the letters. She must have been ready to chop his balls off when she found out what he'd done . . .'

Kemp frowned.

'I'm sorry,' she said, grinning. It was only when her mind was working too fast for her tongue that she slipped up on her language. 'Shall we just say that Amy was a trifle upset? Perhaps it was when she was in that state that Dan Frobisher got the truth in his face . . . After the murder, of course, they were all running for cover. And the letters stopped coming . . .'

'Well, they would, wouldn't they?' Kemp's tone was dismissive. 'They'd served their purpose . . .' He got up from the table. 'Now, can we stop going round in circles? I've got work to do.'

But Mary was stubborn. 'You're surely not thinking the murder of Tony is to go down as an unsolved crime? I'd thought you'd more spunk than that.'

Kemp threw his pen across the table. 'Look, Mary, this isn't a nice, readable detective story, this is real life and that was a real death. There weren't any fingerprints, the weapon wasn't bought at some convenient local shop, it was picked up from a scrap heap and just as casually dropped. There were no convenient fibres clutched in the dead man's hand, no precious bodily fluids for forensics to match up . . . The only blood spilled was Tony's . . .' His voice shook. He tried to stay calm, speak more sensibly. 'It was dark, there were no witnesses. It was like a hit-and-run with no hope of tracing the car . . . It was done at the back of a garage, for God's sake . . . Tyre marks all over the place . . . If a car was used at all. Someone could have been over the hedge and across the field within minutes, and the ground so hard with frost there's nothing for the police to take plaster casts of and go on a merry-go-round of the shoe shops . . .' He stopped, running out of breath and sarcasm at the same time.

She just looked at him, following her own line of thought. 'And maybe there wasn't a connection with the letter-writers,' she murmured.

'What did you expect? A note tossed on the body saying the editor regrets this correspondence is now closed?'

Mary went out to the kitchen; when he was in this mood, she thought, it was no good talking to him.

CHAPTER 15

Michael Cantley was surprised to find Mary Kemp waiting for him in Gillorns the following day.

'Lennox is on the top floor,' he told her, 'having a field day with the auditors.'

'I know. The king is in his counting house . . . But it isn't him I'm wanting to see. He has my full attendance at home.'

Michael was never quite sure how to take the new Mrs Kemp, being unable to shake off the impression of her as Mary Blane, the rather dim Irish secretary Kemp had engaged over a year ago, who had turned out to be far from dim, not altogether Irish, and much more than a secretary.

'I need to talk to you about Mr Lambert,' she said now as she perched herself rather primly on the edge of a chair, 'because Lennox won't . . .'

'Perhaps some coffee,' said Mike, quickly, to give him time to adjust to this sudden visit, and indeed over the ordering and serving of it he did manage to conceal his unease.

'The day Mr Lambert died,' said Mary, who believed in coming straight to the point when there was nothing to gain by going round it. 'I understand he went up to London?'

'That is so. He had business with his own family's solicitors.'

'It was about his parents' estate – I heard it mentioned at the engagement party.'

Well, if she knows that much, thought Cantley, who had more than his fair share of the normal lawyer's caution, there's no harm in her knowing . . . After all, she's Lennox's wife.

'The estate had been finally wound up by Medway, Austin after the two deaths, and Tony still kept his own private affairs in their hands. Despite being a partner here he wasn't

109

the sort to abandon a firm who'd served the Lamberts for several generations.'

Mary put down her coffee cup, and pulled at her skirt with some show of embarrassment. 'You must really be wondering why I've come . . . It's just that Lennox is so concerned. Oh, he may not show it to you, Michael, here in the office, but at home it's becoming a bit of a crisis . . . I suppose that's really what wives are for, isn't it? To listen to their husband's troubles and try to help . . .'

'Well . . .' Mike felt he had no answer to that, so he waited.

'You know he feels himself responsible for Tony's death? That it was all a terrible mistake, and that he was the one who should have been killed, not Tony.'

'Mrs Kemp – Mary . . . We all appreciate how he feels. But it wasn't his fault . . .'

'Try telling him that – you'll get nowhere. Now he's shut down on anything to do with the killing. Doesn't want it mentioned . . . But I can't accept that . . . I didn't know Tony Lambert like you all did but I feel the tragedy of it here in my heart . . .' Mary knew she sounded like a bit part in a Hollywood movie, '. . . for that poor girl, Miss Allardyce . . . I've tried to see her because Lennox couldn't face it . . . but, well, I can quite understand her reluctance . . . She blames him, you see . . .' Mary produced a small handkerchief and a smothered sob, both of which threw Mike off his balance.

'Oh, I say . . . Of course we're all sorry for Miss Allardyce . . . But you can rest assured she has taken it well, although I understand from her brother she may not yet feel up to going on with her studies. You know that Tony has left her everything he had?'

'He did? Oh, I'm glad of that . . . Naturally he could never have foreseen . . .'

'He made the will a few weeks ago, when they first became engaged. That would have been Tony's way. Once they were married she would have got it anyway . . . I suppose he saw it in the old-fashioned sense that an engagement was the plighting of troth.' Michael smiled at the phrase.

'Gee . . . now, I call that really romantic . . . the plighting of troth . . .' Mary paused, almost in reverence. 'And did Tony have much to leave?'

Mike had a good lawyer's proper appreciation of property, so that a certain note of awe crept into his tone as he spoke of Tony's estate.

'The Lamberts had owned a lot of land hereabouts which hadn't much value until the new town came into being. Once development started the price soared and Tony's parents were left extremely well off. Unfortunately they didn't live to enjoy it, but Tony's inheritance was large . . . Even allowing for what the government will skim off there'll still be a cool million for the Allardyce girl.'

Mary was slowly shaking her head in what Mike thought of as a rather Irish manner. 'Of course,' she said, 'no amount of money can ever compensate for the loss of a loved one . . .'

Michael cleared his throat. This was not a language in which he felt at home. Somewhat desperately he changed the subject.

'At least you're not being bothered by any more of those dreadful letters. Lennox tells me there's been no more.'

'Oh, I don't think we're needing to trouble ourselves with them,' said Mary, with a casual air of indifference. 'Inspector Upshire has that side of things already buttoned up.'

'Is that so? You mean, the police know who's responsible?'

'There's evil minds were bent on mischief,' she said, airily. 'They'll come to a sticky end. You seem surprised . . . Did you really see the letters as that important?'

Cantley felt himself floundering, out of his depth. 'The threats in them . . . so like what actually happened . . .'

Mary sighed. 'So you and Lennox are of the same mind. You believe it should have been him got killed that night. That's the burden on his soul.'

'I didn't mean it that way,' said Mike, hastily. 'It's just that there doesn't seem to be any other reason for Tony's death.'

'That appears to be the universal view . . .'

There was a heavy silence for a few minutes as each of them pursued their own line of thought. Mary knew she was clutching at straws. She was always aware of her limitations. You need imagination, she thought, to take this thing further, you need that spark which will light the way forward, you need the flair to see beyond the facts . . . Lennox had that flair, she hadn't . . . In fiction the ideas would buzz like bees

111

in the brain of the arch-detective and hey-presto, the pieces would come together and the crime be solved . . . But she had no head for fiction, her world had always been real and as in the real world nothing was perfect, things didn't work out the way one wanted, and you had to be content with less . . . All the same, she had a dogged determination within her which drove her on to follow even the most unpromising trail . . .

'I've a favour I want of you, Michael,' she brought out at last. 'Could you get an appointment for me with Medway's, the solicitors in London? Don't look so startled. It's just that John Upshire wanted to know if there was anything said that day which would explain why Mr Lambert might have tried to see Lennox at the garage . . . I know he's already got a statement but he thought that if I talked to Mr Medway I might spot something that was missed.'

'You seem to be very well in with the inspector.' Cantley was more amused than startled. 'Are you playing detective?'

'If you mean am I taking over Lennox's role, the answer is no, but John Upshire and I do get on pretty well.'

'And I suppose if I give you an excuse to interview young Mr Medway I'm to say nothing about it to your husband?'

Mary shrugged as she gathered up her bag and her gloves. 'And wouldn't he be doing it himself if he'd the mind to it? As that's closed down for the time being, it's me has to do it for him.'

Michael was smiling as he got to his feet. There was a lot more to this woman than met the eye. 'You're quite the conspirator, aren't you? As a matter of fact, there are some things of Tony's here which should go up to Medway's . . . I could always say you were to bring them . . . Wait a moment, Mary, and I'll arrange it.'

'Call in here tomorrow morning on your way to the train,' he told her when he came back. 'I've made an appointment for you with Donald Medway at twelve . . . and, good luck . . .'

When Mrs Kemp had gone, Mike sat back and wondered why he should be feeling this surge of excitement. It reminded him of moments in the past when Kemp had brought him into one or other of his mysterious cases.

Cantley had been younger then, not so set in his ways, but looking back he now realized how much he had enjoyed these assignments out of office routine, how he had relished working with Kemp, aware of the man's sharper mind and greater understanding of people's motives, and how he had admired – even from the sidelines – Kemp's capacity for getting things right in the end. What a pity it was that that mind was for the moment overthrown . . .

Mary walked home through the small park which was tentatively greening in the late spring. It was almost warm – that tepid lessening of cold she had learned they called warm here in England – so she sat down on a seat under the laburnums to enjoy it.

Like the rest of this part of town, the park was Victorian in origin, a relic of that spacious age when urban land was not measured only in its cost per square foot. It was a leafy oasis, scorned by hurrying townsfolk and shunned particularly by mothers of small children for fear of the bogeymen hiding in the bushes. As the bogeymen of Mary's childhood had been nosy welfare officers rather than the down-and-outs who lurked round the waste lots in her hometown – where in any case the gangs of scavenging kids tended to be more dangerous than any potential rapist – this neat green place away from the traffic held no terrors for her.

It had been some weeks since she had been there and she had forgotten that the park was also used for those with energy to spare. Several joggers had already passed when she recognized one lone figure. The lion cub was out and about again.

The path narrowed in front of the seat and Mary half rose so that a meeting was inevitable, and Anita had no choice but to stop.

'Whoa there . . . Miss Allardyce . . . Anita . . . Come and give your legs a rest.'

The girl stood rocking backwards and forwards on her muddied trainers, as if poised to take off again in a quick sprint. She was chewing at her underlip, undecided as to the propriety of accepting the invitation. Mary reached out and took hold of a hand which was both cold and sweaty. Gently but firmly she drew the girl down on to the seat beside her.

'I'm so glad to see you. We have been wondering about you lately. Are you all right?'

'Sure I'm all right.'

She did not look it. The lion cub had grown up and shed some of her furry glory on the way; the shine was out of the red-gold mane and the bright eyes had lost their candour. Gone too was the chubby buoyancy which had been so much a part of her charm. This was a lioness now, and to Mary's eye, a wary one.

'You're thinner. You don't need to jog.'

Anita shrugged chunky shoulders, a movement that had contempt in it.

'I don't do it to slim, I do it because I like it . . .'

'I can see that you do. Sometimes it is as well to do things that are routine, they help us to forget . . . Are you back at the studying?'

Anita gave her a full look, which was not friendly.

'What do you think? That's what everybody says . . . It'll take your mind off . . .' A mimicry of other voices.

'Well, it might help.' Mary was being her most soothing. 'You've a career in front of you, Anita.'

'Fuck that . . .' The girl tossed back her hair in a gesture as rough as the words. 'What do you know about such things, anyway? You don't strike me as an educated person . . .'

The attack was personal, and calculated to offend, but Mary let it pass. Little smartyboots, she thought, perhaps I've underrated the Australians.

'I appreciate that you lost Tony,' she said, calmly, 'but it must be of some comfort to know how much he thought of you when he left you all his worldly goods.' If there was straight talking to be done it needn't all come from the one side.

Anita stared at her, a rude, unblinking stare.

'I've got no reason to talk to you,' she said. 'You're all the same in this dreary old town, empty heads and clacking tongues . . . I'll be glad to get the hell out . . .'

'Back to the old sheep station – is that really the way of it? You're giving up on the law and all?'

'I can do it as well back in Sydney. The English haven't

the monopoly on it – though to hear them talk you'd think they had.'

'And is your brother to accompany you?'

'If you're so interested, yes, he is. We're both fed up to the teeth with this place. Oh, there's no need for you to look so prissy, Mrs Kemp, you don't fit in here either . . . Bet you get asked the same questions, where d'you come from, who's your family, how long have they been there . . . Makes you sick . . .'

'It's called placing people,' said Mary, pleasantly. 'They do it all the time, even with their own kind. They listen to accents, assess your education and origins so that they can slot you into their feudal system . . .'

Anita seemed surprised that Mary should even know the word.

'Too right it's bloody feudal, it should have been chucked out centuries ago . . .' She stopped, and took a deep breath as if suddenly remembering who she was talking to. 'And I'd be glad if you'd keep out of our affairs. Zack's right when he says it's all your husband's fault what happened to my Tony and you're just trying to get round it by harassing me.'

'Anita. Trying to sympathize is not harassment. You should not spurn the efforts of those who only want to help.'

Something in Mary's tone arrested the girl who looked on the point of taking flight. 'What a funny way you talk . . . One minute you're on about Zack and me having no background as if a fair-sized sheep farm north of Perth wasn't enough . . .'

'Look, I don't give a damn where you and your brother come from so long as you treat the people here right . . . Those clacking tongues you spoke of, why should they bother you?'

'That old Crab-apple, or whatever her name is . . . Now she's one with a tongue like an egg-bound hen. Just because we said we'd be selling the house. What's she expect? I'm not going to live in it so what else is it good for? Zack says it'll fetch a good price on the open market.'

'I'm sure it will,' said Mary, drily. 'Mrs Crabtree was probably sad out of loyalty to the family she's served all these years.'

'There you go again. Family, family, it's all the English ever talk about . . . And that old retainer thing – doesn't it make you want to puke? We weren't going to have her around anyway once we were married.'

Mary looked into the girl's face for some sign of sadness as she spoke the last words, a sorrow for the loss they must bring to mind, but there was nothing in the light-blue eyes or in the set of the wide mouth other than a kind of peevish resentment, the expression of a child deprived of a favourite toy. For the first time Mary took a closer look at the might-have-been, and then smothered the thought that Tony Lambert could be well out of it . . .

'I can understand you wanting to go home to Australia, Anita,' she said, 'but why should Zachary be leaving Newtown?'

'Zack has his reasons. Time to move on, he thinks . . .'

And you can do a lot of moving when your sister has come into a fortune.

'So, the bungalow too will be put up for sale?'

'Zack's thinking of making it over to the Development Corporation, for hospitality purposes, you know. Zack would like to be remembered in the town for his good works.'

Was that a touch of ironic humour? Mary took it as that. 'They could put up a plaque,' she said, and both of them laughed, briefly in harmony.

'Zack needs a holiday, and he's been good to me . . .' Perhaps Anita felt she had been disloyal, consorting as it were with the enemy. 'He paid for me to come over here.' She brooded on that for a moment. 'But I was happier back there in Sydney when I got my degree. I had friends there . . . I couldn't make friends with that lot at the College of Law with their lah-di-dah accents and honours from Oxford . . . To them I was some kind of freak, a pet kangaroo with a billycan . . . Sometimes I wished I'd never come . . .'

'But you met Tony,' Mary reminded her, gently.

'Yes, I met Tony. Zack saw to that . . .'

She was pushing her heels viciously into the soil beneath the seat, as if trying to scrape the mud off her smart trainers. She muttered something which Mary could hardly hear, though it sounded like: 'God, don't you just hate all men?'

Then Anita was up and away across the grass, her little feet pounding the turf, her long bright hair flaring behind her like a comet's tail.

CHAPTER 16

For a brief period the next day Mary Kemp felt out of her element. It was not because this was the city of London, for, under various names, she had lived and worked in many cities: Chicago by its wintry lake, Philadelphia where there wasn't much brotherly love these days, Dublin which had a surfeit of it, and of course, New York, the acme of cities all. She had thought there could be nothing in London that could faze her, but the quiet courtyard to which she had been directed – itself only a few steps from the bustle of the Strand – struck even her prosaic mind with the fancy that here was the very essence of all that separates the Old World from the New.

The air was still, and had a musty smell as if it hadn't been changed in generations, the unswept dust gathered in the cracks between the paving stones seemed more permanently settled than the grey rise of modern concrete on the skyline. Everything she could glimpse through the ancient archways, stone stairs up to old wooden doors, curly iron railings and blank, blinded windows, was waiting for something – possibly eternity. The scuttling figures – they all seemed to be dressed in drab grey or black – brought no sense of life to the scene since they looked painted on, mere puppets of the moment as they hurried about with their briefcases and piles of books.

It has been here for so long, she thought as she stood trying to come to terms with her feeling of dislocation, for she knew herself to be a changing woman who had never known permanence of place. For all the ruined castles and other antiquities she had seen when travelling Britain with Lennox she had never felt moved as she did now by this grave, archaic precinct. I'm not one for the past, she'd told him, history meant nothing to her . . . But here, here in the very centre of his world, she felt the strength of it, the domain of unalterable law . . .

In the shadow of the arch she found a modest nameplate: Medway, Austin, Solicitors. Although advertisement was obviously out of the question, the brass had received daily attention, a little more than a lick and a promise, for perhaps a hundred years. The slate step was crumbling but the mahogany door, which was half open in tepid welcome, shone with the polishing of many handmaidens. Such small elements of tradition registered with Mary, for she had a tidy mind and approved of orderliness.

The waiting room into which she was shown was downright dingy, prints of bewigged gentlemen looked down gloomily on stiff leather chairs and the long table strewn with copies of *Country Life* it was too dark to read. She skimmed through pictures of impressive properties, and reflected that the homes of the English landed gentry had certainly set their stamp on many a mansion down on Long Island where she had nursed. Then, even as now, she had no desire for the unattainable and could look at expensive homes without envy, though she scrutinized their gardens more carefully and decided to cut down to a decent size those bushes in her own which blocked the access to the stream of the Lea.

She was interrupted by Mr Medway's secretary, who led her out of the Victorian parlour into, and through, the clamour of a modern office. This was the engine-room of the firm, and the machinery was working at full tilt, typewriter and word-processor keys clicking away like Spanish dancers under the greenish glow of the winking screens. It looked a more costly set-up than she'd known at Gillorns.

The noise was lost to the high ceiling of the dim corridor beyond, which had worn linoleum underfoot, and more prints along its walls of lawyers dead and gone. Here the doors were chastely lettered: Mr Herbert Austin, Mr Merivale Austin, Mr Medway, Senior, and finally, Mr Donald Medway.

His room was large enough to have contained the whole of the general office in one corner of it. The windows gave on to that quiet square, and pigeons fluttered on the sill

119

outside, settling, pecking and flying off as if they were bashful clients who couldn't quite bring themselves to face the costs of litigation.

Donald Medway was young and fresh-faced, an athletic-looking man with a pink-and-white complexion. He received her small package with gratitude.

'Kind of you to bring them, Mrs Kemp. There was really no hurry. And how is your husband?'

'Working hard,' she said, 'but Mr Lambert's death has affected us all.' It was no more than the truth.

'Coffee? Or would you prefer a sherry?'

'Coffee, please.'

He went over to the tray on a table in a corner and poured out from what looked like a silver service. The cups were delicate, the coffee strong and black. He offered milk and sugar, which she refused.

'You saw him that last day, Mr Medway?'

'Indeed, yes. There was little I could tell the police. Tony was in a happy mood, more so than for months . . . I was only too pleased to see him snap out of it. His parents' death had been a sad time for him. Getting engaged made a new man of him . . .'

'Had you met Miss Allardyce?'

'No. Unfortunately my wife and I had tickets for the theatre the night of the engagement party, but there was no doubt Tony had gone overboard about the girl from the first moment he'd met her. We'd had a college reunion dinner some months ago and I remember him telling me all about her . . . She seemed just right for him as she was a law student and could share his interests. How is she taking things?'

'She's very young. She'll recover . . . It was good of him to leave her all he had.'

Donald Medway leaned back in his chair. 'I had a bit of a tussle with Tony over that . . . He insisted on making the will . . . but as the situation was then there was nothing inherently wrong in doing so. Prenuptial settlements used to be quite the thing, but of course they were made in consideration of the marriage taking place . . . Tony would have none of that. His will was straightforward, everything was to go

120

to his fiancée, and knowing how he felt about her I bet he told her, too.'

'I can understand. He was very much in love . . . And there was no other family?'

'No one. The Lamberts had come to a dead end, if you'll excuse the phrase. There are some far-out cousins on his father's side in Scotland but they're well set up. He'd no need to consider them. I did advise that he wait, for as his wife, Anita would inherit anyway and I understood the wedding was to be in June. But I couldn't move him . . . Tony had an old-fashioned notion of chivalry . . .' Donald laughed, then stopped rather abruptly. 'You will know enough of lawyers, Mrs Kemp, to appreciate they look into every eventuality, so of course I did mention death . . . It was naturally accidental death I had in mind, as who hasn't in these days of daft motorists? It would make no difference, Tony said, if he died before the marriage, that was the whole point of the will — and he assured me he was in perfect health and had no intention of shuffling off, etc . . .'

The lawyer paused, looked out of the window for a moment and when he continued his tone had lost its jollity. 'Tony and I were at school together, and up at King's . . . He was one of my closest friends . . .'

Mary saw that his feelings ran deep, but in the English style they would not be given utterance. It would be tactful not to pursue them.

'The police have got nowhere,' she remarked, flatly.

'I suppose not. From what they said they don't have much to go on. Could have been an attempt at robbery and they hit out harder than they intended . . . Or there was a gang of them stealing cars round that garage and he caught them in the act.' Donald shook his head. 'Far too many of these mindless murders about these days . . .'

It was clear that Medway knew nothing of Lennox's involvement and Mary had no wish to bring it up. She would rather leave him with the same vague, simplistic explanation the police had given.

'You lunched with Tony that day?'

'At the Law Society, yes . . . I was meeting someone there

121

and I took him along as he wasn't going back to Newtown till the evening train.'

'So he was going somewhere else in the afternoon?'

'I suppose he must have been . . . Oh, I remember he said something about Anita's engagement present. He was rather shy and mysterious on the subject . . . A piece of jewellery, I presume.'

Mary considered the suggestion, and didn't think much of it. Surely if it had been jewellery Tony would have given it to his fiancée before the party so that she could show it off . . . She already had a sparkler of an engagement ring on her finger . . . And wasn't jewellery rather old hat these days? The lion cub hadn't seemed quite the type for it . . . What was it Tony had said to Lennox that night? 'It's to be a surprise. She's got no idea . . .' and something about it not being ready . . .

As Mary racked her brains wondering what on earth rich young men gave their fiancées these days (apart from all their worldly goods) as surprise presents, she sensed that Donald Medway was getting restless – though in an impeccably gentlemanly fashion. She had already taken up much of his time and he would have other appointments. She gathered her bag from the floor beside her chair, and prepared to rise.

'I'm sorry,' she said, sweetly, 'to bring it all back to you, Mr Medway, but can you remember anything you talked about with Tony that day which would indicate where he was going when he left you?'

Donald rested his chin on his hand, and looked across at her. Really, Mrs Kemp was a most persistent woman, nice of course, but persistent. She must have a bee in her bonnet somewhere. But out of courtesy he made the effort.

'It's difficult, you know, when old friends meet from time to time – they talk about all sorts of things. Let me think, now . . .' Like any good lawyer, he had an excellent memory.

'Certainly nothing over lunch, of course . . . My friend Marcham was with us then . . . We both came down the steps of the Law Society with Tony and I said goodbye to him as he set off down Chancery Lane towards the Strand. Marcham and I were going to Counsel's chambers – that was

122

in the opposite direction . . . And yet . . . something's coming back to me. Why did I know that Tony would be going down that way? For I did . . . It must have been something he'd said earlier . . .'

'Oh, please think, Mr Medway. It is important.'

Her eagerness had by now communicated itself to him, and caught on.

'It wasn't then . . . so it must have been earlier. But that would be here in my office.' Donald Medway looked round the room as if the walls had listened and could tell him. 'Let me see, now . . . We'd discussed the estate, and some matters of legacies from his mother . . . I've got it . . . Tony remarked that he was seeing Lydia's chap later, he'd get a bus in the Strand . . .'

'Lydia's chap? Who's that?'

'My dear Mrs Kemp, I haven't the foggiest idea . . . It was just said casually when I asked him if he'd time for lunch with us . . . It didn't mean a thing to me apart from the fact that when he walked off down Chancery Lane it must have registered in my mind.' Medway looked at Mary with some admiration. 'You've quite a way with you of getting at a person's memory . . . You'd have made a good barrister. I'm only sorry I can't be of any more help. I've no idea who he meant by Lydia's chap.'

'Oh, but you have been, Mr Medway,' Mary said, getting to her feet and holding out her hand. 'You've been a great help.'

'Have I? All I've done is pluck from the memory . . .'

'A rooted sorrow . . . I've caught my husband's habit of quotation . . .'

They both laughed as he held open the door for her. Returning to his seat he decided that the words she had followed so swiftly had been out of context, and as he repeated them to himself he began to think they had not been altogether inapt.

Mary gave no thought to them as she waited at a bus stop in the Strand. Was this the way Tony Lambert had gone, on the route to Charing Cross, or had it been from the other side back to Liverpool Street? But it would have been far too early for him to go to the station . . .

123

In desperation she got on a bus going west. She scanned the shop windows, the façades of offices and public windows, even the signboards outside cinemas and theatres for some clue to Lydia . . . I must be dumb, she was thinking. The expression didn't give rise to any comment from Donald Medway when Tony said it so it was nothing out of the way, it was just as if he'd said: 'I'm going to see Lydia's young man,' or, 'my friend Lydia's recommended hairdresser, chiropodist, shopkeeper . . .' the possibilities were too endless to contemplate.

In the end, Mary gave up. She had lunch in a restaurant at Charing Cross, and spent the afternoon wandering round the large stores where she gave more time to the household goods in basements than fashion items on the other floors. She was still determined to follow the footsteps of Tony Lambert on his last day in London and catch the five-thirty train to Newtown as he had done, but the hours between continued to rankle in her mind.

She had been warned about the evening rush hours and was early on the platform. Nevertheless, when the train came in and it was every man for himself and chivalry a dead duck, she was swept into the carriage like a parcel on a conveyor belt and lucky to get a seat. She sat primly, drawing in her legs as she used to do on the subway to Brooklyn.

At least here there's something to see, she thought, as the train trundled past the old sheds and grimy hoardings with their scrawls of witless graffiti, gathering speed as the way broadened as if it too was glad to get out of the city.

Only after several stops when the mass of swaying bodies had more or less separated into its component parts did she glance up at her fellow passengers. She immediately recognized the tall figure leaning negligently against a pole, his bronzed head at the level of the luggage rack. Zachary Allardyce's ruddy complexion would have marked him out anyway in the midst of so many pallid faces, even if he hadn't towered above them like a sun-god among pygmies.

He caught her eye, and gave her a wide smile. She was surprised, thinking of their last meeting. Perhaps he has a forgiving nature, she thought, someone with his looks ought at least to have that . . . More likely it was little sister's golden gain had brought him to a better humour . . . Which made Mary wonder if he too had known. Of course he would; Anita was his protégée, she had said as much.

There was no time for Mary to follow this disturbing line of thought for at the next station the seat beside her became vacant, and Zachary came and sat down beside her.

'How nice to see you, Mary Kemp. Been shopping?'

'It's little I've to show for it,' said Mary, smiling and showing her one modest Marks & Spencer bag. She could slide easily into conversation with this man, he was of her own kind.

'Do you always catch this train when you're up in the City?' she asked.

'It's a sardine tin but it's convenient. British Rail's a right con, you'd think they'd run a better service for commuters the prices we pay.'

'Well, it's half empty now,' said Mary, looking round the compartment and out at the marshes of the Lea Valley. 'Look, wide open spaces inside and out.'

Zack snorted. 'Industrial wasteland. Should be put to proper use.'

'Like them?' she said, pointing at a cluster of high-rise flats sticking up like lost teeth. 'I'd prefer parkland . . . So, you're thinking of returning to base, Zachary?'

'Anita told you? Well, things are getting a bit sluggish in the Development Corporation. Between the old stick-in-the-muds and the new conservationists any forward planning's hamstrung.'

'You mean you're not getting your own way?'

'Too right I'm not. For me that signals the time to move on . . . Knocked the Corp for six when I told them I was leaving, but they've known all along I'm not the man to hang around till the pension pay-out.'

'Your eyes will be set on a wider horizon . . . Is it back to Sydney you'll be going, you and Anita?'

'We-el . . . We'll take in a bit of the world, first. There's no telling . . .'

There obviously wasn't so far as Zachary's plans were concerned so Mary changed the subject.

'This is the train you were on with Tony Lambert that day,' she remarked, casually. 'What did he talk about?'

'Stop right there, Mary. I was not on the train *with* Tony. I only saw him get off at Newtown Station and we hardly spoke. He went for his car and I went for mine. Where'd you hear this?'

As she was sitting alongside him, Mary could not see his face but there was a new sharpness in his voice.

'Inspector Upshire told me you'd seen Tony. I took it for granted you'd been together.'

'Take nothing for granted, that's my motto . . . And I thought police files were confidential.'

'Lennox has an interest – as you were at pains to point out to me the last time we met.' Mary, too, could be sharp.

'You and that other woman from Gillorns called at an unfortunate moment . . . Anita was upset.'

'All the more reason why a little feminine sympathy might have helped.' Mary was not going to let him get away with his bad manners.

But Zack Allardyce had dismissed that episode. He half turned in his seat and gave her a hard look from eyes blue as his sister's but at this moment darkened by anger. 'You and that Inspector Upshire ought to be careful what you say . . . I repeat I was not with Tony that day on the train.'

'No need to lose your cool, Zack . . . I understood you were in the same compartment, and naturally I assumed . . .'

'You've seen for yourself how crowded these trains are . . . and once people start getting out and you find yourself a seat you might never see someone who's already sitting somewhere else.'

Mary glanced around and had to admit this was true, though Zachary's explanation seemed unnecessarily detailed.

'I'd just wondered . . .' she said, vaguely. 'Tony was supposed to be getting a surprise engagement present for Anita and I thought perhaps you were in on it . . .'

The train had stopped at the station before Newtown and several people stumbled over Zachary's outstretched legs as they pushed forward to get to the door. Either this was another example of the Australian's bad manners in not drawing back his feet, or he was oblivious to their fellow passengers. He was certainly unnaturally still, and the oath he brought out when the last man kicked his ankle was both unseemly and vicious.

Once on their way again, Zachary sat in sullen silence, his handsome face flushed. Perhaps he was nursing the pain of his ankle, a grudge against the man who'd kicked him, or some larger grievance. Whatever the cause, he had given up chatting companionably to Mary and possibly regretted ever having started. When they pulled in to Newtown Station he opened the door before the train stopped, hopped out, and slammed the door back in her face as she got to her feet.

'I say, what a rude chap! Are you all right?' A gentleman retrieved Mary's bag and opened the door for her.

'Thank you,' she said, stepping down on to the platform. 'That young man, he's maybe got something on his mind . . .'

She wished she knew what it was.

CHAPTER 17

Although calling in at the police station meant making a detour on her way home, Mary was carried as if by impulse in its direction. She was up the steps and into the front office without either appointment or any idea of what she wanted. It would all sort itself out when she spoke to John Upshire.

Unfortunately, he was out, and the uniformed man behind the desk was a constable she did not know. She gave her name, and said the inspector had promised to let Mr Kemp see one of the statements in the case . . .

'And what case would that be, madam?'

'The murder of Mr Lambert. He was my husband's partner. Mr Kemp is unable to come to the station this evening and he asked me to call in, and make some notes.' The blarney came easily once she got started – as it had always done.

Constable Jones hesitated. He had received no such instruction, and Inspector Upshire was a terror for detail. Was it in order to ask for some identification? The woman looked, and spoke, respectable enough but then so did many interfering busybodies . . .

At that moment an inner door opened and Sergeant Cobbins poked his head out, and saw her. 'Why, hello, Mrs Kemp . . . What brings you here?'

Mary gave him the same tale, at ease now with someone she knew.

'You'd better come in and see Detective Sergeant Martin. He's the officer in charge while the inspector's away. It's OK, Bob, I can vouch for Mrs Kemp.'

DS Martin had, until recently, been with the Met. He was a shrewd man who believed in keeping a close mouth where members of the public were concerned. It took a lot of Mary's soft words and wheedling ways to get him to produce the file and the statements in which she was interested.

'It's so important for Mr Kemp to know just what brought Mr Lambert to the garage that night ... Whether it was professional or private business ...'

'The statement given by Mr Kemp says no meeting had been arranged,' said Sergeant Martin in a tone which gave no indication as to whether such a statement should be believed or not. For all he knew, Lennox Kemp was still a suspect. He'd never met him, and his experience of lawyers in general made him wonder if their tendency to lie was out of sheer perversity or a habit they picked up from their clients.

Mary knew exactly what he was thinking because, in her view, cops always thought like that. They never believed anyone until face to face, and sometimes not even then. What was more comforting was that cops on the whole considered themselves much brighter than they were ... How easily this one had been tricked into assuming she had the authority to ask for the contents of statements! It must be something to do with the deferential manner she had put on in his honour, and the fact that she had dropped her Irish-American accent in favour of a homely, but slightly upper-class, one she had acquired at meetings of the local Women's Institute.

Eventually Sergeant Martin came up with what she wanted.

'No, we have not found anybody who saw Mr Lambert after he left the station car park the evening he was killed.'

'But he was definitely on that train?'

'He was seen by several people.' DS Martin riffled through his papers. 'One was a Mr Allardyce.'

'They travelled together?'

'The statement does not actually say so.' The sergeant read part of it out: 'I saw Mr Lambert whom I knew, as we came into Newtown Station. We exchanged a few words as we got off the train and went towards our respective cars. I think we spoke about the weather. We were both hurrying to get home.'

'My husband got the impression from something Inspector Upshire said earlier that Mr Allardyce had travelled in the same compartment as Mr Lambert.'

The sergeant went back through the notes, with a touch of impatience.

'In his first statement Mr Allardyce says they travelled together. Then he changed it to the one I've just read, and said all he'd meant was that they were on the same train.'

Mary shrugged. 'It probably doesn't matter. It was just that if they'd had a longer conversation Mr Kemp wondered if Mr Lambert might have mentioned what it was that took him to Lorimers' Garage later that night. He also thought perhaps he'd met a professional client on the train whose affairs needed an urgent discussion . . .'

The sergeant received that idea with some scepticism. 'Only two witnesses came forward to say they'd seen Mr Lambert that evening, besides Mr Allardyce. One was the stationmaster at Newtown who knew him by sight, and stated he saw Mr Lambert alight from the train in the company of a fair-haired man who we now know to be Mr Allardyce. The stationmaster also says that he saw Mr Lambert drive out alone from the car park about five minutes later – which bears out what Mr Allardyce told us.'

'And the other person who saw Mr Lambert that evening?'

DS Martin hunted through the file; he was getting fed up with this woman, despite her pleasant manner. There was nothing pushy about her but he suspected she was going to sit there burbling away like a half-boiled kettle until she got what she wanted.

'A Mr Andrew Ferguson of forty-five, Victoria Road, Newtown, saw Mr Lambert on the train. Mr Ferguson is the proprietor of a retail footwear establishment in Market Square, and Mr Lambert had dealt with a leasing matter for him. He didn't speak to him on the train, and had nothing to add apart from the fact that he'd recognized Mr Lambert as a fellow passenger. Now, does that satisfy all your enquiries?'

'I guess it'll have to . . .' In making an effort to pin the name and address firmly in her mind, her accent slipped. She gave the sergeant one of her best smiles, the one that lit up her dull features. 'Thank you,' she said. 'You have been so kind. Of course, Mr Kemp should have come himself – I'm only the dogsbody . . .'

When he showed her out DS Martin found himself thinking what nice warm grey eyes she had. He didn't look close enough to see that they were not especially honest.

Mary walked along Victoria Road counting the numbers on the houses. She knew the area, having once had lodgings nearby. She hoped to find Mr Ferguson at home for it was well past closing time at the local shops. When she found the house, he came to the door himself, a sporty-looking little man in bow tie and blazer.

'I think I told the police all I knew,' he said as he ushered her into a narrow hall, impressed by her ladylike manner and unconsciously succumbing to the persistence behind it.

'I'm sure you did, Mr Ferguson, but my husband, Mr Kemp, is trying to get at the state of mind his colleague was in during these last hours . . .'

'Of course. I quite understand. Anything I can do to help. I've been a client of the firm's for many years . . . Mr Lambert's death really upset me.'

Andrew Ferguson showed her into what was obviously a little-used front parlour, and fussed about, fetching a chair and enquiring whether he should put on the gas heater. He was, it seemed, a bachelor man whose cosier quarters lay in another part of the house. 'Don't you be bothering with the fire now,' she told him. 'I'll not keep you a moment. All I want is for you to tell me when you saw Mr Lambert on the train and whether you travelled in the same compartment.'

'Well, as I told that young policeman when I called in at the police station, I'd spotted Mr Lambert getting on at Liverpool Street. I'd been lucky in getting a seat but he was left standing further down the same compartment. When the crowd cleared – about two stations down the line from Newtown, that would be – Mr Lambert got a seat opposite to mine. We just nodded to each other but we didn't speak.'

'Was he alone?'

'He was when he sat down but he was soon joined by someone he knew – a large, rather good-looking chap with a suntan . . .' Mr Ferguson gave a little laugh. 'That's a bit unusual this time of year, so I remembered him.'

'Did they talk together much, Mr Lambert and this other man?'

Andrew Ferguson pursed his lips. 'They obviously knew

each other, that I'm sure of . . . When the tall man sat down Mr Lambert folded up his evening paper as if prepared for conversation. I wasn't paying much attention to them, you know, but I do remember they were talking together, but not, of course, very loudly . . . That train fairly rattles along, you're unlikely to overhear anything people are saying . . . Not that one would listen, anyway . . .' He made haste to correct any other impression his words might have given.

'Did they seem on good terms with each other?'

Mr Ferguson screwed up his little brown eyes in concentration. 'Well, you see, I wasn't taking much notice . . . And the police never asked me any questions like that . . . But, now you mention it, I'd say Mr Lambert and this other chap, they were chums . . .' It was, to Mary, such a very English word that it made her glance keenly at the little man so that he probed his memory still further. 'Yes, I would say definitely chums. Mr Lambert even made a little joke . . . I couldn't help hearing . . . As the train came into Newtown Station, he picked up his briefcase from the rack, and he said something like: "It's all in the bag . . ." Whatever he meant, he was pretty cheerful about it.'

'Now that's just the kind of thing my husband wanted to know, Mr Ferguson. That Tony was in a good mood when he got off the train . . .' Mary rose to leave, and held out a slim, gloved hand. 'Thank you so much for your help.'

As Andrew Ferguson trotted back into the house after showing his visitor down the front steps so that she would not stumble in the dark, he experienced the rosy glow of one who has done a good deed, albeit unwittingly. Mrs Kemp had made him feel he had really helped — so unlike the brisk indifference he'd had from that fresh-faced constable at the station . . . Never even a proper 'thank you, sir', had he got from him. A very nice lady, Mrs Kemp, not exactly a good-looker, but pleasant. Mr Ferguson, who had no great interest in women and tended to be shy of good-lookers, was reminded of his mother . . .

Mary was very late home but as her husband had taken to spending his time in the study these evenings rather than in the sitting room or the kitchen, her absence seemed to have gone unnoticed. At any rate, no comment on it was made. She was good at preparing impromptu meals out of whatever happened to be lying about on the larder or refrigerator shelves so that when she finally called Kemp to the table he might well have thought she'd spent the day among the pots and pans. It was a measure of the distance which now lay between them that he did not enquire where she had been, nor did she volunteer the information.

Conversation over dinner was far from lively and by the time the pudding stage was reached it had stuttered its way into silence. The odd thing was that they were both thinking along the same lines, and for the same reasons. Accustomed to living alone, working out their own thoughts, planning their actions without recourse to the advice of others, neither of them was easy in the open give-and-take of a good marriage, no matter that it was what they both desired. Out of habit each of them drew back from disclosure of their innermost thoughts, even when such thoughts concerned the other person sitting across the table.

Had he known how, Lennox Kemp would have liked nothing better than to share his present misgivings with his wife. He would have told her how the atmosphere in the office was thick with doubt and suspicion and how his sensitivity to it grew more tender day by day. He'd played detective so often in the past and been successful at it that it was no wonder his colleagues were disappointed in him now. They wouldn't have minded if he'd abandoned all idea of work so long as he applied all his intelligence and energy to finding Tony's murderer . . .

Instead, all he'd done was stick his head into a trench of unnecessary routine and been too scared to raise it above that parapet of paper. Only he knew what scared him . . . If he as much as stopped for a minute and looked up, there was Tony, leaning forward in that earnest way he had, pushing up the big spectacles on to the forehead beneath the dark, untidy hair. It frightened Kemp to feel the threat of that presence, too raw for comfort, too new to be a ghost . . .

Had Kemp reasoned it out he would have seen this was no troubled spirit come to haunt him, but simply the effect of place; he and Tony Lambert had spent the greater part of their lives together during the last few years, such is the proximity work brings, and they had shared a friendship outside the office as well. Like the after-image of light which persists behind the eyes even when extinguished, it was too soon for Tony to have disappeared so long as every corner echoed with the sound of his voice . . . The blotter on his desk still seemed to hold the impact of his elbows . . .

All Kemp did know was that if he relaxed his hold on the here and now in the form of safe, tedious work, then the past would swoop back, back to that moment in the dark behind the garage, then the piercing pain, the killing sin . . . And with that he could not cope.

He did not have to be told by Mary or anyone else that his state of mind owed everything to one premise: that he was to blame for the murder, the guilt was his, so that his true feelings for the loss of a friend were curdled by remorse for things left undone, and his natural need to mourn stifled by all the might-have-beens . . . But merely to call a problem psychological in origin was like telling a patient their illness was due to a virus, as if naming the cause effected the cure.

He looked across at his wife. He would like to have told her all this but the old habit of reticence was strong . . . Anyway, she didn't look particularly receptive. The close attention she was giving to domestic trivia showed she too had a lot on her mind.

It was, however, in better shape than his, and quite capable of taking decisions. One was that she should not tell him yet about her recent exploits. Telling might relieve her conscience but it would do nothing to improve their relations. On reflection, she felt her activities to be somewhat amateurish – the adventures of Nancy Drew or whatever was the English equivalent – certainly not the kind of thing lawyers' wives were supposed to get up to. It would have been different if she had really found out something important . . . As it was, Lennox was hardly likely to approve of her going about pretending to be other than she was, although such deviousness came naturally to her.

Mary was beginning to learn that 'fitting in' was something you had to take seriously in English society – particularly in a small town. She had no wish to embarrass her husband, especially when he was in his present fragile state of mind.

Sure, he thought himself unconventional but she suspected that, as with other men who think it a virtue to be a little outré, the disposition was only skin deep, and in any case well overlaid by years of conformity. A little deception might be practised in your line of business from time to time but that didn't mean you regarded lying as an alternative way of life. When Mary was growing up she'd had to gather lies about her shoulders like a cloak for pure protection – it was a habit difficult to shake off.

Surreptitiously she watched her husband now, and was sharply reminded that she must not underestimate him; some of the conclusions she was only stumbling towards might already have occurred to him and been dismissed as false or irrelevant. Who was she to think she could steal a march on him? She'd heard him say that nothing in human behaviour could surprise him . . .

Yet *she* had surprised him . . . once . . .

'What are you smiling at?' Her mouth must have flickered involuntarily.

'Just a thought . . .'

'Am I in it?'

'You surely are. I was thinking about you saying that nothing could ever surprise you . . .'

'I hope I never said anything so cynical; maybe I was showing off . . . What made you think of it?'

'You got the shock of your life when we got married and you found out I was a virgin.'

'Darling, everything about you never ceases to surprise me but, yes, that was the nicest of all . . .' He took her hand across the table and squeezed it gently, suddenly unsure of himself and not able to cope with the rush of tenderness he felt for her.

'I should have been in the rare breeds' show,' she said. 'White American female from the Pennsylvanian backwoods, over thirty years of age, and still untouched by human hand. You took an awful chance, Lennox, asking me to marry you. I'd been wanted by the police, and I could have been a hooker . . .'

'I wanted you more than the police, and I don't think I'd recognize a hooker if I met one. Anyway, as they say in space

travel, it's far better to go where no man has gone before . . .'
He stopped as he saw she was laughing at him. 'Is this supposed to be a serious discussion, Mary, or shall we simply go to bed?'

'Not yet,' she said. 'I have it in my mind to ask you something . . . Do many men fall in love like you did without knowing anything about the other person?'

'I imagine it's rare. People generally fall in love with those they grow up with, or their families moved in the same circles, or else they meet in an office, or in the course of their profession . . . Proximity seems to have a lot going for it . . . Then of course there's social gatherings which in themselves tend to be restricted to people of the same kind . . .'

She made a face. 'Kind and class . . . It all sounds too, too awfully English.'

'Well, we're in England. It's the way things are. Society is a bit stratified . . . I'm sure it's not that different in the States, perhaps rather looser round the class edges with more emphasis on the money than the accent. Even over there King Cophetua would still hit the headlines.'

'Who's he?'

'He married a beggar girl. It's his only claim to fame. Where is this little conversation leading us? Upstairs, I hope.'

'Not yet,' she said again. 'It's just that I got to wondering . . . You and I are probably unique, but someone like Tony Lambert now, he was terribly English, wasn't he? I mean the way he was brought up and all that. If his parents had been alive they'd have wanted to know all about his fiancée . . .'

'Certainly his mother would have. She was very much that sort of lady . . .'

'But she had died before he met Anita Allardyce?'

'If you want to put it flippantly they missed each other by a month . . . I'm not sure that I know what you're getting at . . .'

'I don't know, either . . .' she confessed, and went on, almost talking to herself. 'Of course, like you said, they moved in the same circles, law and property – through that brother of hers . . . The elder Lamberts might have found him a bit pushy . . . But the little lion cub, I expect they'd

136

have liked her . . . The English, they forgive a lot in what they still think of as their Colonials . . . The English I'm talking about are people like the Lamberts; I don't mean your sort, Lennox . . .'

'My sort is about to clear the table, and do the washing-up while you sit there and get on with your wonderings . . . Otherwise I'm never going to get you to bed tonight . . .'

'I'll help you in a minute. Just one more thing . . . If you were a frightfully rich young man who had just got engaged to a bright beloved, what would you give her as an engagement present that would be special to her, not jewellery because she isn't the type?'

'If I were frightfully rich I wouldn't be here at the kitchen sink with you, we'd both be on a world cruise as far from Newtown as we could get . . .'

'No, we wouldn't,' said Mary, absently. 'You like the place too much. But I'm serious about this present that Tony was planning to give Anita. I wish I knew what it was.'

'Oh, that's what all this wondering is about . . . and there was me thinking there was just you and I and the rest of the world outside . . . Come on, Mary, stop having these ideas running in your head. They'll do no good, and they may hurt . . .' Kemp had been diverted by the pleasantries of their small conversation but now he grew stern again.

Instinct told Mary to let it go . . . She had him back, that should be all that mattered, they were on speaking terms, as lovers they would draw even closer . . .

As she hesitated, the telephone rang. Kemp was already on his feet and it was he who answered it.

'Yes, this is Lennox Kemp,' she heard him say. There was a pause.

'Of course, Mr Medway . . . Good of you to ring . . . Yes, I quite understand. These things do come back to one . . . Yes . . . I know who you mean. I don't suppose it's important . . . She did, did she? Well, thank you for calling. Good night . . .'

Mary had skipped hurriedly into the kitchen, and had her hands in the sink by the time Kemp walked slowly through from the hall. Even with her back to him she could sense his anger.

Although he kept his voice level the tone bit like corrosive acid.

'What the devil do you think you've been up to?'

And that was only a beginning.

CHAPTER 18

Being not long wed and so still fairly sanguine as to the chances of the marriage, neither of the Kemps had made any immediate provision for sleeping in separate quarters. The two guest bedrooms and the small boxroom were barely carpeted and scant in furniture and comfort. Nevertheless, Lennox took himself and his old camp-bed into the cramped boxroom as it suited his mood of hurt isolation. To Mary he left the luxury of their double-bed, and perhaps, he might have hoped, tears of remorse . . .

He should have known her better. She took a poor view of tears, and was already planning action on the next day. All right, so she had stepped on his professional toes in approaching Medway, Austin without getting a signed permit from him first. She knew it was the visit which had angered him, not the purpose. By going there she had invaded territory exclusively his – one of those male strongholds where the law was at work – and she had done it behind his back, suborning his colleague, Michael Cantley, on the way.

How petty men are, she thought. How quick to take offence when things are not done according to their previous rules . . . It had been her husband's pride that had been damaged, his *amour-propre* – she'd thought Lennox far too sensible to possess such a thing.

As it was not in his nature to be hot in temper there was no shouting match last night. That she could have dealt with, hitting back with all the force of argument that what she'd done had been for him, and only attempted because of his lack of initiative, but against the chill of his anger, the harshness of his few but biting words, she'd not had even the stammer of a defence. In the end she'd done what she'd always done in the face of hostility – simply clammed up and said nothing. It might have seemed to be sulks but, like weeping, she'd never had time for those. When she'd planned what she would do the next day, Mary slept soundly.

She came down early to find that Lennox had already made himself breakfast and left the house. Somehow, that hurt . . . He could have left a note, but there was nothing . . . She looked round the fresh, lemony-coloured walls of the kitchen and marvelled that so recently she and Lennox together had chosen the shade, watched as the decorator painted, and admired his work when he'd finished. So, a husband and wife could be at one in such a trivial thing yet worlds apart where it really mattered. Maybe she should quit the detective business and get back to being a proper housewife like everyone expected . . . But it was too late for that; she was hooked by curiosity, and must go along with it. She must go on asking questions until the answers came together and settled like a bowl of jello . . .

She glanced at the clock. Only just after eight so there was a chance John Upshire could be still at home. As he was Lennox's friend they had his unlisted number, although it was only for social occasions. Would it be social enough simply to wish him good morning?

'And good morning to you, too, Mary. You've just caught me . . . What can I do for you?'

'I'm going to be away for most of the day, and I was wondering if there were any developments . . . If Daren Roddick said anything?'

There was an uneasy silence at his end. She reckoned the inspector was not too pleased at having such an enquiry on his home line. She was banking hard on the friendly relationship she had been at pains to foster.

'I worry so about Lennox,' she went on softly into the silence, and was astonished to hear a faint whine in her voice. 'You're the only one I can ask about the case for he tells me nothing . . .' In fact, Lennox had told her a great deal the night before, mainly on the subject of minding her own business and letting the police get on with theirs.

'I'm afraid I've nothing to report, Mary.' The inspector was reluctant but having once started, he continued: 'We've had

to let young Roddick go. Nothing we could charge him with
. . . All he'd say was he'd been in the Victoria pub that night,
and yes, there was a bit of a fracas in the car park but that
got sorted out and he went home to his innocent bed. Says
he's no idea where you Kemps live, and wherever it is he
was nowhere near it . . . He's lying, of course, but he's learnt
the family motto off pat – keep your mouth shut when
it's the law and they can't touch you. He's the sullen kind
and the only spark of life we get out of him is when Amy
Frobisher's mentioned. Then he goes bright pink and
mumbles they were at school together. They've been a lot
of other places together since, in my opinion – but that's not
illegal . . .'

'Amy's his soft spot,' said Mary with some satisfaction, 'but
I'm real sorry Daren's out in the town again . . .'

'What did you expect? That we'd rough him up till he
confessed to every sin in the book? Come on, Mary, you
know there's more plod than punch in police work. Which
reminds me, it's high time I put in my share this morning.'

'I'm sorry, John, I didn't mean to keep you.'

'Don't fret about young Daren. He's not going to flee the
country; we can lean on him again whenever we like. Give
my regards to that husband of yours . . . I think you worry
unnecessarily – I'm sure he's all right really.'

'Depends from where you're looking,' said Mary, bleakly.

As she put the phone down she saw the note Kemp had
made the previous evening – the gist of Donald Medway's
unfortunately timed call. For all his astonishment and final
anger, habit had seen to it that the conversation was recorded
accurately.

*As I told your wife . . . Tony had said he was going to see Lydia's
chap. It came back to me later . . . his mother's will, some legatee
of that name. I checked it. Lydia Beresford of Newtown . . . No
idea at all what it was about . . .*

Lennox had written the name in capitals, but of course
both he and Mary knew who Lydia Beresford was. She was
an old friend of theirs, as she had obviously also been of the
late Mrs Lambert. Her number was in the address book when
Mary looked it up.

Mary got herself some coffee and made toast. Since her

conversation with the inspector she knew this was going to be a very long day.

Lydia Beresford's telephone was finally answered but not by her.

'I'm sorry, this is Polly Burt speaking, Mrs Beresford's cleaning lady. Mrs Beresford's on holiday.'

'When will she be back?'

'She's got nearly a week to go. Is there any message?'

'No, thank you, Mrs Burt. I'll ring her later . . .'

It irked Mary that there wasn't going to be a quick answer to the question of who Lydia's chap was. That query had come to a full stop – but other lines were open . . .

Mrs Robsart was relaxing with her feet up in the back parlour, worn out, she complained, with the early morning's struggle to get newspapers delivered and cope with customers collecting theirs from the shop on the way to the station. She was pleased to see Mary Kemp again, gave her an excuse to rest a bit longer before taking on another stint.

'He can get on with it,' she said, nodding in the direction of her husband. 'I've been on me feet since half past five. Like a cuppa tea?'

It helped the chatter, so Mary accepted.

'The thing is,' she said, 'I'm on my way to town to catch the Liverpool train. My aunt up there, she's had to go into the hospital.'

'Liverpool? Well, now isn't that strange . . . They say there's a lot of you Irish up there . . .' It was spoken of as fact, and nothing intended otherwise. 'Hope it's not serious?'

Mary put on a solemn face. 'It could be, Mrs Robsart. Auntie's getting on in years . . . Maybe that's the reason why she wants me up there. It's a long journey but she's the only relative I've got left . . .'

'Then you have to go. Will you be staying overnight?'

'Oh, no, nothing like that. I'll get the late train back. But what I was thinking was, I'll not need to be long at the hospital so there'll be time to spare. I wondered if you'd like me to call and see your Amy while I'm up there. I know you're concerned for her.'

Mrs Robsart's face lit up. 'Now that's a kind thought, Mrs Kemp . . . As a matter of fact, Amy's asked for some of her school stuff, the commercial course she did, because she says there's the chance of a job. I'd got them ready to send . . .'

'I'd be happy to take them along.'

'If you're sure it's no trouble? They're here in this plastic bag, some of her certificates and her Pitmans shorthand book. It would be ever so kind of you . . .'

Mary eagerly took the bag which would give her the entrée into the Frobisher home.

'Shall I phone our Amy and say you'll be coming?'

Mary gave this suggestion short shrift. One mention of the name Kemp and Amy would be out of the door and into the Mersey . . .

'No, don't do that, Mrs Robsart. If you let me have her number I'll ring her from the station when I arrive. Oh, is that her address?'

She took the slip of paper from Mrs Robsart. 'Fazackerley? Why, that's the very district where the hospital is . . . How very fortunate.'

'I had young Daren Roddick round here asking for that address,' Mrs Robsart grumbled, 'but I says to him, no, you leave Amy alone, she's got a new life up there and she's not to be bothered with folk from here . . . I mean, we owe it to Dan Frobisher not to have no more trouble . . . He's stood by her, spite of everything, and now she's got this chance of a job, she'll want no hangers-on from the past.'

This was probably more true than Mrs Robsart knew. It was a relief to be told that Daren hadn't yet got her address or telephone number . . . All the more reason for Mary to act fast, so she took her leave of Mrs Robsart and set out for Newtown Station.

Compared with her extensive travels in the States, any journey in England looked a mere doddle to Mary – at least on the map. You got in one of their toy trains and were towed across the coloured counties in no time. In practice, of course, it wasn't like that and took much longer because you had to get to a mainline station before you could start.

Once on the Intercity, however, and having nothing to do except look out of the window, she enjoyed herself, intrigued by the number of tiny green fields there were in this country, even in the industrial Midlands, and amused by the churches that dwarfed the villages, the funny bosky little woods and the patterns made by solitary trees in the flat water meadows.

It was afternoon before she reached Liverpool, a city of legendary status in the unwritten history of the Blanes. According to her mother, umpteen of the family had sailed from that port in days of yore when the ferries brought them over from the old country to board the great liners for America – where they'd sunk without trace since none of them had been heard of again. All that remained were her mother's memories, and a bundle of dog-eared postcards with pictures of the high-hulled ships with their coloured funnels – red for Cunard, cream for White Star, and yellow for Canadian Pacific with names like *Montcalm* and *Montclare* . . . Despite it being a land of opportunity, the Blanes had not been destined to make their mark in the New World – unlike the Reagans and Kennedys, the Blanes were the lesser Irish . . . Just the same, Mary would have liked to have seen the Mersey out of which they had sailed with such hope, but this was not the time for a sentimental diversion.

She took a taxi from the station and paid it off at the address she had been given. She told the driver to come back for her in an hour and a half, for she had no wish to be marooned in this desert of middle-income semis where Daniel Frobisher had parked his child-wife. Mary was taking a chance that she was home and her husband not; surely at this time of day any self-respecting crime reporter would be out chasing it up.

Amy Frobisher did indeed look like the child-wife Mary had envisaged, though she was much prettier. She held the door ajar as she regarded her visitor with clear turquoise eyes which were far from childlike. While she was working out whether this was a charity collector (no box in evidence) or a double-glazing salesperson (not smart enough) Mary stepped forward, smiled gently and held out the plastic bag with the name ROBSART'S CORNER STORE prominently displayed.

'Amy Frobisher? I'm Mary Blane, a friend of your mother's. She asked me to call in with these books you wanted. I'm only here for the day to visit an aunt in the hospital at Fazackerley . . .'

144

'Oh . . . Well, you'd best come in . . .' Startled but somehow reassured by the plain looks of the woman, and the rather common accent, Amy opened the door wider and ushered Mary into the hall which was done out in beige with white trim. The builder had obviously found it cheap to buy paint in bulk so the same blameless decor held throughout all the downstairs rooms, which were shown off by Amy with pride so that the visitor could carry the message back home to mum that our Amy was doing well. There was certainly nothing here to jar the nerves; even the Frobisher furnishings tended to be neutral to the point of anaemia.

'D'you mind the kitchen?' said Amy, finally, having judged her guest to be in the category a kitchen would suit. 'I was just going to have a cuppa when you came.'

Here the beige was deeper but the white still white, though the dishtowels were checked coffee and cream – like the duvets on the beds upstairs. Single beds, separate rooms, Mary noticed when she had been shown round. Marriage, she thought, is a right lottery, there are always winners and losers.

'You've a lovely home, Amy,' she remarked. 'You don't mind me calling you Amy? I really feel I know you, the way your mother talks of you so often when I pop into the back shop. Soon's I said I'd to come to Liverpool to visit Auntie and I said I'd see you, she was all for it. She's ever so glad you're taking up with your school stuff again . . . I gather you've the chance of a job?'

Playing the gabby old pussycat, Mary gave Amy time to get used to the idea that here was a friend of her mother's – and a good friend at that, for it wasn't everyone got asked into the back of Robsart's shop – who was only in the district a short time so Amy might as well be nice to her, even though she'd not much time for anyone over the age of thirty-five – and that went for her husband as well.

'I shan't be staying long,' said Mary – which nicely rounded off Amy's goodwill towards her; if the old trout was only here for an hour or so she could put up with her. 'I'm getting the evening train back to London.' She explained she had seen her aunt in Fazackerley hospital; the elderly lady

145

was now off the danger list and had been pleased to see her but too tired for much conversation.

Once the tale of the mythical aunt had been told and commiserated upon, Amy in her turn complained of the neighbours, none of them young, and all of them stuck-up. 'Can't wait till I get a job,' she went on, 'but Dan says it's got to be a good one, and he should know, being in that line himself.'

'Is it a reporter you're thinking of becoming, Amy? Is that why you're brushing up your shorthand? You'll have a type-writer, of course . . .'

'Oh, I've junked that old thing, it's a word-processor I've got now,' said Amy, proudly, 'and it's a journalist I'm to be . . . They say I've the talent for it. At school I'd always get the top marks for my essays, and when I had my trouble and went for counselling they all said writing things down was the saving of me . . . I suppose Mother told you about my trouble?'

Mary nodded solemnly. 'You went through a terrible time, my dear. I'm glad to see you've come out of it well.'

Amy certainly looked the picture of health. She was not the waif one might have expected from all one had heard. She had sleek fair hair and the kind of translucent skin which looks delicate and flushes easily, but in Mary's view the girl was probably tough as an old boot, and quite capable of manipulating everyone around her. And there had been scores of them: social workers worried about her mind, church workers concerned for her soul, doctors and nurses for her body, all of them trying to keep her within their own terms of reference. To someone like Amy Robsart, who craved attention like others craved drugs, all this cuddly counselling had come as a godsend.

Mary was remembering something Mrs Robsart had told her about Amy as an infant: 'She was a screamer. If she didn't get her own way she'd scream and scream. Soon's she got what she wanted, she'd stop like you'd turned off a switch . . . And what she usually wanted was just attention – anybody's attention . . .'

The ploy that had been so useful in Amy's childhood was still in working order, although in adult life the screamings were necessarily quieter. She had found other ways of attracting attention. The role she was now acting out on Mary was the real-life heroine in some television documentary, possibly called *Coping with Crisis*, and as she retold her personal tragedy what came over most strongly was how deeply she was already immersed in the part. Her counsellors had a lot to answer for . . .

She had reached the point where the baby had had to be removed from her care. Her eyes, which were set wide apart so that they left space for a lot of naked emotion in between, glistened. Then she reeled off medical terms with great fluency for she had had a receptive ear when she was the subject for discussion as a patient.

'They were all so worried about me,' she said, turning her blue-green gaze on Mary but seeing beyond her a crowd of viewers, 'because I'd got postnatal depression with complications . . . I couldn't bear to look at the poor little thing, and as to feeding it . . .' She shuddered. Then she drew herself up. 'They said when I left the hospital I'd have to go into therapy. That was psychoanalysis, you know . . . Ever so interesting. The full course took nearly two years before I could cope with life again, and come to terms with what had happened. Of course my family never understood, they didn't want me going to a shrink 'cos the neighbours would talk about me being out of my mind. As if I cared what they said . . . Anyway, my shrink – he's really called an analyst and ever so understanding – he said like I was to let my feelings out the only way I knew by writing them down, not keep them in and getting repressed.'

'Sounds good advice,' said Mary, thinking that Amy had probably manipulated him too, massaging his ego like a pro. It may not have been done in the fleshly sense, yet the accomplishment would have brought satisfaction to both parties.

She let some admiration into her voice when she said: 'What you have been through, Amy! I know little of this kind of thing but I've friends in America who go to therapists like you go to dentists here in England.'

'That's what I told Dad and Mum, but they didn't understand . . . I said being in therapy didn't mean you're heading for the loony bin . . .'

Amy had a brisk way with words and a matter-of-fact attitude to her past problems which indicated that either the therapy had worked or she hadn't really needed it in the first place. Mary favoured the latter alternative. Not that she lacked sympathy for the girl. All Amy had ever needed in her short life since coming into the world as the youngest of a large and not particularly caring family was attention.

Perhaps a teenage pregnancy hadn't been the best way to go about getting that attention, but marriage and a healthy baby might well have satisfied the hunger for it, and to the child at least Amy would have been the centre of his world for years to come . . .

When it all went disastrously wrong it was no wonder Amy had kicked out in anger and frustration. The irony was that the method she chose to give vent to her silent screaming – a method which used some writing skill and a fertile imagination – had had the blessing of her analyst. He, poor man, could have had no idea how thoroughly his advice had been absorbed.

'More tea? Do have a piece of that cake. I only bought it this morning . . .' Amy was being the bright young hostess entertaining a visitor in her new home. Mary felt pity and understanding for her but time was running fast and other considerations outweighed the natural tenderness. It was the moment to bring the performance to an end.

'You've the makings of a good journalist, Amy,' she remarked, conversationally, as she took a slice of Marks & Spencer's sponge. 'It's a great turn of phrase you have in those letters. Did you post them yourself all over London?'

'Oh, I never did the posting, that was up to Nick . . .'

'Nick . . . He does rather get about a lot to all these different courts, doesn't he?'

Amy's mouth was still open as if to swallow back the words that had come out. Her little hand began slowly to thump on the table. She stared at Mary for a second or two then shifted her gaze as the hot tears welled up in her eyes. The pink colour kept coming and going, leaving her cheeks patched red and white like a painted doll. She could neither move nor speak, the only sound was the rapping of her small fist on the tablecloth.

Mary was patient. She had more to gain by keeping silent, so she waited.

Eventually Amy brought both of her shaking hands up to her mouth and through the fingers she stammered: 'You . . . you . . . know Nick Stoddart?'

'Oh, yes, I know Nick. He told me all about his part in the letters so you're free to speak out.'

Relief flooded into the girl's face, and speech burst from her like a bubbling spring. 'Oh, if Nick told you . . . then it's all right. It was just him and me, just a game, like . . . He got interested in my therapy, he said it was more fun if I wrote letters . . .' Her voice trailed off, and she looked puzzled. 'But Nick said no one else would ever know . . .'

'And no one would have if some eejit hadn't sent them to the paper . . . It wouldn't be you, now, would it?'

Amy couldn't get the words out fast enough. 'Of course it wasn't me . . . How could I? I never had them once Nick sent them off. It scared me when he told me they'd been posted . . . I'd never meant that . . .'

Mary's calm grey eyes regarded her in silence for a moment.

'I think I believe you, Amy . . . Well, up to a point . . .' She made a soft clucking sound like a mother vexed with her offspring. 'What a pity Daren had so much to say when the police picked him up . . .'

The little clenched fist stopped beating and plugged itself into the mouth. Over the knuckles Amy mumbled: 'The police have got Daren?'

' 'Fraid so. That lad's a right eejit . . . I don't suppose Mr Stoddart would like the job of defending him.'

Mary's aim was to pile confusion upon confusion, keep the girl in a state of such bewilderment that she didn't know what she was saying. After all, this was not a court of law, there were no set rules . . .

Amy was quick enough to latch on to Mary's last remark.

'Nick wouldn't give a damn what happened to Daren . . .' she said bitterly, 'not after he found out who sent them to the paper . . .'

Mary shook her head solemnly. 'Daren's in trouble over that break-in . . . Says you put him up to it . . .'

149

Then temper flared. 'He's a liar ... I never did! Just because you have a giggle about something, like it would be fun to put the wind up somebody, he goes and says I put him up to it! I've finished with Daren Roddick after this –' Amy suddenly stopped. 'How do you know all this, then?' The spurt of anger had for the moment put away her fears, and set her wits working.

'I have the confidence of the police, Amy, as I have of Nick Stoddart. He wishes to keep out of it, and I'm sure he told you that when he came up here to Liverpool.'

Amy was beginning to regard Mary with something approaching awe. This woman had knowledge of things only known to Amy herself and a few others, and the trouble was you couldn't tell whose side she was on. The one thing Nick had stressed when he'd had she and Daniel together the night he'd come rushing up from the south was that if anything got out he would deny he'd ever had any part in the letters. 'It's your word against mine, Amy, and if it ever came to a court of law you'd not have the chance of a snowball in hell ...'

When he'd gone, Dan had said the same thing. 'He's right, you know, people will just say you're trying to implicate him because he's another lawyer and you've got it in for lawyers ... You'd get off lightly if there were any charges ever brought. Your analyst would help you, say you just got carried away and the social workers you had, they'd be witnesses to your state of mind ... Like I said when we moved from Newtown, Amy, we've got to put the whole thing behind us.'

Amy had to admit that Dan had been wonderful. Not at first, not when she'd had to tell him about the letters, the night he'd come home from the paper and said he was going to investigate them for this man Kemp. She'd had to tell him the whole story, and about Daren bringing her the empty briefcase and boasting how clever he'd been with what he'd found in it ... Dan had hit the roof that night ... But he'd stood by her, and when that other lawyer got murdered and everything was in such a muddle, it was Dan who'd whisked her away so she shouldn't think about it any more, and get upset, and maybe ill in her mind again ... That was the way Dan saw it, and there was something comforting in his view, something she could always fall back on if things got really rough. You've been a victim, he'd said, and that was what her counsellors had told her, too, and that's what makes you act the way you do but once you've come to terms with it and not repressed anything, then you'll be all right . . .

And now here was this woman – who looked pretty much like one of the social workers she'd had – telling her that Nick Stoddart now didn't mind her talking about the letters, and there was stupid young Daren getting picked up by the police . . .

Later, as her homebound train clattered over the points, Mary conceded that it had not been a fair contest. Amy Frobisher was basically honest, she might have her fantasies but falsehoods did not spring lightly from her tongue, and the influence of her many counsellors was such that she truly believed that confession was good for the soul. She might embroider here and there, embellish plain fact with fancy bits, but barefaced lying of Mary's sort was beyond her. Even by the time the taxi driver had come to the door to collect Mary, Amy Frobisher still had no idea who her visitor was other than Mary Blane, a friend of her mother's, and also of Nick Stoddart.

'It was all Nick's idea to send the letters to this Kemp person. I'd never met him. I wanted them to go to that bitch in their office, the one that told me to go away and have the baby . . . Bloody fine advice that was, and more fool me to take it . . .'

'The lady was not to blame,' Mary had told her severely. 'She had a strong belief . . .'

'Then she should have kept it to herself.' Amy had not been mollified. 'Now, Nick, he was different . . . more understanding. I was scared of him at first. Well, I'd had to go see him after that fool Sharon's mother put in a complaint. But Nick soon squashed that one, told her to drop the whole thing 'cos I was a victim of circumstance and meant no harm. Then we got kind of friendly and he asked me out a few times . . . He said I'd been silly dropping those notes in like that on Sharon, I'd be better staying anonymous . . . The idea of the letters just grew out of that somehow . . .' Amy had been vague at that point, and reverted to how wonderful Nick had been and how grateful she was to him.

That this gratitude should take the form of allowing him to make love to her came as no surprise to Mary, but she took a personal delight in learning that Nick Stoddart's wonderfulness stopped at the bedroom door . . .

'We went to his place most times,' Amy told her, 'as it wouldn't be good for us to be seen out, he said. Well, I went along with that . . . didn't want Dan knowing, did I? Anyway, Dan often worked nights so it was easy seeing Nick. I'd bring takeaways, and he'd get the wine, and we'd have a right giggle doing those letters . . . 'Course he always wanted to go to bed afterwards . . . Well, they do, don't they?' She had included even her unprepossessing guest in this general feminine opinion, which Mary took as a compliment. 'But he wasn't much cop there, I can tell you . . . Tried too hard, like they do when they're old . . .' Mary tucked this gem away to repeat to Lennox if the time ever came . . .

Amy Frobisher had been more discerning than Nick Stoddart had possibly realized. 'He'd some old score to settle with this Kemp bloke,' she'd said, 'but he never let on to me what it was . . . Sometimes when he'd got all excited, like, about the threats he was making, I thought to myself, it's you needs the therapy, Nick, but I never dared say it to his face . . . I never dreamt he'd really post them . . . When I saw it in the paper I nearly died. I went round to his place and I says to him: "Be it on your own head, mate, but I'm off . . ."'

Mary considered this to be the expurgated version. She knew the fat must have been really in the fire the moment Daniel Frobisher learned that the threatening letters he was so anxious to investigate had been partly written by his little wife. Amy wasn't clever enough to get away with it once the letters got talked about; it was no wonder the pair of them had fled from Newtown . . .

But it had not been the murder of Tony Lambert that sent them running for cover – at least not as far as Amy was concerned. In speaking of it, Mary had come up against blank incomprehension. Astonishing though it seemed, Amy had made no connection between the affair of the letters and the killing. Whether it was because Daniel had deliberately played it down – and it was her husband now whom Amy took as her mentor – or whether her mind could not, or would not, take in the two events together Mary found it difficult to decide . . .

'That chap got mugged at the garage?' Amy had asked when Mary tentatively raised the subject. 'Yeah, I knew he worked at Gillorns but it wasn't him Nick had it in for . . . Anyway, wasn't he beaten up by some gang of car thieves? That's what I heard . . .'

Amy's ignorance of the true circumstances was so transparent that Mary did not pursue the matter. By this time the girl was so much into confessional mood that one didn't need to be an analyst to know that the beans had all been spilled and the sack was empty.

In the end she was gentle with Amy.

'I have to go for my train now,' she said when she heard the taxi driver at the door. She went out and told him to wait a moment.

When she came back into the coffee-and-cream kitchen Amy was still seated at the table. She was chewing the corner of a napkin, and beginning to look agitated again as her mind ranged wildly over their conversation.

'Don't worry, my dear,' said Mary, putting an arm round the girl's shoulders, 'none of this is going to go any further. I'm just glad we've cleared up a number of points . . . Best to get things off your chest,' she went on, thinking, when in doubt talk in clichés. 'You'll feel all the better for it . . .'

As she left, Mary had been well aware that poor Amy Frobisher was in no way better for the afternoon's talk. It would take some time for her to work out what it had all been about . . . and there'd be Daniel coming in for his supper.

Mary shuddered as she imagined the reception he would get; no hot meal and a deal of tears . . . Or was Amy made of sterner stuff? She might be relieved now it was all out in the open, but Mary knew Dan would hardly be pleased at the manner of that relief nor the identity of Amy's visitor. The briefest description by Amy and he'd know instantly who it was . . . Mary had a pang of contrition for the way she'd tricked the girl but in the detective game as she played it there were no rules.

No rules either in the IRA. The bomb was not a large one and nobody was killed or injured, but the mainline stations in London were closed for hours . . . Mary's train sat and sulked . . .

CHAPTER 19

Daniel Frobisher was not the only hard-working bread-winner to go supperless that evening. When Lennox Kemp arrived home at seven o'clock he found neither food on the table nor wife in the kitchen. In the short term these were minor irritants since he had decided, magnanimously, to forgive Mary anyway and hoped to effect a reconciliation. He poured himself a drink and went into the study where he worked for an hour or so on some unnecessary drafting which might have been better done by young Franklyn – and should have if Kemp had been giving proper attention to his articled clerk.

By half past eight Kemp was not only hungry, he was also bleakly angry. Hunger could be easily assuaged by a visit to the freezer and operation of the microwave oven, but as he sat down at the bare kitchen table – putting on a cloth would be giving in to some feminine principle – and looked at the pretty but possibly tasteless shepherd's pie, his mood deepened and rage rose up in him like a tide of molten lava. Any attempt at rational thought splintered and broke on the twin prongs of anger and anxiety . . . It was no use him arguing that Mary had the right to lead her own life without referring back to him in everything she did – no more than that he should inform her of all the details of his own working day – for by now reason was gone out of the window . . .

He was troubled by the irrationality of the anger he felt towards his wife. There were so many conflicting elements to it; regret for the way he had spoken the previous night, justification for the way he had spoken (how dare she usurp his authority, use his own office as a pretext for an approach to another solicitor she didn't even know?), a heartfelt desire to make up and an equally heartfelt refusal to give an inch . . . And all the time a loud crying in his mind: where the hell are you, Mary, at this time of night, without a word, without a sign?

Kemp could not remember having felt this way before. Life had certainly never gone smoothly for him: a first marriage that went terribly wrong, a fall from grace in his profession and the humiliating aftermath, long years working in a menial capacity which his intelligence often repudiated . . . These things he had ridden out, keeping himself sane and in control by an ironic detachment and a stubborn belief in his own integrity. That integrity, which in the past led him to seek justice for others while reserving his own view that it was possible life wasn't meant to be fair, was what was now at risk . . .

He scraped the remains of the quite blameless pie into the wastebin, made coffee and poured himself a brandy. By doing these small mechanical things he hoped he might bring some order to his thought processes which seemed to have gone to rack and ruin.

He carried the tray into the sitting room and switched on the imitation log fire which they both hated but had not yet got round to replacing. Because the central heating did not appear to have been turned up all day – when on earth had Mary gone out? – the house was cold. He pulled the fireside table over towards his armchair and settled down to collect his thoughts which certainly needed to be gathered in from all directions.

Instead of reminding him of how self-sufficient he had been in his bachelor days, Mary's non-presence only accentuated the loneliness which had been the other side of the coin. He found himself resenting the pull she had on him, yet at the same time he longed for her to be there across the fireplace in her usual chair . . . For one terrible moment he regretted his marriage, then hastily retracted the disloyal thought. He knew the cause of these vacillating emotions which were novel to him; love was the cause, love was what had weakened his self-sufficiency, made him tender to these passing vagaries of temper which had never upset him before.

Hadn't he read somewhere that Plato called love a serious mental condition? 'Love casts out intelligence . . .' Well, I'll

156

go along with that, thought Kemp, suddenly restored by this amateur diagnosis of his present indisposition. He was angry with Mary because he loved her, he valued her closeness and wanted more of it, he didn't want her to be independent, flitting about on her own and having ideas that didn't include him, he wanted her by his side or on a very short leash . . . As he was being led to these conclusions he became more and more appalled. So, that was it; he was a man like other men – where his wife was concerned he was simply a male chauvinist at heart. It was a sobering thought and pulled him up sharply. He had considered himself to be a tolerant man, amiable and not possessive, one who would be easy in the give and take of marriage, yet here he was chafing at the bit because his wife was out and hadn't told him where she was going . . . And it had been he who had left the house that morning without a word to her because he had slept badly in the discomfort of the boxroom and blamed her for that, too . . .

He realized he'd no idea how Mary Madeleine would take that sort of behaviour in a husband. Was it possible that she would simply walk out?

That was a real heart-stopper. He sprang from his chair and raced upstairs. Despite her personal wealth – which was new and possibly ill-founded – Mary had few clothes, just one or two good but quiet suits, the rest casual separates, some nondescript, others startlingly colourful as if bought on a brave but transient impulse. Altogether they took up but half of a wardrobe, and nothing seemed to be missing save the blue jacket and denim skirt she wore most days. The only shoes not on the rack were her sensible black loafers; whatever had taken Mary out, it was not to any well-dressed occasion. Her anorak had gone from the stand in the hall but that was not surprising for the day had been chilly.

Kemp returned to the sitting room, poured a second cup of coffee and another brandy. He felt he was making headway with his thinking. If it was love that swung his moods between resentment and remorse, anger and desire, then that was a rational enough explanation for him to understand and all he had to do was stay calm until Mary came home when he would greet her quietly and ask about her day instead of shouting: 'Where the hell do you think you've been?' which was what a baser instinct demanded of him . . .

He took his tray into the kitchen and washed up. In the process he struck the cup against the tap and broke it . . . That was another thing, he had been breaking a lot of things since Tony's death. Maybe this was the moment to think about that too if self-examination was going to fill in the time before Mary's return, for it would be pointless to go to bed where he would sleep even worse than he had the night before.

He tidied up the kitchen just for the sake of something to do, and walked out into the hall where the big clock which had belonged to his father gave him an unwelcome grin and told him it was after midnight. Where was she at this hour, and without a word from her? He had not thought there could be, in his disordered head, sufficient space to let in another emotion but when it came it flooded out everything except fear. What if she never came back, what if there had been an accident and she was lying unconscious in some casualty department while they cut away her denim skirt, her white blouse?

Kemp had been in tricky situations in the past, known fear and seen it in others but never before had he experienced such blind, stupid panic – blind because it led nowhere and stupid because it arose from neurotic imaginings. Love and matrimony, it seemed, had combined to make him vulnerable to every toss of life's coin . . .

This sort of language is no good, he said to himself, and he went back into the sitting room and replaced the brandy bottle in the drinks cabinet, closing the door with a decisive snap. Whatever else, he would not take the drinkers' way . . .

He sat down in the armchair and continued on his self-imposed course of psychoanalysis until he finally came up with a solution; what ailed him was a guilt complex. The last time he had felt as miserably insecure as he did now was immediately after the Law Society had passed judgement on him and chucked him out of his profession. The guilt then had been real enough; misappropriation of Trust funds was stealing no matter what fancy words you used to cover it . . . There may have been virtue in the motive (he'd done it to save the face of Muriel, his first wife – there, love again to blame!) but the act itself was nonetheless criminal.

Guilt too had unseated his reason when he found Tony Lambert's body. Guilt for not being there, for not taking the threats seriously, for not heeding the warnings, and for the simple fact that it was his best friend who lay dead in his place.

And now guilt for the way he had spoken to his wife, not only last night in cold temper but in the weeks since the murder, for shutting her out from his innermost thoughts, for treating her like some meddling stranger.

Finally, there was the guilt he felt for his behaviour to his colleagues in the office whose recent mistrust of him was well merited, guilt for his unforgivable inertia in not going out to find Tony's killer, guilt for leaving undone those things which he ought to have done, guilt for hiding his head in the sand because to look at things too closely might damage his ego . . .

His ego now reduced to a blob of jelly, saddled with a new guilt complex and tuned into its relevant anxieties, Kemp had dropped into a state of body for which depression was too simple a word. He asked his alter ego where do we go from here, in the manner of a patient told the Latin name of his disease but not given the pills to cure it, but that Smart Alec of an analyst had already packed up and gone . . .

Still, Kemp did feel they'd come a long way together and, glancing at his watch, he was not surprised to find the journey had taken up yet another hour.

This reminder of the passing of time unfortunately undid all the good work of therapy and threw him once more into that same sea of panic out of which he had been trying to struggle by process of mind . . . This time he decided he might as well sink. Mary was dead. She would never have left him so long without a word if she had not died. Mary was dead and there was no hope for him . . .

Waves of despair were beating so heavily about his ears that it was some time before he heard the phone.

'Was that funny noise you speaking?' said Mary. 'Sorry I had to wake you up at this unearthly hour but . . .' She went on to explain about the bomb scare and why her train had

159

to sit outside Euston for so many hours. She didn't say where the train was from and he didn't ask. All he could think of was how sweet the sound of her voice. It set off a singing in his head like celestial music.

'. . . because I'd missed the last train to Newtown I've come here to the Station Hotel for the night. I'll be out first thing tomorrow.'

'No . . . Don't do that . . . I'll get in the car and come up . . .'

'What, now? You must be crazy . . . It'll be three in the morning before you're here. Besides, they'd never let you in, you're a dead ringer for an IRA man . . . Are you still with me, Lennox?' For there had been a long silence at the other end of the line.

Kemp wasn't saying anything. He was standing in the hall with the phone nuzzled under his chin and a silly grin on his face. If she had been reciting the alphabet backwards he wouldn't have cared so long as he could go on hearing her voice.

'Lennox? Are you all right? Is it another woman you've got there?'

The joy of sudden laughter.

'I left it too late to book one . . . Oh, Mary . . .'

'What?'

'Just, oh, Mary . . . What's the number of your room? I'll join you for breakfast.'

'Two-one-three. What about the office?'

'To hell with the office. You get some sleep and wake up all fresh and . . . I love you . . .'

'I love you, too . . . If I'm to be all fresh I'll need some clean undies . . . trains at night are grubby. You'll find them in my drawer, and would you bring the blue blouse that's in the airing cupboard?'

'I'll bring you the jewels of Ophir and the hanging gardens of Babylon . . .'

'I'll settle for the clothes. Have you been drinking?'

'Only at the fountain of wisdom . . .'

'I thought as much. Make sure you sober up before you drive up here tomorrow . . .'

CHAPTER 20

'What did you tell them at the desk downstairs?' asked Mary, helping herself to toast and marmalade.

'That I'd just flown in from Sri Lanka.'

'I don't know where that is. I told them my husband was arriving from Miami.'

'Outside of the United States, your geography's terrible.'

'I did see a map once at school, but I learnt most of it sitting around in airports. The families I travelled with knew where they were going and Nurse just went along like a piece of extra baggage. It was all one to me whether we were off to Martha's Vineyard or the Florida Keys . . .'

'I always took you for a travelling lady . . . Is that why you've still got itchy feet?'

She looked at him then, across the little breakfast table. Behind them the bedclothes were rumpled. Kemp had come at seven and it was now after ten . . .

'I only went to Liverpool,' she said.

'Not a patch on Martha's Vineyard . . . Want to tell me about it?' Kemp poured coffee for both of them and was surprised to find himself thinking he could do this every morning of their lives in hotels all over the world and never be tired of it . . .

'No reason why not,' she said. She told him about her visit the previous day, only leaving out some of the shadier details of her deceptions which might show herself in a poor light.

She need not have worried; the only light Kemp was seeing his wife in this morning was rose-coloured. He still had not quite got over the traumatic effect her absence had caused, and was content to gaze fondly at her whatever she was saying.

'I was going to John Upshire with all this,' Mary ended. 'What do you think?'

161

Kemp considered.

'Yes, tell him everything you've found out from Amy Frobisher. No action will be taken, of course.'

Mary stared at him. 'Why ever not? Surely it's criminal to send such letters?'

'It is, but can you see Nick Stoddart admitting he posted them or that he helped Amy to write them? If a case was brought he'd fight it and Amy would be the only prosecution witness. Can you really see her standing up to cross-examination, bringing up that stuff about her baby all over again?'

Mary thought about it. 'No, I can't,' she admitted. 'Amy would go to pieces and it would look like she only involved Stoddart because he was just another of the lawyers she hated . . . But he can't be allowed to get away with it.'

'Oh, he won't,' said Kemp, grimly. 'I shall drop hints to Nick Stoddart that I'm well aware of the part he played in the letter-writing, and that the police also have their suspicions . . . Let him sweat that one out. He'll suffer the uncertainty of never quite knowing when some bit of evidence will surface, and he might be pounced on . . . Of course, the police may choose to proceed on what we've already got, but I don't think so . . . I'll make sure the inspector sees it my way. After all, I'm the one who was affected by the letters . . .'

'Now that we've got that little matter tidied up,' said Mary, carefully, 'can we talk about Tony's murder without you leaping up and down?'

She had chosen her moment well. Without knowing the cause, she realized that in the last twenty-four hours her husband had changed. Gone was the edgy tetchiness which both worried and inhibited her, now he was relaxed, easy to talk to . . . Something had happened to him but she would not probe into it; she rarely attempted to analyse either herself or other people; now she was simply pleased that the change in him was for the good. It could not be entirely due to her discovery of the letter-writer's identity, since Lennox had even arrived at the hotel that morning as if about to begin their honeymoon all over again . . .

'Well, now . . .' He was leaning back dangerously in the

only rather small boudoir chair the hotel provided while she had the dressing-table stool, but he looked at ease. 'If we are to suppose that Amy and Dan Frobisher, plus Nick Stoddart, are guilty of nothing more than causing mischief and covering it up, then the killing takes on a different aspect.'

'When you start talking in paragraphs,' she said, happily, 'I know your brain is working again . . .'

'It never really stopped. It was idling in neutral . . .' He didn't care what she thought of his brain; in his present euphoria he would have scooped out the contents and handed them to her on a plate.

It was some time before they tore themselves away from the Station Hotel which, for Kemp at least, had taken on a soft-edged golden glow – the kind of scene a movie cameraman lingers on to the detriment of the narrative.

'Here they used to say Harwich for the Continent, Paris for the incontinent,' he announced cheerily as they emerged from the doors into a throng of late commuters striding purposefully towards uncertain goals. 'And these are just the privileged few,' he added, taking Mary's arm to steer her through the bustle of briefcases. 'The early birds are already caged up . . .'

'What nonsense you talk,' remarked Mary, who was perfectly capable of getting through crowds unaided. She did not quite understand this mood of his, which seemed to be one of high elation as if he'd just won first prize in a lottery. She wasn't going to ask the reason for it but would simply accept that the atmosphere between them was suddenly clearer.

Kemp would not have told her, not then, anyhow. Perhaps later when he was feeling more sensible, when the memory of last night's panic had dimmed a little . . . When he thought about it now it still could grip him by the throat.

As each of them was in a relieved and amiable frame of mind the normally tedious journey home through City traffic and the long roads of urban Essex assumed an air of holiday. They even stopped for lunch at the Epping inn where they had once dined romantically after an afternoon spent exploring Kemp's beloved Forest. 'Exploring?' Mary had scorned the word and talked of the woods of Maine. 'A piece of scrubland and a few trees and you call it a forest!'

But she had been impressed when he showed her the house that stood on the green near the hornbeams, the house with the white gate where he had lived with Muriel and which he had lost because of her . . . So, over that candlelit dinner he had talked of the past, and they had both spoken of Muriel, one thing led to another and by the time coffee was brought he had proposed and she had accepted . . . It had seemed the most natural thing in the world.

'Any regrets?' he asked her now.

'Of course not . . . I'm the luckiest of ladies. What about you?'

Her husband's reply was fervent; last night he had glimpsed the abyss of life without her.

She, who was inclined to be uneasy when led into sentiment, hurried to change the direction of the conversation.

'Shall we both be going to see John Upshire this afternoon? I do feel it can't wait.'

'Aren't you the great one for rushing about, Mary? Did you never think of standing still a while?'

She reddened, partly at the deliberately Irish way he'd put it, but more that he had jabbed a nerve.

'It's true, I suppose . . . I'm always after the next thing . . . I blame it on my deprived girlhood. If you sat still in our house you'd soon get a rap round the ears . . . You'd to move fast to dodge Smith's fatherly hand. When I finally ran away I just kept on running . . .'

'Until you bumped into me, and I told you to stop.'

She put out a hand impulsively and covered his. 'I know what you're trying to say,' she said. 'That we're together and nothing else matters . . .'

'That's it. Now to answer your question. Yes, we will both go and see John Upshire, but there's to be none of this dropping in after office hours . . .' Kemp had not been entirely blinkered to Mary's little ploys. 'We will do it the proper way by making an appointment with the inspector.'

If Upshire was surprised to see the Kemps together at the station that afternoon he gave no sign of it; not for him to comment on what seemed to be a mutual rapprochement.

Nevertheless, he was pleased for he hadn't liked his anomalous position in the space between them.

Kemp gave the field to Mary since it was in essence her story. When she'd finished Upshire merely grunted.

'I thought it was something of the sort,' he said. 'The way young Daren clammed up and looked guilty as hell . . . She's been a right little bitch, that Amy Frobisher, getting these three men dangling round her just to satisfy her ego. All that psychoanalysis stuff gets my goat . . . I don't give a damn what it's done for her, all I know is she's wasted a lot of good police time which couldn't be spared . . . This whole mess about the letters only muddied the waters of the murder enquiry. Not that I went along with the idea they were connected in the first place . . .' He cocked a wise eye at Kemp.

'They may not be entirely unconnected. It may be the publicity given to the letters triggered something . . .' Apparently Kemp's mind was not yet quite up to relinquishing some measure of responsibility.

'You still harbouring that notion of mistaken identity?' asked Upshire.

'Well, Tony was about my height and build, the coat he had on was like mine, and of course there was the place chosen for the killing.'

'It probably wasn't chosen beforehand,' said Mary, who was careful about exact words. 'Somebody could have been following Tony and saw an opportunity.'

'Then they couldn't have picked a better spot,' said Upshire, gloomily. 'Scattered gravel to hide footprints, and as for a weapon . . . That heap of scrap over by the hedge was for taking up by the skip the next day, there were enough bits of rusty old iron, lengths of lead piping and sharp-edged metal to furnish an armoury . . . My men took the whole pile apart and there's at least half a dozen likely weapons that could fit the wound, according to the pathologist. Waste of time, anyway, the killer would have gloves on . . . same as everyone else that frosty night . . . When I say we haven't a clue, I do mean just that.'

'If we discount the threats in the letters, and it wasn't me they were after but Tony, then we have to look at motive,' said Kemp, 'and find out why he was there at the garage at all.'

The inspector grunted. 'If you think it matters,' he said, dismissively. Then he went on, in a more diplomatic manner: 'It's really a question best answered by yourself or one of your colleagues, but now the matter of the letters has been sorted out I'm beginning to go along with the Super – this was the work of muggers, Mr Lambert was an easy mark in that isolated place but they were disturbed, probably by your Miss Stacey's car turning into the forecourt so they'd no time to get at his wallet or his watch. Could be they only meant to stun him but whatever they used for a weapon was sharper than they thought . . . What's the matter, Mrs Kemp?'

For Mary was staring at him, aghast.

'So all you're looking for is a couple of burly villains in boiler suits who just happened to be passing?'

Kemp got hurriedly to his feet. 'I'm sure you've got a busy schedule, John, and we've kept you from it long enough. Don't take any action on what we've told you about Amy Frobisher unless I give you the go-ahead – you can tell the Super I'm content to let it lie . . . Oh, and I wouldn't mind having a dekko at the Lambert file before we go. Just to refresh my memory . . .'

John Upshire didn't remind him that he hadn't even glanced at the file before, it was Mary who had been given access to it. But this was a time for male solidarity.

'Sure, Lennox, it's all yours. I really should be on my way – I've a meeting out at County Hall in half an hour. I'll be seeing the Super so I'll drop him a word about the letters . . . no immediate action. But for my own satisfaction, I'll have young Daren in again. The scribbles of a sick girl may be no big deal but attempted arson's something else . . .'

'That's right, have a go at the small fry . . .' Mary muttered but the inspector went on as if he hadn't heard . . .

'Sorry I've got to go out, Mary. That was a most interesting story you had to tell . . . While your husband goes through that file I'll get Constable Jones to make you a nice cup of tea . . .'

He hastened to the door, throwing Kemp a glance of

166

commiseration as he passed. Mary, who saw it, was further exasperated. 'Cup of tea, indeed! Let's humour the little lady . . . Men!'

Kemp took no notice. He was riffling through the statements and other papers in the file the inspector had handed to him. As far as information went, it was meagre and he had finished reading by the time PC Jones arrived with two mugs of the station's favourite tipple – a dark, inscrutable brew of high tannin content.

'You could dye your lace curtains in this,' said Mary who, in the face of determined male teamwork, had decided to calm down. She knew now that her outburst to the inspector had been a mistake, she didn't need Lennox to reprove her for it, and in fact he had not done so.

He pushed the file back into place on the desk, sipped his tea and grimaced.

PC Jones put his head round the door. 'Everything all right, Mr Kemp?'

'Yes, thank you. We're finished here. Tell me, Mr Jones, how do you make this tea?'

'Ah, now that's a handed-down secret . . . There's not many gets to know it . . .'

'I should hope not,' muttered Kemp as he and Mary went for their car. 'I trust they're an endangered species, at that . . .'

Not till after a good dinner – '. . . to make up for last night's starvation . . .' – did Kemp allow one word to be said about the case. Interesting, though, that he thought of it that way now, whereas before it had been something in the back of his mind, and to be avoided.

Mary and he were tentative in discussion at first; his the more meticulous analysis of facts while she kept to the practical side. She did not seem to have much in the way of womanly intuition, which surprised him, but she was certainly stubborn about some things.

'You keep harping on that present Tony was giving his fiancée. Why do you think it so important, Mary?'

She had thought it out carefully. 'Because it bridges that gap. Something happened between him leaving Donald

Medway, and him ending up at the door of your car – and I don't just mean a railway journey. He said at the party he was getting something for Anita. The call he was going to make in London that afternoon was to "Lydia's chap" – whoever that may be. Well, it's my guess that's where he collected the present.'

'Well, all he had with him was his briefcase . . . That was on the table at his home. The police brought it to us the next day to check whether any of the papers in it concerned our clients. They didn't, they were only the final accounts on his parents' estate that he'd been going through with Donald Medway. No sign of any present for Anita . . . I didn't personally look at the papers, of course, I let Michael do that, but he assured me there was only family stuff – nothing involving clients. That was all that interested us. Anyway, I think Tony's gift to Anita was to leave her everything he had – surely that was enough.'

Mary shook her head. 'No, Tony was referring to something far more specific. Anyway, Mr Medway said the will was made a month ago – when they first got engaged – and she knew about it so there would have been no surprise for her in that . . . I still think it was a stupid thing to do . . .' Mary added, meditatively.

'What, make such a will or tell her about it?'

'Both. I can't think how any man could have been so trusting . . .'

'That's because you have no romance in your soul.' After that glimpse into the pit, the yawning emptiness of a life without Mary, Kemp had all the confidence of the born-again, able to speak boldly of things hitherto hedged with scepticism. 'Tony was in love, and because he had reached an age when he might have thought it would never come, he tumbled in head first . . .' Just as I have done, Kemp was thinking, and it's got nothing to do with marriage, I would have signed over all I possess for no other reason than out of love . . .

'He a grown man and behaving like a callow kid?' exclaimed Mary, only half following her husband's line of thought. 'Well, I still think he was foolish. But to get back to that briefcase, now. Mrs Crabtree said it was on the table in the hall when she got in . . . I wonder if Tony opened it, took something out and looked at it . . . It's the sort of thing you would do if you'd bought something and you wanted to take the first opportunity to look at it properly. He couldn't do it on the train, for it was crowded, so he waited till he was home . . . I should've asked Mrs Crabtree if the case was open when she found it. I'll go and see her in the morning.'

CHAPTER 21

Ember Village liked to cling to what was left of its rural past, but the bright new bungalows along the highway outshone the dull red brick of the older houses and made them seem irrelevant, standing back as they did, avoiding the traffic rather primly. Emily Crabtree's cottage was neither the one thing nor the other. It had been built immediately pre-war on the edge of the Common in the first uneasy stage of Ember's expansion and still retained a look of surprise at finding itself there at all.

Lennox, in his new mood of cooperation had provided Mary with an excuse for her call – a form from Medway, Austin in connection with the annuity which required a signature. That, Mary reflected, was an advantage of their present working relationship, no need now for her to wheedle her way round his office staff, nor lie about her activities – though it might be difficult to break the habit.

Once business was out of the way, Mrs Crabtree produced tea and seedcake. 'Morning coffee's just a fad,' she said, firmly. 'There's nothing like tea. Coffee's all right in its place, and that's after dinner . . . You like caraway seeds?'

'Love them.' Mary was prepared to like anything on offer this morning. 'You settled in, then?'

Mrs Crabtree looked round her parlour complacently. It was neat, clean, tidy and crammed tight with furniture, pictures, ornaments and other articles which defied description. There wasn't a vacant spot on carpet, wall or even ceiling from which tethered ferns and flowering cacti fought for air-space.

'My nephew, he fixed them hooks.' Emily nodded up at them as at some vast engineering feat. 'It was a squeeze getting all my stuff in, I can tell you. I'd my own things, see, from my housekeeper's room at the Hall . . . Well, some had to go but you get attached to things, don't you?'

Mary, who had never in her life been attached to more than a piece of hand luggage, nodded. 'You do indeed,' she said, 'and it's the familiarity with them's such a comfort when they're around you.'

'Different with kitchens . . .' Mrs Crabtree sniffed, giving such places their due but only so far. 'I'm real glad of all the mod cons in there . . . Mr Tony had it all done up for me when he bought the cottage.'

'It was a great loss, Mrs Crabtree . . . Such a kind man, Mr Lambert – and there's the police no nearer catching his killer . . .'

'They never do catch muggers,' said Emily Crabtree, with the gloomy certainty of those who haven't the experience but read the papers avidly. A brief discussion on modern youth and crime was inevitable before Mary could steer the conversation back on course.

'No, I'd no regrets on leaving Copt Lodge. Tell you the truth, the place gave me the willies after that night. The Allardyces wanted me to stay on but all they wanted was a caretaker, and that's not my style at all so I said I'd rather pack it in. They were good about the furniture – anything I wanted, they said. 'Course, they'd had the dealers out for the best bits . . .' She gave a little laugh to show she took it lightly. 'Same with the pictures, but I did take some that were favourites of Mrs Lambert – flowers and girls in long dresses . . . Old-fashioned, but I like them.'

'So do I,' said Mary, who'd never really thought about it. She got up to look more closely at one over the fireplace, a Victorian beauty with cherries in her hat. Beside it hung what seemed to be a parchment of some kind in a gilded frame.

'Ah, now I'm really glad I got that,' Mrs Crabtree exclaimed, seeing Mary's interest. 'It was Mr Tony's present to his parents on their golden wedding – five years ago it would be now . . .'

'What is it?' Mary peered at the dim script but it was difficult to make out much because of the shine on the glass.

'Wait now, and I'll get it down.' Mrs Crabtree took the

frame from the wall and laid it reverently on her lace table-cloth. 'He had it done special-like for them. I'll never forget the look on his mother's face when she unwrapped the parcel. She was so pleased . . . Well, she being a Courtenay herself, of course, and they go back further than the Lamberts . . .' She stopped, sensing that she had lost her audience. Mary was staring at the article, unable to hide her puzzlement.

'It's the family tree,' Emily explained, 'of the Lamberts . . .'

Mary looked at it with some awe. 'My word,' she said, 'I've only seen things like that in the history books. I thought they were only for kings and queens.'

'Bless me, no . . . they're all the rage with some folk nowadays.' Mrs Crabtree's nose lifted in scorn. 'Lot of snobbish nonsense, I call it . . . Fine for the proper gentry as has a right to their name but not for the likes of us, Mrs Kemp . . .'

'Of course not,' Mary hastily agreed. The Blanes had been inclined to boast they were descended from the High Kings of Tara – but then so did the whole indigent population of Ireland, squireens to a man . . .

'It was that Mrs Beresford at the library who got Mr Tony interested in the pedigree, and he hit on the idea to give it to his parents as a present.'

'A good thought for a son to have,' said Mary. 'Thank you for showing it to me, Mrs Crabtree. Now let me put it back up there for you . . .'

'Thank you, my dear . . . Have another cup of tea . . . I do like talking about the family – there's none around here that's interested any more.'

The flow of reminiscence about life up at the Hall in more spacious days did not interfere unduly with Mary's own thoughts as she waited for an opportunity. It came with a tale of the Lamberts' household pets.

'And would that be the same cat the window was left open for that night?'

'Yes, that's Timmy . . . Fancy you remembering him . . . The police didn't seem interested, though they were quick to take away the briefcase that had been on the table.'

'Was it open when you got back, Mrs Crabtree?'

'Oh, yes, the catches were off and the lid up like as if he'd taken something out and left the rest. Wasn't my business to look, of course, but I did see it again just before the police took it because they asked me if there was anything unusual about it. I said, no, and there wasn't that I could see – just his usual things: papers, folders and the like, then that adding-up machine – a calculator, is that what they call them? – his notebooks and a holder for his pens . . . If there'd been anything out of the ordinary, I'd soon have noticed . . .' Mary was sure she would – Mrs Crabtree had a good eye.

'So there would have been room for something else,' she observed.

Mrs Crabtree was dubious. 'I shouldn't have thought so,' she said, 'unless it was very small . . . You think he could have been carrying something he took out of his case, and that's what he was mugged for? They got no money, and never even took his watch – that's what the police said . . .'

Mrs Crabtree may have been elderly but her mind was as free from dust as every corner of her cottage.

'I think it possible,' said Mary. 'He did mention to my husband that he was getting a present for Miss Allardyce that day.'

'Mebbe it was a bit of jewellery, like . . . That poor girl, my heart goes out to her, but she's young and she's got a lot of spirit. I can't blame her for wanting to sell the Lodge – it would be too much in the memory. They'd be on the phone to each other near every night when they weren't meeting . . . He'd always phone her if he'd been out all day, and she'd be home studying . . .'

'But he didn't phone the night he got killed,' said Mary, 'for the police say there weren't any calls from the Lodge.'

Emily Crabtree sighed. 'It's a mystery why he went out . . .'

Mary would have to leave it like that, and it was time for her to follow another idea which had begun to buzz in her brain and required room to expand. On the bus ride back to Newtown, all around the council estates, she gave the idea space . . .

Tony Lambert must have been gratified by the success of his gift to his parents; why should a similar notion not come to him about his fiancée? Not of course the Lambert pedigree

173

– that had already been done, and anyway would not have been appropriate. But what if, prompted by his mother's friend, Lydia Beresford, who did that kind of thing, he had decided to give Anita a framed scroll depicting the Allardyce family from their roots in the Old Country to their present representatives in the Antipodes?

Mary had no idea how such things were done, nor had she been able to take a long enough look at the Lambert record so proudly displayed above Emily Crabtree's fireplace to see what it contained. What a pity Mrs Beresford was on holiday, now she would be just the one to tell all about it . . . Well, in her absence the library would have to do.

Since coming to England Mary had found such places astonishingly stocked with information. She would not have been so astonished had she been in the habit of frequenting libraries back in the States, but as a child in her hometown Mary had all too often been seen off these premises by officious ladies in charge:

'Out you go, you lot' – pointing to the door – 'we don't want dirty Smith fingers on these good books . . .'

Only clean, decent children in proper shoes and white socks were welcome in the library of Vineland township – or indeed in any of its public buildings, except for the state schools and juvenile courts who had to deal with the others in the course of duty, their proclivity for truancy and their aptitude for crime. Though Mary's name had been Blane she was dubbed Smith with the rest of the tribe since it was the man called Smith who had married her mother.

'How can you be so ignorant . . . !' It was not the rudest thing that had ever been said to Mary but it scored high for her experience this side of the Atlantic. Sitting now in a small room off the main library, she was suddenly thrown back thirty years; she could have slid to the floor and crawled out, fast.

And yet her initial introduction to Newtown Library had been pleasant enough.

'I'm sorry Mrs Beresford isn't here,' said the girl at the desk. 'She would have been only too glad to help with any enquiry about family history . . .'

Mary was about to turn away, disappointed, when the girl

174

called her back. 'There's a friend of hers, a Mrs Brunt-Evans, in there now . . . I really don't know whether she could help you . . .' There was a certain lack of enthusiasm in her voice, as if she doubted the wisdom of her own recommendation or the double-barrelled lady was something of a monster.

Which was exactly how Mary saw the person who had looked up at her entrance. The large face was equine or horse-like depending on whether you were fond of horses or not, and the manner of her address was forthright to the point just short of rudeness.

Mary stood her ground against the accusation of ignorance. 'On this subject, yes,' she admitted, 'I've not had the experience . . .'

She was given little time for further explanation as Mrs Brunt-Evans's great voice boomed in her ears telling her – and everyone else in the library – that breeding was too important a subject to be ignorant about, and breeding meant getting your family history right for a start . . .

'I bet the scientists who discovered the DNA didn't do it by studying the finer points of heraldry,' Mary interrupted, standing up for herself and hordes of lost Hibernians. 'And, anyway, it's only a bit of information I'm after.'

Mrs Brunt-Evans looked again, this time more closely, at her visitor who must be from outer space since she'd never heard of St Catherine's House and yet, by the manner of her speaking, was no fool. Mrs Brunt-Evans did not suffer fools gladly, as she was heard to say often and loudly.

'I'm sorry,' she said now, coming down an octave and in a more kindly tone, 'it's just that I can't imagine anyone . . . But, of course, you are perfectly correct, we all have our areas of ignorance . . . And by your accent you are an American which would explain this one. I find Americans are a very mixed lot . . .' She made them sound like a bag of broken biscuits. 'In far too many of them the strength of their desire to know their antecedents is only equalled by the strength of their conviction that they were all titled.' Mrs Brunt-Evans snorted. 'A most unlikely happenstance . . .'

Mary tucked the word away for future use, and said: 'I'm not here on my own account. I am only interested in a family tree which was researched by Mrs Beresford.'

'You know Lydia Beresford?'

'I am acquainted with her, yes.' When in Henry James country you use the idiom.

'Oh, then you must be disappointed to find she is not yet back from holiday.' Both Mrs Brunt-Evans's face and tone of voice lowered themselves more to Mary's level. 'Is it possible that I may be able to help you?'

Horse-face had recognized one who, at the very least, shared acquaintance of a kind. Mary reflected briefly on the very English habit of putting people into little boxes: those you know, those who know you and those whom those you know, know. It was all very tidy and had probably been so since the Middle Ages when the population was of manageable size and could more easily be boxed up.

'Perhaps you can,' said Mary, with some hesitation, 'if only in a general way. English families, now I can understand what you do with them, looking up records and things as you've explained, but what about people who have emigrated, perhaps to the colonies?'

Mrs Brunt-Evans's laugh rattled the paperclips. 'You're not supposed to say "colonies" any more. I'm surprised at you – an American . . .'

'But an ignorant one . . .' Mary gave a small smile of self-deprecation. 'It was an Australian family I had in mind. How would you go about tracing them?'

The enquiry set the woman's hobby off at a gallop as she expounded the methods by which Australians might be tracked down like kangaroos in the outback regardless of whether their passage from the Old Country had been voluntary, assisted or by earlier force majeure.

'Very interesting,' Mary murmured. 'To think there are all these records, by sail, by steam, by air . . . Tracing a family like that sounds very hard work and would have to be paid for if you didn't have time to do it yourself. What if my Australians wanted a permanent record, like a family tree?'

'Ah, then they would consult a professional.'

'A professional?'

'Yes, we're only amateurs. There's some chap in London Lydia uses for that kind of thing. I've got his address somewhere if you're really interested.'

176

She began turning over papers on her desk. 'Here he is – on the back of one of our local family history magazines.' She passed it over to Mary. 'Do keep it, my dear. It might just get you doing your own family.'

I doubt it, thought Mary, thanking her all the same. 'Mr Charles Blakeney,' she read. 'I see he advertises his services as a genealogist.' What pleased her more was that he operated from an address in the Strand.

'A genealogist is a person who traces family pedigrees,' explained Mrs Brunt-Evans, kindly teacher to willing pupil. 'Mr Blakeney will produce a work of art on parchment or vellum should the subject be worthy of it – which in the case of Australians seems hardly likely, meaning no disparagement of your friends, of course . . . He could produce a mock-up scroll of sorts, I suppose, if they really want something to show off, but coats of arms are rare in such families . . .'

'Oh, I don't know,' said Mary, gathering up her gloves and bag, 'they might fancy crossed cricket bats and a recumbent sheep. I was only joking,' she added hastily, seeing the bleak look on the other's face. 'Thank you for your time and patience, Mrs Brunt-Evans, you have told me just what I needed to know.'

'I'm glad to hear it.' The response was gruff; to Mrs Brunt-Evans, family histories – even of people from the Antipodes – were matters not to be taken frivolously. For the moment Mary agreed with her; the visit to the library had paid off. It had only been a hunch in the first place.

Back home she could hardly contain her excitement as she pulled off her gloves to dial the telephone number. She sat, still in her outdoor clothes, and waited.

'Mr Blakeney?'

The voice was elderly but clear. 'Yes, this is Charles Blakeney speaking.'

'Gillorns, solicitors of Newtown here. I have your name from a Mrs Beresford. It's concerning a client who used your services not long ago . . .' Mary paused. A semblance of authority never did any harm, and the personal note here would have taken too long to explain.

'I know Mrs Beresford. Who is this client you speak of?'

'A Mr Lambert. Mr Tony Lambert. We act in the matter of his estate.'

'Dear me . . . I wasn't aware the young man had died. Of course I remember him; I did some research into a family for a friend of his quite recently.'

'That is just what this enquiry is about, Mr Blakeney. Was the family name Allardyce?'

'Yes, that was it. I am saddened to hear that Mr Lambert has died. An accident, was it? He seemed in good health to me . . .'

'A tragic accident, I'm afraid.' There was no need to take that any further. It was helpful that Mr Blakeney had not known of the death – there was no reason why he should: just a mugging, and outside of London at that, and as far as the police were concerned they did not know of the connection. Because he was taken by surprise Mr Blakeney had not had time to be suspicious of the call. In fact, surprise made him more voluble.

'A tragedy indeed for his young fiancée. He told me the family tree was for her. That was why I had worked exclusively on it for some weeks.'

'Which brings me to the reason for this enquiry, Mr Blakeney. We were aware you had prepared this record but we cannot trace any payment having been made. Naturally, as executors for the deceased we are anxious to settle any outstanding claims before distributing the assets of the estate . . .'

In her nursing days, sitting in the rooms of the rich, often by the bedside of the dying, Mary had half listened to many a whispered conclave among relatives who waited, hushed and hopeful, so that now she could rattle off the words without bothering too much as to their exact meaning. The sound of them was usually impressive enough.

'That's quite all right,' Mr Blakeney was saying. 'Mr Lambert had already paid my account. All he had to do the day he came to see me was pick up the finished product . . . And very pleased he was with it . . .' The voice trailed off. 'Oh, dear me, what a sad thing.'

'Would it be a heavy parcel? I mean with the frame . . .'

'I don't frame my work.' Mr Blakeney was brusque;

evidently his toes had been stepped on. 'That is for the client to do should he wish.'

'I do apologize. I am ignorant of such things. Would that be a Wednesday Mr Lambert called?'

Mary mentioned the date which the old gentleman confirmed. Now he seemed reluctant to let her go.

'Mr Lambert was very pleased with the work. Of course he knew a good deal about family histories. He'd done his own some years ago so naturally we discussed the Allardyce pedigree . . .'

'Had it been very complicated?' Mary's voice must have betrayed the eagerness she felt for Mr Blakeney picked it up at once, sensing an interest outside of her original query.

'Bless you, no . . . It was very simple because it followed a pattern common to such Australian families. Great-grandparents both from crofter stock in Scotland, travelling to Australia in the eighteen-forties, and settling there, doing a job they knew – raising sheep. The next generation well established on the land and prospering. But their descendants, the youngsters of today, they're different – they're highly educated and they seek a more sophisticated lifestyle which often brings them back to this country – full circle, as you might say . . . That was clearly what happened in the Allardyce family.'

'No black sheep, then?' Mary prompted, hopefully, but keeping her tone light to soften impertinence.

But Mr Blakeney only laughed. 'Nothing like that, all pure merino wool. Not that we don't come across that kind of thing in our line of work – persons our clients would prefer to ignore, but whatever their character we don't ignore them, we hang them out on the family tree along with everyone else . . . But, I'm sorry, I must be keeping you . . .'

'Not at all. I find it very interesting, Mr Blakeney.'

'Even the names remained the same in that family: the grandfather had been Zachary and I gather that is the name of Anita's brother. Anita – well, the original of the name was always plain Ann or even Annie, but modern girls prefer something a little different. Yes, Mr Lambert and I had a very pleasant chat that afternoon he called. Oh, dear me, to think of him gone . . . Do you know, I can see him now just as he

179

left my office, he snapped his briefcase shut, put the envelope in his pocket, and gave me such a cheerful farewell . . . A young man, newly engaged, with his whole life before him . . .' The old man's voice shook as if he had had an intimation of mortality.

Mary was struck by conscience. 'Please don't be upset, Mr Blakeney. The accident to Mr Lambert was sudden, he would have known nothing. I'm sorry that I had to tell you the bad news . . .' Her explanation seemed lame, even to herself, in the face of the elderly gentleman's concerned sincerity.

'I know, I know, these things happen . . . They can't be helped . . . But it has been nice talking to you, Mrs . . . Ms?'

'It's Mrs Kemp of Gillorns . . .' She could no longer bring herself to lie, and anyway, she had got what she wanted. 'Thank you for your help, Mr Blakeney. I shan't have to trouble you further.'

Mary made herself some tea and carried it into the sitting room. She had much to reflect on. She had solved the puzzle of Tony's present to his fiancée. Where was that present now? She was sure that it had been removed from the briefcase when Tony arrived home that night; it would have been the natural thing to look at it right away. What then? When the contents of the case had been checked by the partners at Gillorns their only concern was whether there were clients' matters in it – Tony's own family papers would have been left intact. If the family tree of the Allardyces was still there it would have gone exactly where it was meant to go – to Anita. But if Tony had taken it out of the briefcase before rushing out into the night, what had he done with it, and where was it now?

Mary sipped her tea and gave her thoughts full rein. It was disappointing that no great revelation had come out of the tree itself, like a light behind a cloud. She had so hoped for something; that Zack and Anita weren't Allardyces at all but strays from the Sydney waterfront, that the sheep station was a myth . . . But no, even that was in place like a little cardboard house on the prairie stocked with well-fed baa-lambs and home to Zack and Anita's decent, grey-haired parents.

Had Mary been honest with herself – which in her present

excited frame of mind she was not — she would have had to admit that she had disliked Zachary Allardyce from their first meeting. He reminded her of those brash young men she'd encountered in rich New York families, as confident in their Brook Brothers suits as in their Harvard education and papa's stake in Wall Street. She had viewed them, she thought, dispassionately at the time but there had always been at the back of her mind that niggling sense of outrage that they should have so much and be careless of it while others who had less cared more.

She tried to rationalize her feelings. After all, she didn't feel the same hostility towards Anita; in fact, she quite liked the girl, all that animal energy so attractively packaged you could warm your hands at it. No, the Allardyce she disliked was Zack, but there was more to it than mere dislike. Had he not behaved suspiciously that time she met him on the train? He'd been upset because she suggested that Tony Lambert and he had travelled together the night Tony was killed, he had denied it, yet that little man in the blazer, Ferguson, had said they did and they'd been deep in conversation before the train reached Newtown Station. Why should Zack be so sensitive about it if it was just a small thing? And when Mary had brought up the subject of Tony's present to Anita the big Australian had been reduced to sullen silence . . .

The more Mary thought about it the more she became convinced that Zachary Allardyce had something to hide about the death of Tony. It would explain his inexplicable behaviour the day she and Sally had called. He could not bring himself to face them; it was not on account of his sister, though he had made that an excuse. No, it was because he, Zack, had something to hide and he was afraid . . . Afraid of what? That he would give himself away?

Mary's thoughts were travelling on a narrow road but they were travelling fast, not looking to right or left. What if something had been said in that conversation between Tony and Zack on that evening train to Newtown, something which must not be allowed to go further?

Mary knew that she ought to talk her theory over with her husband but her mind backed away from what would inevitably be his verdict. With his ridiculous English sense of fairness he would say: 'Mary, Mary, your prejudices are showing . . .' And he would tell her in no uncertain terms that dislike of a person was no reason to fit them up for a murder. Under his bland stare all the beautiful fabric of her theorizing would shred itself of meaning. She'd watched him do it to others; she wasn't going to risk it happening to herself.

Anyway, Lennox wasn't here and ideas about what she should do next kept jabbing at her like needles. She was annoyed with John Upshire for giving in to his superiors by putting the Lambert case away in some file marked 'mugging by person or persons unknown', and, despite his newly awakened interest in the killing, Lennox too seemed to prefer this easy way out. Perhaps for him it was still the death of a friend which was important rather than the hunt for his killer. She found this attitude difficult to understand in the face of his reputation as a seeker after justice, yet she would allow for it. But it would not stop her acting on her own if she felt urged to do so.

She glanced at the clock and was surprised to find it was already mid-afternoon; thinking sure took up a lot of time. She had not had any lunch but somehow that didn't seem to matter. What she needed was action . . . She had to find out the truth about that blessed family tree of the Allardyces.

CHAPTER 22

Mary got the taxi to drop her at the gateway to The Leas even though that meant a long walk up the drive. To take a taxi right up to the door seemed pretentious and, anyway, it wasn't her style. Also, it would draw attention to her, and that was the last thing she wanted.

The drive curved to get itself up the hill, and each time she rounded a clump of bushes she caught a glimpse of lawns on either side stretching away in well-ordered stripes like satin dresses in old pictures. Mary had high hopes of her own lawn in the back garden which went down to the river, but thought it unlikely the grass would ever look like this; here money had obviously been spent to some purpose.

She hoped that Anita would be home and Zack out at whatever business still held him in Newtown. Anita was the softer target, she would get the information out of her first before going on to tackle Zack . . . Mary had not formulated a precise plan, she would play it by ear – at least that was the way she put it in her mind.

Her ring was answered promptly by a maid, not in uniform but certainly a domestic by her demeanour, and local by her accent. 'Yes, Miss Allardyce is in . . . Who shall I say?'

Mary skipped in smartly as the maid stepped aside. Once safely in the hall she gave her name.

'Mrs Kemp . . .' The girl repeated it. 'I'll go and tell her.'

Anita must have been working in the conservatory for it was from that direction she came, carrying a plant pot. Its contents didn't look at all healthy, if not yet dead there seemed little hope of recovery. Anita on the other hand looked better than when Mary had seen her last. The mane of the young lioness shone reddish-gold in the sun striking through the glass as Mary followed her into the conservatory.

'I'm chucking half of them away,' she said, unplugging the

183

poorly plant and throwing it into a bin already full of others similarly afflicted. To Mary's admittedly unbotanical eye it looked like a case of simple neglect.

'Is it that they're not wanted?' she asked, gazing round at the empty shelves.

Anita shrugged. 'Our purchasers have other ideas,' she said. 'They think plants ought to be kept in their proper place – outside . . .' She gave a grimace like a monkey. It was extraordinary, Mary thought, that all Anita's gestures and expressions recalled creatures of the wild, though fortunately neither kangaroo nor wombat.

'What are you grinning at?' She had a cub's quick perception. 'And what on earth are you doing here?'

'Sorry about the smile. Just something I thought of . . . Why am I here? Well, actually it's to ask a favour . . .'

'Come and sit down somewhere comfortable. It's freezing out here. This bloody climate – why don't they all just emigrate?'

She led the way through to the enormous sitting room which Mary remembered from the night of the party. It looked a lot less festive now. Obviously a removal was in progress. Pictures had gone from the walls, some still left standing around on the floor like a bewildered bus queue awaiting transport, ornaments instead of being neatly displayed were stacked end to end on table tops, and rolled-up rugs sulked in corners.

'You're on the move, I see,' said Mary, stating the obvious but hoping to get information out of it.

'You can say that again. What a bore it all is . . . Zack's a great one for collecting stuff; there's far too much of it. Let's sit down, shall we, and talk about this favour you want.'

There are small furry animals that are friendly. They ingratiate themselves by coming up for a pat and a biscuit, there are others who will scorn the biscuit and bite the hand that holds it, and there are those that are simply neutral – they haven't made up their minds. Anita Allardyce, Mary decided, was one of those. Of course it might be she was just practising a lawyer's caution (after all, she must have learned something up at that college).

184

Mary had no time to speculate further; Anita was waiting for her to put her cards on the table.

'Someone told me that there's a family tree of the Allardyces,' she said, trying to keep the tone casual. 'And I was wanting . . .'

Anita made a throaty sound between a growl and a chuckle. 'You can't be serious. Not you, Mary Kemp . . . You're surely not going to hunt up your pedigree? Zack tells me you're an Irish-American, but I can't see you in there with the Kennedys.'

'It's not for me,' said Mary. 'I think that's a lot of nonsense myself, and so did you last time we spoke about the English obsession with their ancestors. But all I wanted to know was, did Mr Blakeney get the tree finished in time . . .'

'In time for what?' The little cub was quick to pounce and the words came sharply.

'Why, for Tony's death,' said Mary.

There was a pause. Mary watched the girl's eyes. They were set so wide apart they gave an impression of wariness as if she expected to be jumped on from either side.

'I know that tact isn't your strong point, Mary, but don't you think that's a bit insensitive, even for you?'

'I'm sorry . . . It was only that Mrs Beresford had recommended Mr Blakeney in the first place so she felt responsible . . . She was going away on holiday so she asked me to find out whether you eventually did get the family tree.'

There was another pause after this farrago of truth and lies. A small frown puckered Anita's brow below the fringe of yellow hair. There was a faint line of down along her upper lip, a mere brush stroke of flat hairs which glistened now as the pink tongue came out and moistened them.

'I've never heard of any Mr Blakey, or whatever his name is. Mrs Beresford, yes, one of Tony's more boring friends, but she's got nothing to do with me.'

'All I'm asking . . .'

'I know what you're asking, and all I've got to say is I don't think it's any business of yours whether we have a family tree or not. In fact, Mary Kemp, I think you've got a nerve coming here . . .'

'I'd say more than that . . . I'd call it bloody cheek . . .'

185

How long Zachary Allardyce had been standing there Mary didn't know. The door into the hall was behind her and had been left open. He now advanced into the room followed by a short thickset man who looked embarrassed. As well he might, for both Allardyces stood in front of Mary, blue eyes flashing and tempers up.

'I'll handle this, Anita.' Zachary put out a restraining hand. 'What the hell does she want here?'

'I'm not a "she",' said Mary, tartly. 'I've a name of my own and it would be manners if you'd use it. I'm here on a perfectly proper errand for Mrs Beresford.' She made no move to vacate her seat.

'Like hell you are.' Zack continued to stand over her in an attitude of barely concealed menace. His height, his breadth of shoulder as well as his compelling personality were supposed to make people shrivel up and give in. Mary ignored him.

'Good afternoon, Mr Blackett,' she said to the other man, whom she recognized as the estate agent who had dealt with their purchase of No. 2, Albert Crescent. 'We've met before.' She would like to have told him that he was a godsend in her present circumstances. His being there would take some of the heat out of the situation, and in fact it did allow her to tell the tale of Mrs Beresford's concern for the Allardyce family tree for a second time. The telling of it went so smoothly that she was beginning to believe in it herself.

Zack, possibly influenced by having an outsider present, did at least take a step back while Anita plumped herself down in a chair again and looked to her brother for a lead.

'Look here, Mrs Kemp,' said Zack, only slightly less belligerently, 'we're getting fed up with you interfering in our affairs. What right have you to question Anita about our family tree?'

Mr Blackett was still standing about, nervously clutching a notebook and papers. At the mention of something so intimate as a family tree he took fright. 'Perhaps it would be better if we finished the inventory later, Mr Allardyce . . .'

Zachary turned on him. 'For God's sake, man, sit down. You know there's no time to do it later. Anyway, Mrs Kemp is leaving.'

Mary sat back in her chair, fastening herself more securely to the seat of it. She was not going to leave this house until she saw the family tree, or got thrown out. Mr Blackett was her guarantee that would not happen. She beamed at him. 'How is business, Mr Blackett?' she said. 'This must be a fine sale.' She looked round at the dimensions of the room. Fine sales meant fine commissions for Blackett's.

He only nodded, and furtively at that. He was rarely at a loss for words, his line of work depending on his having a good flow of them, but here he found himself between Scylla and Charybdis paddling furiously to stay in midstream. The commission on The Leas would be gratifyingly large, so long as the Allardyces didn't pull out at the last minute. On the other hand, Gillorns put a lot of business his way and Mrs Kemp's husband was senior partner in the firm.

Mr Blackett decided he'd better keep out of things so he withdrew to a seat by a side-table where he laid out his papers fussily and bent his head over them to pinpoint his neutrality.

Zachary Allardyce had not succeeded in his career simply by his intimidating personality – particularly in local government where there were plenty of others like him – so he knew when to change tactics. He recognized in Mary Kemp a stubbornness to match his own.

'This Beresford woman,' he said to Anita. 'Is she someone you know?'

Anita shrugged. Since her brother had taken charge she seemed to have lost interest. 'I've probably met her. She was a friend of Tony's mother.'

'And was it through this Mrs Beresford Tony got the idea of having the family tree done?'

'I suppose so.' Anita swung her muscular little legs over the side of her chair and stifled a yawn. That done, she addressed Mary in a tone at once kindly and only slightly contemptuous. 'I really think it's time you went. You're only wasting our time and your own.'

'I've plenty of it,' said Mary cheerfully, 'and you still haven't answered my question. Did you get your family tree safe and sound?'

'Of course we got it.' Zack was putting up with no more

of this nonsense. 'That answers your question, so you can now go on back to Mrs Beresford and tell her . . .'

'Oh, but I'd so much like to see it,' said Mary, at her most charming – rather for the benefit of Mr Blackett than either of the Allardyces, as she could sense that his ears were trembling for all that he was scribbling away like mad. 'If you wouldn't mind,' she went on with an appealing smile. 'I'm so ignorant about such things . . .'

'Amongst others, I'm sure,' said Anita, matching her tone in sweetness. 'Now do go away as Zack says, and you can reassure Mrs Beresford and that Blakey man that all is well.'

Mary was stumped. Although she had learned that the Allardyce family tree really did exist and they had it, she was obviously not going to get a look at it unless she got a search warrant. In the meantime everyone was looking at her, including Mr Blackett who had at last raised his head from his notebook in which he had been busy scribbling nothings.

It seemed she was expected to go quietly; it would be worse than bad manners simply to go on sitting there . . .

She was saved by the entrance of the maid who came in on cue as if in a stage play.

'How many cups of tea will it be, Miss Allardyce? Are they all of them staying?' Her eyes swept round as at a multitude clamouring for teacups.

'Oh, I'd love a cup of tea!' Mary cried, putting her bag and gloves down again. 'Just the right time in the afternoon, too . . .'

The maid looked at her as if she was mad. It was after five and she'd waited long enough in the kitchen for the summons to bring in the tea.

'Oh, let them all have tea,' said Anita, wildly. 'It's getting more like the Mad Hatter's tea party every minute. Just the tea, Debbie,' she told the girl. 'We don't want cakes and things . . .'

'There aren't any, miss. With you leaving so soon like you said, there's nothing in . . .' Debbie flounced out, raising her eyebrows as she passed Mr Blackett as if to say: 'Some people!'

'I didn't realize you were leaving us so soon,' said Mary, conversationally. 'Are you both returning to Australia?'

Either the brother and sister thought the other would answer or together they were determined to freeze her out for no one answered. Zachary strolled over to Mr Blackett and began discussing the inventory of household effects. Anita got up and began fiddling with some of the ornaments on the top of a china cabinet.

To be thus studiously ignored by the other three people in the room was a trial of patience to Mary who was made to feel like the worst type of gatecrasher. Resolutely, however, she sat on.

One part of her mind was telling her the Allardyces had every right to deny her a glimpse of their blessed tree, she wasn't after all a close friend of theirs. But if they really wanted to get rid of her and get on with Mr Blackett's business they'd only have to give in to her request. The more they stonewalled the more suspicious Mary became.

'I'm sorry if I seem to be a nuisance . . .' she began.

'If you were at all sorry you'd be gone by now,' said Anita, coldly, putting down a porcelain figure with unnecessary force and coming back to her chair. 'As it is, we're supposed to humour you. What exactly is it you want with the family tree?' she added with more curiosity than she had previously shown.

'I'm interested in it because collecting that pedigree from Mr Blakeney was one of the last things Tony Lambert did . . .'

Now that it was out, straightforward and without the lies and subterfuge, Mary felt relieved. Her bald statement certainly had the effect of gaining immediate attention. Zachary left Mr Blackett and came swiftly over to tower once again over Mary's chair.

'What are you getting at?' he demanded.

'Just that Tony brought your family tree home with him from London that evening you were with him on the train not long before he was killed. Didn't he mention it in his talk with you?'

'You keep wittering on about me being on the train with Tony. I've told you once and I'll tell you again, we were not together.'

'A witness says you were, Zachary. He saw you talking with Tony on the train.'

'Whoever it was is lying. I did exchange a few words with Tony that evening, that was all.'

'Enough for him to tell you what Anita's present was . . .' Mary was trying to see his expression but his back was to the window and his face in shadow.

'Are you playing at being some kind of detective?' The note of amused curiosity was still in Anita's voice.

'No, I'm just asking questions,' said Mary, calmly, 'and if your brother has nothing to hide he won't mind answering them. You say you've got the family tree, well, why won't you let me see it?'

'What a cheek!' Zack was in explosive mode again. 'Are you suggesting this has got something to do with Tony's death?'

'I'm not suggesting anything, but since you've brought it up it does seem strange that he should bring home your family pedigree, have a look at it, then dash out on a freezing night and get killed . . .'

'I thought it was a mugging, whoever did it was surprised in the act and ran off empty-handed. That's what the police think. And yet you come here trying to involve us!' Anita was obviously outraged; she tossed her golden mane and clenched her small fists as she leant forward and confronted Mary.

'That's the easy theory,' Mary told her, still keeping an eye on Zachary. She thought she detected some hesitation in his manner since she had mentioned a witness on the train. Now he pulled up a chair between Mary and Anita, and sat down.

'Leave this to me, sis,' he told her once more, the way he had probably done all her life. 'I can handle Mary Kemp.' He turned to Mary, narrowing his eyes and speaking in the kind of reasonable voice an executive might use to sell an unsaleable product.

'I think I know what's bugging you, Mary, and up to a point I sympathize. Tony Lambert was your husband's partner and friend, and he had good reason to believe Tony had been killed in mistake for himself because of those threatening letters. I understand that Lennox Kemp has suffered a kind of breakdown as a result. So you're looking for a way out of his problem, any way . . . And you've fastened on me . . . You don't like me so you want to make trouble for me . . .' He paused, and leaned back. 'Yes, I did talk to Tony on the train, and yes, he told me that his present to Anita was our family tree. It was too personal a thing to put into my statement to the police, it had no bearing whatsoever on what happened to Tony subsequently . . . At first I simply forgot, then by the time I'd remembered it seemed silly to go back on what I'd already said . . .'

If Mary had not been so driven by her own conviction and her dislike of the man she would have recognized Zack's explanation as not only possible, but a considerable concession, particularly coming from someone like him who wasn't given to waffle. As it was, however, she jumped on the weakness in it.

'So you lied,' she accused him. 'You lied because there was something in that family tree which might make Tony think again about his engagement to your sister.'

'What are you saying?' Anita's face puckered up in distress as she forced out the words. 'What terrible thing are you saying?'

'I'm sorry, Anita . . .' Mary told her. Probably the girl had meant no harm, possibly she did not know what her brother was capable of. Only Zachary knew that.

'Go on, then,' he said now. 'Get it out in the open, whatever it is you're hinting at . . .'

Mary sat still. She was so certain in her own mind; all the pieces fitted, the pattern was complete.

This time the entrance of Debbie was not so timely. She wheeled in a tea-trolley with a great deal of clatter, effectively filling the ears of those in the room expectant upon something less mundane. Debbie herself was not aware that her arrival came as an anti-climax, although the sudden cessation of talk might have alerted her.

'Milk? Sugar?' She dispensed her wares in total silence. 'I found some biscuits, Miss Allardyce, it's all that's left . . .'

'All right, Debbie . . . Hand them round, please.' Anita seemed the only one to find the maid's presence a boon.

Zachary had found the line of action he meant to take,

and no interruption was going to stop him. 'Go on, Mary,' he pressed her, 'don't just hint at things. Spit it out . . .'

Suddenly she was aware that he was baiting her, daring her to say more . . . She had not prepared herself for this. In films she had seen, the crime fiction she had read, there was always a showdown, even in her own real-life drama there had come a time of reckoning when villains were unmasked, and justice triumphed. That was supposed to be the scenario . . .

This was it . . . Or was it?

Looking across at Zachary Allardyce, he was still the hotshot high-flier of the Newtown Development Corporation planning department, the flamboyant Australian tycoon who could teach those hick Englishmen a thing or two about buildings, the owner of this fine house, guardian of his lion cub of a sister and all her money . . . Nothing had changed . . .

Mary was startled at the havoc Zack was causing to her thought processes. Sitting directly under the glare of his eyes was like being out in the midday sun of the desert – it addled the brain.

And he was goading her.

'Cat got your tongue,' he gibed. 'What's this notion you and that husband of yours have cooked up between you to get him out of the mess he's in . . . ?'

He half turned towards Anita. 'Don't worry, sis, I think I know what this is all about. It's some kind of personal animosity the Kemps have against me. Isn't that it, Mary?' He brought the full force of his eyes on her as he continued: 'You need to draw the attention away from yourselves because it's just possible that Tony was mistaken for Lennox that night, and if Lennox had acted quicker over those letters it might never have happened . . . And neither of you wants to live with that so you're looking for a scapegoat. Tell me, is this charade your idea or did your husband put you up to it? His own past isn't exactly clean, perhaps that's why he can't resist casting aspersions on others . . .'

The last straw need only be a light one. Mary didn't care what Zack thought of her, she had put up with plenty of insults in her youth, but for him to slur Lennox, that did it

. . . Allowing no space for caution and taking no time for thought, she spoke out.

'Zachary Allardyce, it was you who killed Tony Lambert. You killed him because there was something in your family pedigree which might prevent his marriage to your sister. But if Tony died before he could break off the engagement, Anita would still inherit. You followed Tony home that night from the train, he took out the family tree from his briefcase and his first thought was to get advice – from Lennox. You were outside Copt Lodge when he came out and you followed him again, this time to the garage where you killed him. You had to do it before he could tell anyone . . .'

Mary's words were falling into a deep well of silence. It seemed to go on and on as if it would never be broken. Then she heard the little sounds: Anita's indrawn breath, the tinkle of spoons from the trolley where Debbie stood, Mr Blackett's nervous cough and the rattle of his cup as he felt for the saucer with an unsteady hand.

Zachary was still staring at Mary. There was such utter disbelief in his face that she was struck dumb. But she had said enough.

At last he moved. He pushed his chair back, and walked over to the table where Mr Blackett sat. 'Is it still in the same drawer, Anita?'

'Yes, the right-hand one. She could have seen it, only . . . Well, I didn't see why she should . . . But if it could have stopped her saying this awful thing . . .'

'Excuse me, Mr Blackett.' Mr Blackett moved his chair and Zack pulled open the table drawer.

As soon as she saw the long, narrow cardboard cylinder, Mary knew . . . 'A holder for his pens' . . . That was what Emily Crabtree had said . . .

Something into which you might put a rolled-up scroll to avoid getting it creased . . . Mrs Crabtree had seen it in the open briefcase . . .

Zack slid the parchment out and handed it to Mary. 'See for yourself,' he said, tersely.

She took it, hands shaking beyond her control. His very calmness, the quietness of his voice after its previous roaring, all these were having an effect on her. After her accusation, what had she expected? Bluster, angry denials, more false-hoods, some incoherent blundering to pin down her certainty of his guilt? But not this cold unconcern which yet had behind it some obscure satisfaction.

She glanced over the writing on the scroll but she didn't really have to look at it any closer to know that it was all there as Mr Blakeney had said. There were no blanks, no bastards, no lines of doubt between the Zachary and Annie Allardyce who had lived and died in the last century, and the present Zack and Anita. There were lots of other people on the tree, of course, many names, marriages, births and deaths, but none of them relevant. The blood line was direct, those who were, proudly, 'of Mauchline Farm', the name which had obviously been given to the original settlement by the great-grandparents to remind them of the Ayrshire town they had come from . . .

Besides compiling the record in his fine copperplate writing Mr Blakeney had added curlicues and flourishes of his own so that the whole thing was indeed a work of art. Turning it over in the vain hope that there might be some secret on the back, Mary saw the simple initials *C.B., Genealogist* to demonstrate the authenticity of the family tree.

Wordlessly, she handed it back to Zachary. His eyes were glittering like blue ice; to avoid them she stooped for her bag . . .

'Don't go yet,' he said. 'This is only the start . . . I want you to listen carefully to what I'm going to say. Mr Blackett?' The estate agent got up and crossed the room. By the hunted expression on his face he would rather be anywhere else than here.

'Do you have your diary with you, Mr Blackett?' asked Zack.

'Of course. I always carry it.'

'Then would you mind looking up a date for me. It was a Wednesday . . .' He gave the date of Tony Lambert's death.

Mr Blackett took out his book and riffled through the pages. 'Yes,' he said, 'I've got it . . . It was the night of the Newtown Chamber of Commerce dinner . . . Why, you were there, Mr Allardyce. At our table . . .'

'Precisely. And the dinner was at the Castle Hotel starting at eight o'clock. Am I right?'

Blackett nodded. 'You had a drink with myself and my wife about seven-thirty in the bar — that's when we found we were at the same table.'

'And I was with you all evening?'

'Well, you had to be, didn't you, Mr Allardyce? They got you to thank the speaker . . . He did rather go on a bit . . .'

Zack threw out his arms as if in appeal. 'Then I couldn't have been following Tony Lambert from the train, or killing him at the back of Lorimers' Garage, could I? The police said poor Tony died about eight o'clock . . .'

'Why, that was the night you gave me a lift to the town,' Debbie cried out, in great excitement. 'Remember? You'd hardly time to change your suit coming in from the train and then you were out again, and I was going down for a bus . . . I couldn't forget that night because of what happened to Mr Lambert. I think it's sick to bring it all up again . . .' She glared at Mary.

'Well, thank you, Debbie.' Zack gave the girl a huge smile of charm and candour. 'I never thought I'd need an alibi and here's one that's watertight. Isn't that what they call them, Mary Kemp? You should know, you're the wife of the great detective.'

Zachary Allardyce was enjoying himself. So might he have done when at the business end of a shotgun hustling trespassers off his land.

'I think you should leave now, Mary,' Anita said, firmly but with a hint of sympathy. She picked up Mary's bag and gloves and handed them to her. Mary felt numb, as if she'd been given an anaesthetic but with the full knowledge that pain would follow later. However, she was not to escape so easily.

'She's not leaving yet,' said Zack as he loped over to the desk in the corner where there was a telephone. He glanced at his watch as he dialled. 'I hope the old man's still in his office . . .'

'Mr Cedric Roberts, please. Zack Allardyce here . . .'

He began whistling softly through his teeth while he waited.

'Mr Roberts? Glad you haven't gone home . . . I want you to do something for me . . . I need a writ issued . . . for malicious slander . . . Yes, I know it's a very serious matter but so is the accusation which has been made against me. The writ is to be served on Mrs Mary Kemp . . . That's right, the wife of Lennox Kemp. Yes, I know who he is . . .'

There was a pause as he listened. 'Yes, in the presence of witnesses . . . Mr Blackett, you know him . . . the estate agent. Miss Deborah Ford, our domestic, and my sister . . . Yes, I understand. Of course there was malice . . . As I told you when arranging for completion of the sale, Anita and I are leaving England shortly but I want that to make no difference to this action I'm taking against Mrs Kemp. It must be pursued with all vigour . . . Yes, I'll give you the details in the morning . . . Ten o'clock? Fine by me.'

'Do you have to, Zack?' exclaimed Anita when he put down the phone. She sounded horrified.

'I've no option . . . You may not want to return to this country but I may work here again, even come back to Newtown . . . What has been said in this room in front of other people, it has to be given the lie if I'm to have any reputation left . . .'

Anita's eyes met Mary's. There was the slightest uplift of her reddish-brown eyebrows, as if to say: 'Men, and their precious reputations!' but even this mark of feminine solidarity could do nothing to ease Mary's discomfiture.

'I'll call you a cab . . .' There was a little of her usual animal perkiness left in Anita's face. She was the only one showing any warmth to Mary and Mary was grateful for it, but nothing could take away the bitterness . . .

She shook her head, and walked steadily through the hall to the door . . . Afterwards she couldn't remember how she got there nor the long walk to the bus stop. She had shut down all thought, closed off all parts of her mind so that it was as an automaton that she boarded the bus, paid her fare, climbed the stairs and sat letting the lights of the ring road flash past her unseeing eyes.

Only the brilliant neon sign above Lorimers' Garage brought her sharply to her senses. She remembered being on this bus route before. She leaned forward now to look

196

out of the opposite window, and saw across the darkened field the outline of Copt Lodge, its empty windows staring out above the shadowed gardens.

CHAPTER 23

'I'm not an invalid,' muttered Mary, later that evening.

Her husband took no notice. He was bringing in the coffee and already there were two large brandy glasses on the tray. It was Lennox who had cooked the dinner, made her eat some of it and even washed up afterwards.

'I'm not an invalid,' she said again, but weakly as if in fact she was . . . Lennox had treated her as one from the moment she had come home, stumbling through the door, her hands shaking so much she couldn't get the key out of the lock. He had taken one look at her, guided her into the sitting room, helped her off with her gloves and coat, and finally pushed her down gently on to the sofa and brought her a drink.

'Now, tell me the worst . . .' he had said.

To stretch it out on the rack by lengthy explanations, justifications and excuses would have been too terrible . . . So she simply told him baldly in two paragraphs.

Lennox said nothing for some time. She watched his face, saw the sudden frown, the pursed lips, but above all, she watched his eyes – grey, like her own, opaque, not given to overt expression – for in his eyes she would read her fate. What she had done was so awful for herself, the consequences to both of them so fearful it took all her courage to face him. She just wanted to curl up and die . . .

Then she saw the corners of his mouth twitch. It was a rueful smile but it was still a smile. He gave a little shake of his head.

'Mary, Mary, so contrary . . . When you go off on these jaunts of yours paddling your own canoe . . .'

'I know . . . I end up in shit creek . . .' She had given up on Henry James and gone back to Brooklyn; after what she'd done to this man of hers it would be better if she'd never left. 'Will Zachary really go on with this slander thing?'

Kemp shrugged, but he wanted her to have no further illusions.

'Probably. He's not known for backing down . . . Anyway, it'll take months, and old Cedric Roberts isn't a bad sort. We might be able to come to terms, perhaps an apology and a fairly large sum of money.'

Mary was aghast. 'But Zachary Allardyce doesn't need money!'

'Of course he doesn't. That's not the point. He'll give it to charity and make a big splash about it . . . You've a lot to learn, Mary Madeleine . . .'

Chastened, even humbled, Mary could only listen as he attempted to show where she had gone wrong without inflicting further damage. Carefully he went through the steps she had taken two at a time instead of first making sure she had a foothold, and pointing out why she had arrived at a totally wrong conclusion.

It was a good tactic on Kemp's part. Naturally he had been shocked – much more than he showed – by the implications of what Mary had done. At this point particularly where his firm was concerned he could well have done without yet another embarrassment of a personal nature. But his first thought had to be for his wife.

She had received a stunning blow, enough to rob her of all self-respect, all confidence in herself, and for a loner such as she that could be devastating. Sympathy was of little use. Until he had come along and married her, Mary had never in her life been the object of anyone's regard, never mind concern for her wellbeing; she wouldn't know how to cope with sympathy. He was no psychologist but he guessed the only way forward for her was to concentrate on something so crucial that it would take from her mind all thought of the deed already done, and in any case irretrievable, and put in its place an idea worthy of her commitment.

'. . . so, you see, Mary,' he ended this exercise in home-spun therapy, 'what you and I have to do now – and we have to do it together – is find who killed Tony Lambert.'

She cottoned on fast. Whether she knew what was in his

mind, that he was doing it for her sake, didn't matter, she grasped the chance he was giving her.

'So you don't think it was just another mugging?' she said, eagerly.

'It may turn out to be that in the end,' said Kemp, cautiously, 'but there are too many loose ends lying about . . . You were right to give more attention to Tony's last hours than the police did, even though you dropped a clanger in the end . . .'

'I was so sure it was Zachary Allardyce,' said Mary, miserably.

'Forget it. You just don't like Australians with good muscles and a deep tan. What you forgot was evidence. You were making bricks out of straw in your rush to find him guilty.'

'He was going to leave the country soon . . . I didn't think there was time . . . I'm sorry . . .'

'That was no excuse for crashing in like an avenging angel. Think first, fight afterwards, the soldier's art – and it should be yours too if you ever want to make a detective.'

He handed her a brandy. 'Help you to loosen up, because I want you to sit there and give me a detailed record of just how you reached the conclusion you did, even if it was wrong.'

After over an hour Mary felt as if she'd been put through a wringer and hung out to dry. Everything she'd done, every thought she'd had, every suspicion she'd harboured even for a fleeting moment, all were hauled out by her husband's persistent probing, then scrutinized, sorted and stacked to his satisfaction.

They had been back as far as the letters . . .

'I always thought they were a kind of side issue,' said Mary.

'You didn't want them to be the main one because you needed to spare me . . . You wanted the killer to be someone who knew it was Tony, even though he was beside my car and wearing a coat like mine. You looked for a motive, and there was the money so you plumped for Zachary who you didn't like.'

Put like that, Mary had to admit he had a point, but she could be stubborn. 'Now the letters have been explained away,' she said, 'I've still a thing about them that lingers

... Something you said once ... One of your quotes ... Something about "between the thought and the deed" ...'

'Between the acting of a dreadful thing and the first motion,' Lennox quoted.

'That was it ... Well, it has bothered me, that gap between the thought – which was the letters – and the deed, which was the murder. I didn't think the connection was straight, there was a muzzy feeling about it ... I can't explain properly. It was as if there were two lines which had nothing to do with each other, and suddenly they came together.'

'You think the letters could have been the trigger but it wasn't necessarily anything to do with them when the shot was fired – metaphorically speaking? – Hmm ... I'll tuck that idea away ... In the meantime you went after Zack Allardyce because you disliked him even more than you disliked Dan Frobisher or Nick Stoddart.'

Lennox was laughing at her; she must be at least half forgiven. 'That wasn't the way of it at all,' she said. 'You make it sound as if I'd got it in for all menfolk ... It was Nick's hostility to you that coloured my opinion of him. As for him being a murderer ... I don't know. He's an intelligent man, I think it would take more than revenge as a motive ... Besides, he got his kicks from watching the effect of those letters on you. As for Frobisher, I scarcely know him. He tried to protect Amy from her foolishness – that's in his favour – but I don't know how far he'd go ... He'd nothing against you that we know of, nor against Tony either ... I suppose now the police have the facts about the letters both these men will get some attention. They didn't before ...'

'They weren't connected before ... It will be interesting to hear where they were at the time of Tony's death. They've had lots of time to concoct alibis,' Kemp added, sardonically.

'That reminds me,' said Mary. 'Those statements I saw in the police file, Zack's only took him as far as saying good night to Tony in the station car park. Didn't they ask where he was for the rest of the evening?'

'Haven't you twigged it yet?' Kemp sounded amused. 'Blackett wasn't the only person to see Zack in the bar at the Castle around seven-thirty. The Chief Constable was the guest speaker at that dinner. What were John Upshire's men supposed to do? Ask the Chief if his eyesight was good or how much did he have to drink!'

'Oh . . .' Mary put her hand to her mouth. 'And there's me thinking maybe they'd been a bit lax in questioning the Australians . . .'

Kemp gave a short laugh. 'Zachary didn't need Blackett's alibi, or the girl's. He only put that show on for your benefit. And, another thing, you realize by now that in the quick turn-around he had between getting home and leaving again there was never time to have any discussion with his sister about the blessed family tree.'

That cursed tree more like, thought his wife, yet she was reluctant to let it go. 'Tony Lambert went nowhere else in London that afternoon,' she said, slowly. 'Only to Mr Blakeney's . . . Then he's on the train, chatting normally, from there to the car park, again everything seems normal, then he goes home, puts his briefcase down on the hall table, opens it and dashes out into the cold night . . .'

'Leaving the family tree still snugly rolled up in its container.' Kemp finished the sequence for her. 'So, it wasn't that which sent him off in a rush to find me . . .' He thought for a moment, trying to visualize it.

'Tell me, Mary, as accurately as you can, just what that elderly gentleman, Mr Blakeney, said on the telephone . . .'

Mary obliged, although she couldn't see that it would take them any further forward. She was beginning once more to have misgivings about Zachary's threat of an action for slander. From what she had now learned about his position in the community, his prestige or whatever it was called, he might well say she had damaged his reputation . . . It was all very well for Lennox to hope something might be arranged, a compromise reached – the lawyers' talk she had despised – so that the terrible mistake be hushed up and forgotten, but nothing could take away her own guilt, her sense of failure, something which had gone disastrously wrong. She could see only gloom ahead . . .

Her husband sensed the change in mood. Perhaps the beneficial effect of the brandy was beginning to wear off.

202

Mary was no drinker, and now, looking across at her white face, he could see she must be dreadfully tired.

'Time you were in bed, my love, and no getting up tomorrow. You've had a hard day, and what you need is rest . . .'

'Is it peace and quiet then that you're suggesting? Maybe I should be taking a turn at the housekeeping, become a proper housewife and cuddle up to the cooker and the sink for a change . . . ?'

'There's no need to go to extremes,' said her husband placidly, as he put out the lamps. 'You can cuddle up to me tonight, and tomorrow you stay home where you can come to no harm.'

CHAPTER 24

Mary had been a good sleeper since the day she was born. She had absorbed the need for sleep with her mother's milk and had it nurtured by her mother's fear for all her children; if they cried too loud or moved too slow they felt the hand of the father – in Mary's case the stepfather. To be asleep was to be safe and out of his sight. Even now she could still curl up and die each night to awake revived and ready to do battle with whatever the day might bring.

This morning, however, she would be cautious. She was not so set in her independent ways as to take no heed of her husband's advice. It made sense. A day at home on household chores would give her breathing space. She had been shaken, and although she didn't have much imagination her stomach churned when she thought of the possible court case in which she would stand accused of slander.

Don't think of it at all, she admonished herself as she set to work on washing, cleaning and cooking. That should take care of the morning, and in the afternoon, well, there were those shrubs needing cutting back at the bottom of the garden. When Lennox came home in the evening he would find a sparkling house, a tidy garden and a casserole on the table – just like the television adverts where happy housewives greeted happy husbands in happy homes after they'd had a hard day in the office.

Mary was already wrong in one surmise. Lennox wasn't in his office. He'd gone there for an hour to make certain phone calls but by mid-morning he was on his way to London.

Mr Blakeney was expecting him, as Gillorns had phoned to make the appointment, but the old gentleman was considerably puzzled. He led Kemp through long corridors into what was a cubby-hole in much larger offices.

'It's sufficient for my modest needs . . .' he explained. 'I'm sorry you've had to come all this way. Let me get you some coffee while you tell me why this little matter of my account should be so much trouble to the executors of poor Mr Lambert . . .' He fussed with an electric kettle, two cups and a carton of milk while Kemp explained the situation. He saw no reason for subterfuge, there had been a murder, Mr Blakeney's office was one of the last places the deceased had called at . . . Yes, an investigation was in progress . . .

Men of Charles Blakeney's years are less shockable than Mary had supposed. Kemp told him just as much as he needed to know, trailing the cloth of a mugging to evade further questions.

'Because Mr Lambert worked for my firm we had to make sure none of our clients' papers had been taken. No, his briefcase wasn't with him, it was still at his home and, yes, the family record you prepared for him was still in it.'

'I'm glad Miss Allardyce would have that at least . . . Now if it had been a piece of jewellery he was giving her as a present that would have been a reason for mugging . . .'

Kemp shook his head. 'Mr Lambert seems to have had nothing with him of that nature. By the way, Mr Blakeney, I think you said he put the family tree into his briefcase and the envelope in his pocket. What envelope might that be? Your account?'

'Oh, dear me, no . . . Mr Lambert had already paid my account weeks ago, by post – and it was properly receipted then. I told the lady who phoned from your office – Mrs Kemp . . . Was it your wife? Such a pleasant voice – Irish, I thought?'

'Irish-American, I think it's called . . . About this envelope, sorry to go on about it but if it wasn't your account, what was it?'

'It came in with the record from Sydney. I must explain, Mr Kemp, that when I research a family in Australia I use a friend there to check the local sources. I've known Barry Curtis for many years, and he is a great help with shipping records and passenger lists. He did some work for me on the Allardyces and when he sent in the entries that envelope was enclosed.'

'Would that be his bill?'

'No, of course that came as well and had been incorporated in Mr Lambert's account when he paid it earlier. I reimburse Barry for his expenses when an accumulation of money is due to him. The envelope he sent was in fact addressed to Mr Lambert – I had told Barry the name of my client – and it was marked personal so naturally I didn't open it. I presumed it was a notice of some of the other services Barry provides – he's a shipping agent for a cruise line . . . Really' – the old man paused – 'I didn't give the envelope any thought . . . I may have remarked to Mr Lambert it was probably an advertisement for a cruise, perhaps Barry was thinking of a honeymoon . . . Oh, dear me . . .'

Kemp had felt it before; that twinge of excitement which would come at some stage of an investigation, the flicker of cognition at something heard or seen, sooner or later it would come. Only in this case it had come late. He had only himself to blame for that. He should have been up and about to find the thing earlier but he had succumbed to self-pity, allowed himself to be sickened by an indulgent sorrow at Tony's death which had robbed him of spirit.

It had been left to Mary . . .

Charles Blakeney could see by the look on Kemp's face that the envelope had indeed been important. 'If it matters . . .' he stammered, the knowledge suddenly striking him that this concerned murder, 'if it matters, I can give you Barry Curtis's telephone number in Sydney . . .'

Both men looked instinctively at their watches.

'Nearly twelve here,' said Kemp. 'How many hours' difference?'

'Ten,' said Blakeney, promptly. 'It'll be late evening there but it's Barry's home number I have.' He got up and took out a notebook from the shelf above his head. 'This is it.' He scribbled the number on a piece of paper and handed it to Kemp. 'And there's my phone . . . I'll just go downstairs for a moment.'

Kemp didn't know whether the old man really had a call of nature or whether he was just being tactful. Kemp took up the telephone and dialled.

It never ceased to astonish him how easily one could speak

over continents, bridging the oceans by a thread of sound.

It was a woman's voice that answered. 'Oh, you want my husband,' she said when he made the enquiry. 'Hold on . . .'

'Yes, Barry Curtis here . . .'

'I'm speaking from London, from the office of Charles Blakeney.'

'Nothing wrong with the old man, I hope?'

'No, he's well. It's about a piece of research you did for him a short while ago. Family called Allardyce . . .'

There was a long pause. Because of it, and because the voice up till then had sounded frank and free, Kemp felt once again that tingle in his nerves.

'Who am I speaking to?' Now there was a guarded note.

'Would you prefer to talk to Mr Blakeney himself? I can assure you I have his permission to approach you in this matter. '

'No, that's all right. Just so's I know who you are.'

Kemp gave his credentials, both as a lawyer and a friend of the late Mr Lambert for whom Charles Blakeney had the work.

The man in Sydney seemed satisfied. 'You say the late Mr Lambert? Has he died?'

'I'm afraid so, Mr Curtis. That is why I have to trouble you for some information . . . There was an envelope enclosed when you forwarded your records to Mr Blakeney . . .'

'Yes . . .' The acknowledgement came cautiously.

'I wonder if you could tell me what was in it . . .'

There was silence for a moment. 'You mean you haven't got it?'

'It arrived all right, and Mr Blakeney handed it over to Mr Lambert unopened as it was marked personal. After that, well, I don't know what . . .'

Barry Curtis cut him short. 'Did he marry the girl?' The words fell harshly on Kemp's ear; they were peremptory and to the point.

He made his own negative reply quietly, then he waited, and listened . . .

Mary was always being caught on the hop by the English weather. There had been a raw, chilly spell for some days, a denial of spring, setting back green shoots and leaving buds closed and sullen. It had been one of the reasons she had taken a taxi up to the Allardyce residence – she hadn't wanted to arrive with a nose pink from cold. She didn't want to think about that now as she walked down her long garden under a milky-blue sky and felt on her shoulders the benison of warm sunshine.

Her morning had gone well; rooting out the dust, polishing furniture, scraping carrots and chopping onions, it had all been oddly satisfying and – almost – remedial. Now for the outdoor therapy . . .

She made for the garden shed. She considered these installations as being peculiarly English in that they signified to the owners even of the most modest bungalow or council house the importance of the land itself, the very soil on which the buildings stood. She perceived that garden sheds were like altars where the men of the house could worship their masculine gods, their spades and rakes, shears and mowers, away from the influence of females . . . They were havens where tools could be sorted, blades sharpened, plants potted and plans laid, perhaps for a lawn, a patio or a new path – projects that might never happen but were pleasant to think about.

She needn't fear that Lennox would ever seek sanctuary in such a place; he had an office to go to if he wanted to sulk, and anyway, he was no gardener. Back in his childhood, he had told her, when periods of affluence alternated with periods of poverty in a ratio of perhaps three to one in favour of the latter, there had been gardens, and indeed gardeners, but he himself had never owned as much as a window-box. Unlike Mary, whose girlhood had been even more bereft of grass and growing things, Lennox had no interest in this present garden which she thought had great possibilities. As for the garden shed, he'd only been in it once and that was the day they'd bought the house.

They had taken over the garden shed just as it stood – and it had stood a long time. It was brick-built and sturdy. A little larger and it could have housed the entire Smith family a lot more comfortably than the two-room shack in which she had been brought up back in Vineland, Pennsylvania.

Amused by the thought, she went into the shed, fetched thick gardening gloves, and hesitated over shears or pruning clippers, finally taking both. The path down to the stream at the bottom of the garden was almost obscured by hollies and laurels, and some other shrub of a headstrong nature with limbs like wrought iron and leaves tough as cowhide.

Although she was slight of frame, years of nursing had given her strong wrists and what she lacked in stature she made up for in determination. After an hour or so she had made a difference, a glimmer of water could be seen through the undergrowth, and a small vista opened up which in summer would give this part of the garden some purpose.

A while back at the end of the winter she had cleared the stream of debris, and now the water flowed freely between green banks where clumps of torn crocus grew, planted there years ago and defying the long neglect. There were bluebells too in the long grass, darkly purple now as the shadows lengthened.

She tackled the last clutching arm of a bramble revitalized by spring, and decided she'd done enough. She pushed the pruners down into the pocket of her jacket, gathered up some of the cut branches to put on the heap further up the path, and started to walk back to the house.

The low sun dazzled her eyes so that at first she did not see the figure standing on the edge of the lawn.

'I hope you don't mind . . . There was no one home . . . I came in by the side door . . .'

With the strong golden light behind her Anita's frizzled hair stood out round her head like the glory on a painted saint, but there was nothing else the least ethereal about her as she stood foursquare, chunky in her jogging suit, wholesome as Southdown lamb.

'I've never been in your garden before,' she went on.

'I don't suppose you have,' said Mary. 'It's nice to see you here,' she added, belatedly, unsure of her ground.

'You've more space at the back of your house than it looks . . . And isn't it beautifully private.' She glanced over Mary's shoulder. 'Does that path go far?'

.n to the stream. Lennox says it's the River Lea, but
.ve my doubts. A river can't be that small . . .'

'It can – in this wee country. Can I take a look?'

'Of course you can. I'll show you.'

They went together down the path which was just broad
enough to take them side by side. Mary began to feel there
was something pleasantly companionable about this un-
expected visitor.

'I've been clearing a way through,' she said, holding back
a branch to let Anita past, 'so that in the summer we can
use this lower lawn like the original owners must have done.
Look, there's flower beds and pampas grass . . . There's even
some old steps going down to the water . . .'

'Perhaps they had a boat,' said Anita, going to the edge
and prodding the mossy stones with the toe of one of her
yellow trainers.

'It's never the boat you'd get in there,' Mary scoffed,
'unless it was the toy of a child! It's only deep now because
of the rain last week, usually it's no more than a puddle . . .'

'It's deep enough,' said Anita. She squatted down on her
haunches beside the stream and began poking in the water
with a piece of wood she'd picked up from the grass.

'Did you want to see me about something?' Mary had
come to the realization that this was an odd visit, and there
must be a reason for it. 'If you come up to the house we'd
maybe have a cup of tea . . .'

Anita didn't answer, but Mary felt there was the friendli-
ness of a shy animal in her presence; perhaps she'd come
with an olive branch from her brother and was uncertain
how to introduce it.

'Oh, look . . . tadpoles . . . thousands of them . . . Over
here, Mary . . . !'

Mary walked over and looked down into the greeny-grey
water. Surely she would have known if there had been tadpoles there? Didn't they turn into frogs?

Anita was so close to her they were brushing shoulders,
she could smell the girl's perfume, something fresh but sporty
and probably expensive. Mary felt a sudden lurch against
her and saw a ripple of yellow in the stream as Anita's foot

slipped on a mossy stone. She grabbed her arm. 'Hey, watch it . . . You could've fallen in there . . .'

Anita straightened up. 'Phew . . . I could have, at that . . . Damn, that's a pair of trainers ruined.' She rubbed the shoe on the back of her pants leg. 'It would have been so easy. I might have drowned . . .'

'No way . . . Not in that amount of water, not unless you'd hit your head first.'

'You're so reassuring, Mary.' Anita tucked Mary's arm into her own and proceeded up the path. 'Now, how about that tea?'

But they had only reached the level of the garden shed for Anita to be diverted. 'I say, what a poppet of a place . . . You could let it to the homeless.'

'Well, it sure gives me a bit of conscience sometimes . . . Wait now while I put these things away.' Mary brought in the shears, put the pruners down on the bench. It was dim in the interior when the door swung shut behind Anita.

'Do you know how to use all these things?' she asked Mary, as if amused by the very idea.

'Nope. But I'm learning fast.'

Anita skipped across the dusty floorboards and settled herself on a stool. 'England's like toy-town, you know,' she remarked, looking up at the shadowy forms of garden spades, rakes and forks hanging on the walls, 'and this is toy furniture. Back home these things are three times the size and they're used for real men's work . . .'

'I wouldn't know,' said Mary, putting away the shears. 'We took over the whole lot when we bought the house, and most of it's rusty anyway. Do you hanker for the outback?' Shooting the odd sudden question at Anita seemed somehow the natural way to take her.

'You must be joking . . . Zack and I will pay the old folks a visit now and then but it's not a scene either of us want to linger in. How did you hear of Mr Blakeney?' Anita, too, had her way with the abrupt enquiry to lift the conversation out of the trivial.

'Lydia Beresford's a friend of mine, family history is her hobby, and Charles Blakeney is her chap in London.'

'Nice chap, is he?' Anita put the question casually.

211

'I've only spoken to him on the phone, he seemed very pleasant and courteous. Did you never meet him at all?'

Even in the half-light Anita's eyes were luminous as she turned them on Mary, luminous, wide and innocent. 'How could I? I never knew he existed till Mr Medway handed us the family tree and said a Mr Blakeney had done it and the account was paid.'

'So you'd not an idea what Tony's present to you was going to be, Anita?' Mary softened her tone; it was the same as when they had met in the park; she wasn't sure if Anita's flippant manner was real or a cover to hide deeper feelings.

'Not until I heard it from Big Brother . . . He did tell Zack on the train – you got that bit right . . .' She paused and gave her throaty chuckle. 'Bet you hoped Zack and I were bastards or that Ma and Pa were illegal immigrants!'

Mary felt her colour rise, even though the girl had made a joke of it. She had shown no animosity towards Mary during this visit, a visit which could have been an awkward one, and still had not been explained.

'I'm sorry,' she murmured. 'I'm afraid I had it in for your brother.'

'So I noticed.' Anita gave a slow grin which curled her upper lip and showed her small white teeth. 'Men can be pretty awful at times and Zack really does go on as if he's one of the master race. He was quite chuffed about having that pedigree.'

'And you were not?'

Anita shrugged. 'It was a nice idea of Tony's but no big deal to me. I was never keen on family history, ours or anybody else's . . .'

'Me neither,' said Mary, rather pleased to be sharing even a disinterest with this tawny young lioness for whom she was beginning to have a real liking. It wasn't the first time they had found themselves on common ground – a fellow feeling seemed an absurd expression in the circumstances, kindred spirits more like.

'A pedigree is so frightfully, frightfully English' – Anita put on such an affected drawl that it had them both laughing – 'like being top dog at Cruft's . . . I wonder how your

212

Mr Blakeney managed the Australian end. I mean, the Allardyces have been settled out there for yonks . . .'

'Oh, he'd have a man,' said Mary, mindful of the tuition she'd had from Mrs Brunt-Evans. 'It would probably be someone in Sydney who'd look up the shipping lists and things for him . . .' She remembered something else too. 'I wonder if that would be his bill that Tony put in his coat pocket just before he left Mr Blakeney's office. I reckon that was what it was.'

Anita had slid down off her stool and was wandering about aimlessly among the clutter of implements. 'My, what a lot you know about these things, Mary,' she said, without turning round. It was uncertain whether she meant family histories or garden tools. 'A man in Sydney . . . well, well . . . What a lot of trouble to take over one undistinguished farming family.'

'And not a Royal in sight,' said Mary briskly. 'Now what about that pot of tea? Come on up to the house.' She went to the door and Anita followed her out.

It was dusky now in the garden for the sun had disappeared behind a line of poplars.

'Damn!' Anita exclaimed, stooping down to examine one of her running shoes. 'I've lost a lace . . .'

'You must have pulled it out when you dried your shoe after slipping into the stream. You can always get another lace . . . You said the shoes were ruined anyway . . .'

'But these were special,' Anita wailed. 'I paid the earth for these trainers. Besides, I can't walk in them without a lace. It'll only have fallen in the grass down there. Come and help me look . . .'

Mary was none too pleased – she was dying for a cup of tea. Really, she thought, crossly, as she led the way once more down the path to the stream, these sports people, they're as bad as fashion freaks – they must have their matching colours, brand names, the whole works . . .

She made for the place where the ruined steps went into the water. She bent down to look in the long grass, was conscious of a shadow, a shattering blow . . . mud . . . green slime in her face, then nothing . . .

CHAPTER 25

When Mary struggled back into consciousness she was lying on the sofa in her own sitting room, the homely touch of a blanket at her chin.

'She'll do . . .' She heard a male voice that she didn't know. Someone was looking into her eyes, his face swimming in front of them. 'She can have that cut seen to later, but she's OK for the time being . . .'

The person moved away and into her blurred sight came a man she did recognize – Inspector John Upshire. 'What are you doing here?' She managed to get the words out slowly. She felt so weak that when she put a hand out to him it fell back. She tried again: 'What happened to me?'

'You were hit on the head, and almost drowned.' John Upshire pulled a chair to her side, and sat down. 'The doctor here has pronounced you fit for the land of the living . . . and the paramedics who brought you in have gone. They treated you here as they didn't consider you were bad enough to go to casualty.'

'What? How bad do you have to be to get in there?'

Upshire looked a bit uncomfortable. 'Well, actually it was me said you'd be better at home – if they agreed, medically, so to speak . . . I did have the OK from Dr Matthews . . .'

'My head hurts . . .' She felt it with a hand becoming a little stronger now. 'It's got a bandage on it . . .'

'So it has, Mary. You've had a nasty crack on the back of it where she hit you, but fortunately it was only one blow . . . It was pushing your face into the water and holding you down that did it . . .'

'Did what? Drowned me?' As recollection returned Mary was not sure that it was welcome; there was a stench about it as well as the suffocating weed, and the green slime . . .

'That was what did it for us,' the inspector was saying

214

with more than a hint of satisfaction in his voice. 'Attempted murder – no getting away from that . . . She thumped you with your own heavy pruners, then into the stream she goes and pushes your head right down into the water . . . And right in front of witnesses, too . . .'

'You mean you were watching?' Mary struggled to sit up. John Upshire arranged a pillow behind her, and very gently leaned her back upon it. Out of a disordered scatter of thoughts and emotions it came to her that he had once nursed a sick wife.

'Of course we weren't watching,' he told her when he saw she was comfortably settled. 'What do you take us for? We'd only just come into your garden. It was my sergeant who got to you first and pulled you out of the water. He didn't bother about Miss Allardyce, he knew the rest of us were on his heels and could deal with her.' John Upshire's hand went to his cheek where there was a fresh scratch. 'A right she-cat, that one . . . took two of my men in the end . . .'

'I'm having some difficulty with this . . .' said Mary, weakly. 'How did you know?'

'Your husband, of course. He phoned from London . . . early in the afternoon. Trouble was, we wasted time going out to The Leas, and talking to Zachary . . .' Upshire shook his head. 'If it hadn't been for Lennox . . . He got in touch, you see, once he'd found out. When we told him she wasn't at her house he thought she might have come here, and if she had, then you were in danger . . . There was nothing he could do up there in town and no train till after four . . .' Upshire looked at his watch. 'He'll be here any time now. I sent a man to the station to tell him you're all right.'

'I can't make head or tail . . .'

'I'm not too clear about it myself, Mary, but it's as well he managed to convince us . . . We'd got no reason to think Miss Allardyce meant you harm.'

Mary felt round the back of her head. 'But why me?'

'All Lennox would say was that if you as much as mentioned that envelope you were doomed . . . Didn't make sense, but that's what he said, and the way he said it, well . . .' John Upshire shook his head. 'He was like one demented in that phone-box . . . We had to listen. We came

215

as soon as we could, and what we saw, we saw – and will say in court . . .'

Mary closed her eyes. 'I've thought so much,' she whispered to herself, 'I've talked so much, what have I said? The envelope . . . I still don't understand . . .'

She felt like going back to sleep, it was more comforting being asleep, you didn't have to think about anything . . .

The outside door in the hall slammed shut. Lennox Kemp was across the room and had Mary in his arms before Upshire could move from his seat. He did so now, and turned away; the scene, for the moment, could do without his presence. He went into the Kemps' kitchen and explored the whereabouts of tea, coffee, cups and saucers . . .

When he returned to the sitting room the emotion of reunion had passed, although they remained absorbed in each other. John Upshire coughed, put down the tray, poured and handed cups.

'The English answer to everything,' murmured Mary. 'Thanks, John.' She was grateful for the ordinariness of it, it somehow diminished the recent horror without depriving her of her innate curiosity. She looked at the two men. 'Well, which of you is going to tell me?'

'It has to be him.' The inspector was happier on his feet, walking about the room, cup in hand, conscious of a job well done, even if not altogether understood. 'I only know the half of it . . .'

'It was all in your own theory, Mary,' said Kemp, 'except that you got the wrong Allardyce. When Mr Blakeney handed over that envelope from his friend in Sydney – his name's Barry Curtis – he thought it was just an advertisement for a world cruise, you thought it was a bill . . . You were both wrong. It was a personal letter to Tony Lambert – who Curtis didn't know except what Blakeney had told him, that he was a young man about to marry a girl called Anita Allardyce. Now Allardyce isn't a very common name and there was one Anita who came out in the family tree, a young student who just happened to have been a flatmate of Barry Curtis's daughter when they were both at university in Sydney. Call it coincidence if you like, call it fate, but that was the way it was . . .'

216

'What exactly did this Barry Curtis know about Miss Allardyce? You didn't spell it out to us on the phone today, but I warrant it was something pretty disgraceful.' Upshire put his cup down on the tray, his face stern.

'She didn't have a police record, if that's what you're thinking,' said Kemp, shortly. 'Just that her relationship with his daughter was a lesbian one.'

Mary looked at her husband, and gave a wry smile. 'I could have told you that ages ago,' she said, 'about Anita. She couldn't help being chummy even when she didn't want to . . . Why, this afternoon in the garden she was all for making up to me as if we were buddies . . .'

'To find out if you knew anything about that envelope, whether Mr Blakeney had mentioned it when he spoke to you.'

'Which he had, though I hardly knew it . . . Oh, it's a right eejit I've been . . . I mentioned the envelope to Anita, said I thought it was a bill.'

'And Anita knew you'd go on mentioning it. She'd seen you at work before with your persistence . . . Somehow you'd keep on till you found out what it really was . . . That envelope with the letter in it which she must have taken from Tony's pocket after she killed him. He was bringing it to show to me . . . Anita knew no one must see it . . .'

'So, she's a lesbian, our Miss Allardyce,' said Upshire, as if that explained everything, 'and she was going to marry young Mr Lambert . . .'

Mary stared up at him. 'Hey, wait a minute,' she said. 'OK so she's lesbian but that's just the way she was, like you're heterosexual . . . It's not a criminal offence to be a lesbian. You surely can't take it as a reason for . . .'

'Of course not.' Kemp had interrupted her. 'If that had been all . . . I'm afraid there's more,' he went on, grimly. 'What Mr Curtis said in his letter to Tony was that two of Anita's partners were seriously assaulted by her when they tried to break off the relationships, one was his daughter who ended up in hospital with a broken nose. Anita did it with a cricket stump. The other girl was pushed through a patio door and was badly cut . . .'

'But you said she'd no criminal record!' exclaimed Upshire.

217

'Neither she had. No complaint was ever entered. That was why Mr Curtis wrote that personal letter to Tony; he simply wanted to warn him about the girl he was going to marry.'

'Surely these girls' families would have made a fuss,' Upshire persisted. 'There must have been newspaper reports, that kind of thing could hardly go unnoticed.'

Kemp shook his head. 'You don't understand, John. These young people couldn't afford to get their names in the papers even as victims of assaults in these particular circumstances. It would have all come out, they would have been tagged for life. Remember, they were taking law degrees and hoped to make the law their career. I don't need to tell you that the law is the most conservative profession . . . In fact it was their families − including the Allardyces − who agreed it should be hushed up, not even the university authorities got wind of it, according to Mr Curtis . . .'

'And Anita was conveniently shipped off to England,' murmured Mary. 'Botany Bay in reverse . . . I suppose Zachary knew?'

'That his sister has lesbian tendencies? Yes, he probably knows but thinks it's something you get over like measles in childhood, nothing marriage to a fine young Englishman won't cure. He was all for getting her married off, problem solved as far as Zack was concerned.'

'I find that very cynical of him,' said Mary, thoughtfully, 'but I also understand him. Would he know about the assaults on those girls, though?'

'He'd no reason to. Remember he was here in England at the time. I doubt if the parents would tell him, and Anita had every reason not to . . .' He turned to the inspector. 'How did Zachary Allardyce take your visit today?'

'Badly,' said Upshire, tersely. 'He made it clear we were interfering with his packing . . . No idea where his sister was, saying goodbye to an old friend, he thought.'

Mary drew in her breath sharply and found it still hurt.

'That's not even funny,' she said, indignantly.

There was a bleep on the inspector's mobile phone and he went over to the window to answer it. 'Speak of the devil,' he said, putting the instrument away. 'He's down at the station now, they'd told him about Miss Allardyce's arrest . . . I'd best get down there.'

Kemp followed him out into the hall.

'I don't need to tell you, John . . .' he began. Upshire cut him short. 'Just be thankful we were in time . . . The attempted murder will stick . . . Don't know about the other . . .'

'There'll be confirmation from Sydney. I said to Mr Curtis that we'd be discreet, but once I'd told him we were talking about murder he was eager to cooperate. He's willing to swear to the contents of his letter to Tony Lambert, and is sending a fax. As for other evidence' – he shrugged – 'a search of The Leas might come up with at least the envelope, but I doubt it – she'd destroy everything. All the same, she told a lot of little lies – What she was doing that night, for instance – and the maid bringing her a cup of coffee about nine . . .'

The inspector looked slightly shamefaced. 'We slipped up there, I'll admit, but I can't blame my men. There's brother Allardyce out dining with the Chief Constable, and his sister just lost her fiancé and in tears . . . It never crossed their minds to question – what's the girl's name? – Deborah Ford . . . Even when I saw the reports it would never have occurred to me that Anita Allardyce would have anything to do with the murder. The sergeant who took her statement noted she'd no car and that was enough to keep her out of it; it's a good way from The Leas to Lorimers' Garage . . .'

'Not if you run like the wind,' said Kemp. 'Not if you go cross-country; you have a look at a map, Newtown isn't completely built up yet out there. But there's a job your men can do to redeem themselves, someone must have seen her, she'd have to use streets on the last lap . . . And don't blame yourself for slipping up. I made a bad error . . . It must have been Anita who phoned Tony that night just after he got in from the train . . .'

'Well, there were no outgoing calls from Copt Lodge that night – it was one of the first things we checked . . .'

'I think there was an incoming one, and it came from The Leas. If so, it'll show up on their account. I'm to blame for this blunder . . . When I phoned to break the news to Anita that Tony was dead, she cried out that she'd talked to him earlier in the evening, he'd made his usual phone call, she said . . . He told her he loved her, and that they would see each other the next day . . .' Kemp put a hand up to his forehead as if either to aid his memory or to wipe it away. 'Of course, I was hardly listening, the state I was in . . . It should have registered later but it didn't because I couldn't think about that night with any degree of calm . . .'

'We all had a lot on our minds at that time,' said the inspector, gruffly. 'We all made mistakes . . . Questioning both the Allardyces shouldn't have been taboo whatever his connections . . . Anything special you want me to ask Mr Allardyce now he's down at the nick?'

'Only what he told his sister between arriving home that evening and going out again. From what Mary says, Zack was quite excited about that pedigree, I think he couldn't keep it in – he told Anita right away . . . Perhaps it made her nervous, anything coming out of Australia was bound to do that, and there might have been a mention of a man in Sydney who helped with the records. I think that's why she phoned Tony as soon as Zack had gone, instead of waiting for his usual call . . .'

'And by then he'd read the letter? God, that would have been a conversation worth listening to!'

'This is all pure surmise, of course,' said Kemp, hastily. 'Anita Allardyce is the only one who knows what was said, and she's not going to give anything away . . .'

'She's already done that.' The inspector knew exactly where he stood, and it was official. 'She was caught trying to murder your wife, that's enough for me – and for a jury, I'll warrant.'

'So, I'm to be the one she gets done for . . .' Mary was sitting up in bed later that night. 'Well, there's irony in that. I hope John Upshire's grateful.'

'The doctor said you were to rest,' her husband remarked, removing the supper tray.

'There's things I want clear in my head before it's ready to lay down on the pillow. Have I got it right, now? Anita killed Tony?'

'I'm afraid so. Whether it was premeditated or in sudden

panic we may never know . . . She certainly hadn't much time to think . . .'

'She would be thinking with her feet,' said Mary. 'But how would she know where he was that night?'

'I've been trying to work it out . . . Tony had the envelope in his overcoat pocket. When he arrived home he put his briefcase on the table, and started to take off his coat. Now, when I take off a coat I go through the pockets first, and I think that's what Tony did. He finds the envelope and even though he thinks it's only an advert, he opens it . . .'

'I'm with you so far,' said Mary, slowly, 'but I don't have the imagination to get the next bit.'

'You're lucky . . .' Kemp observed, drily. 'I had the whole thing from Barry Curtis on the phone, and believe me, it wasn't pleasant hearing. His daughter means a lot to him and what Anita Allardyce did to her and the other girl was frankly appalling. In his letter to this unknown young man who is going to marry Anita, I shouldn't think he minced his words. Call it revenge if you like but he wanted Lambert to know the truth, and he didn't spare him . . .'

'What would be your immediate reaction if you had read that kind of thing about someone you loved?' Mary wanted to know.

'My first thought if I was very much in love would be that it couldn't possibly be true. Then I'd want to find out if it was . . . But there's no telephone number in the letter, and anyway, it's probably the middle of the night in Australia . . .'

'I know what I'd do,' said Mary. 'I'd phone my beloved for an explanation – any explanation – hoping the letter was all lies.'

'But before Tony does that, she rings him. She must have been anxious as soon as Zack told her about the family tree. She's impatient to know if anything else came out of Australia at the same time . . . Perhaps in a way she was prepared, although what Tony said to her on the phone must have terrified her . . .'

'She'd lie through her little white teeth,' said Mary, who knew about such things. 'I know I would. She'd tell a tale about how this man Curtis had a grudge against the

Allardyces, that his daughter's neurotic and the whole story in the letter is a lie from beginning to end.'

'But no matter what she told him,' said Kemp, slowly, 'Tony's not going to let it rest there. That was not his way. He would want to get someone else's opinion right there and then. He remembers I'm at the Law Society meeting and will be collecting my car from the garage sometime after eight . . .'

'Would he tell her that?'

'Who knows? It's already half past seven by now, but it's a cold night, he wouldn't want to hang about . . . I think he stayed in his house as long as he could bear the waiting, then he set off across the field, the letter in his pocket so that he could show it to me . . . Anita may have seen him and simply followed, or he told her he was coming across to see me so she went to the garage. I reckon Anita could run that distance in twenty-five minutes – it's downhill and she was very determined . . . that letter meant the end of all her hopes, not only money and marriage but possibly her career as well. Whether or not he believed what Curtis put in the letter, Tony would check it out, and being the way he was, he would be scrupulous. He might well take the view that although she'd never been charged, her offences were serious enough for him to see it as his duty that she should never get articles anywhere – never mind in Gillorns. Oh, no, not because she's lesbian . . .' he went on, as Mary raised her eyebrows. 'Tony, I think, would be more hurt than angry at that aspect of her nature, but because of the violence she obviously couldn't contain . . .'

'I knew the cub had claws,' said Mary, with some reluctance, 'but I didn't realize how she could turn and rend with them . . . I always sensed the animal quality she had but thought it was the cuddly kind. I was wrong, she had all the instincts of a predator who would never give up her prey once the teeth were in it . . . Those poor girls learnt that to their cost . . .'

'Well, at least you're one that got away,' he observed complacently to her all but recumbent form.

Mary gave him a long look. 'I'm not of Anita's kind,' she

said. 'And in this matter I was the victim of my own stupidity. I'll know better the next time . . .'

'Heaven forbid there should be a next time,' said her husband, firmly. 'I'm going to domesticate you and keep you as a household pet.'

He could tell she was asleep because no response came to what, in her ears, must sound the highest provocation.

He stretched out his legs, contentedly. It had been a tiring day, the afternoon journey between London and Newtown the longest, most exhausting he had ever known. As the train trundled from station to station – the 'Shoppers' Special', it stopped at every wayside halt – his desperation had grown so huge it was all he could do to stay aboard and not leap off and hire a helicopter.

Twice lately at the thought of losing her, his panic had nearly choked him . . . Would it be like this always now if she was out of his sight? Was this what middle-aged love was all about? If you're given a second chance at it, don't push your luck . . .